MICHIGAN VS. THE BOYS

MICHIGAN VS. THE BOYS

CARRIE S. ALLEN

KCP Loft

KCP Loft is an imprint of Kids Can Press

Kids Can Press gratefully acknowledges the financial support of the Government of Ontario, through Ontario Creates.

Published in Canada and the U.S. by Kids Can Press Ltd.
25 Dockside Drive, Toronto, ON M5A 0B5

Kids Can Press is a Corus Entertainment Inc. company

www.kidscanpress.com

The text is set in Minion Pro, Arial Narrow and Aceituna.

Edited by Kate Egan
Designed by Emma Dolan

Printed and bound in the United States, in 6/2019
by LSC Communications.

FSC
www.fsc.org
MIX
Paper from responsible sources
FSC® C132124

CM 19 0 9 8 7 6 5 4 3 2 1

Library and Archives Canada Cataloguing in Publication

Allen, Carrie, 1976–, author
Michigan vs. the boys / by Carrie Allen.

ISBN 978-1-5253-0148-3 (hardcover)

I. Title. II. Title: Michigan versus the boys.
PZ7.1.A44Mic 2019 j813'.6 C2018-905844-7

To my CC girls —
and to all girls who know what
ice smells like at 4 a.m.

1

It's the hardest I've ever worked for an A. Late nights. Focused studying. Constant testing.

Raw skate bite on my ankles and puck-shaped welts on my ribs.

I hold the palm-sized embroidered A up to my shoulder, even though I'm wearing a tank top instead of my hockey jersey. "How's it look?" I ask Brie.

"It goes great with mine. Matching accessories." My best friend pushes her chest next to mine, sporting a gold C safety-pinned to her cashmere T-shirt. They'll look even better when we get them sewn on our jerseys. "Of course, I expect to be addressed as Captain from now on, Mich."

She's only slightly joking. Brie has the right enthusiasm for a captain. But I suspect my A is supposed to stand for Anti-Brie instead of Assistant.

"Aye aye, Captain," I say.

She shoves my shoulder with hers. "And we'll call you Ass Cap."

I shove her back. No retort from the girl whose parents named her after her home state.

"Congratulations," Coach says, leaning back in her desk chair. "You earned them."

Yes, we did. We get to run this team for the next two years. I smile, thinking of the upcoming season. I can practically smell the damp air and propane fumes of the rink. My quads ache in anticipation of the killer workouts I've got planned for them. Last season we finished a respectable fourth in the league, but this year we're bringing home hardware.

Brie's grinning but I doubt she's daydreaming about playoffs. Ten bucks says she's mentally creating the playlist for our first locker room dance party of the season.

"Katy Perry," she says, bumping my hip with her own. Coach rolls her eyes but I laugh. We're a good team. I'll lead the drills; she'll lead the conga line. Besides, I'll admit I've had our team's welcome-back movie night planned for months (*Miracle*, followed by *Mystery, Alaska,* with Ambassador's BLT pizza and a box of Mackinac fudge I've been hiding from my brother since July).

I'm ready to sprint to the rink this very minute. Or at least bum a ride off Brie.

"Does this mean you want us to start captain's practices right away?" Brie asks. It's only the first day of school and our hockey team doesn't usually start captain's practices until late September. But it's never too early to get in the weight room.

Coach hesitates. "This means that I want to know the team is in good hands."

Brie waves her manicured fingers in the air. "The best!"

There's something in Coach's tone that freezes me in place before her sparsely decorated desk. Beside her laptop, she always keeps a current team picture and a framed, signed Julie Chu puck. And they aren't there now. In fact, the desk calendar has been torn off to a blank sheet, and the whiteboard on the wall, usually crowded with lines and drills, has been scrubbed clean.

"Why? Where are you going?" I ask. Brie's breath catches and she grips my forearm.

"I have …" Coach exhales and flicks at the cracked laminate corner of her desk. "I am taking a new opportunity."

She doesn't sound excited. I try to read her face and wonder what's appropriate for me to ask. As usual, Brie's words are faster than mine and she ignores that line between coach and athlete.

"What? Where?" she demands. "Why would you leave us?"

Because we're a small-town team of sixteen girls who win some and lose some, and unless you grew up here, you don't stay in the Upper Peninsula forever. Coach did not grow up here.

She averts her eyes and stands. "I don't want you guys to be late for your meeting with Mr. Belmont. He'll talk about it there. I wish I could explain …" She comes around the desk to hug me, an unusual gesture for a woman whose coaching whistle never seems to come out of her mouth.

"Good luck, Michigan," she says firmly before she lets go. "I mean it, the team is in good hands with you."

Our new captain still stands with her arms crossed, that lower lip slipping farther out by the second. Brie doesn't do well with "I wish I could explain." Coach shoots a look at Brie. I take the hint.

"Principal Belmont, Brie. Hope you're not in trouble," I quip.

She snorts. "Yeah, right." There's no trouble Brie could get in that Daddy can't fix.

As we leave, Coach's brows are pulled together. I can't tell if she's angry or sad. But I am not looking forward to Belmont.

Partly because the man is half-creep, half–Napoleon with a vengeance. He was probably always creepy, but the vengeance part had to have slipped in when he had a miserable high school career and decided to spend the rest of his life making other high schoolers miserable.

But Creepy Napoleon aside, now I'm sure something's wrong. Did Coach get fired? It's more likely that Brie's Pomeranian learned to skate than Coach got herself in trouble.

As we near the cafeteria, I slip the A into the front pocket of my jeans. Brie not only keeps her C on, but puffs her chest out proudly.

"You earned that," she says, pointing to my pocket. "Flaunt it, baby."

I shrug, even though I'm still grinning over my new role.

"I'm serious, Mich. I don't care which of us has the C."

I roll my eyes at her.

"OK, I totally care. I want the C. But I can't do this without you. I wouldn't want to. You're the Anti-Brie."

My mouth slides open. "Oh, my God, I was just thinking that."

"Come on, Ass Cap." She links her elbow in mine and pulls me through the cafeteria doorway. Our hockey team is squished around a long laminate table filled with backpacks and purses and first-day-of-school gossip. Strangely, the boys' swim team is here, too, sitting at their own cafeteria table.

I slide onto the bench next to Jeannie. "Are we in trouble?" she asks me. Jeannie wouldn't recognize trouble because she's never been in it.

"Not that I know of. Why is the boys' swim team here?"

Kendall leans across the table. "Did I miss some crazy party with them or something?"

"Like you'd miss a party," Jordan tells her. Kendall looks proud rather than insulted.

Brie eyes the swimmers. "I'd be up for a crazy party. Those boys have definitely been working out this summer."

Principal Belmont's shiny balding head draws my attention to the cafeteria entrance. He hurries to the front of the room, flipping through a thick bound notebook. He doesn't look angry, like we're about to spend my junior year in detention. He's not even looking at us. "Is anyone missing from your teams?"

Brie, having been captain for approximately three minutes, stands and takes a head count. "All of our team is accounted for." She flounces back down next to me.

"We're all here," says a voice from the swim table. Jack Ray. We've never spoken, but I know who he is. Everyone does. Jack Ray is an amazing swimmer. Olympic trials amazing. Going-to-Berkeley-for-free amazing. But he acts chill about it, so no one makes a big deal.

Oh, and he's also hotter than noon on Mercury.

"I won't beat around the bush," Principal Belmont says, cradling his notebook to his suit jacket. "We're facing large budget cuts this year. We're halving our arts department, we're making do with outdated technology and we're limiting the library's intake significantly. In looking at our budgets closely, we knew we would have to make cuts to extracurricular activities as well. It's only fair, when academic programs are cutting back. We can no longer justify —"

"You're cutting our team?" Brie screeches. She stands, smacking both palms flat on the table.

Jerk doesn't even flinch. "The school has decided it would be wiser to cut underperforming teams than to make smaller, detrimental cuts across the board to all programs."

My core stiffens at the insult. Or maybe it's soreness from the punishing workout this *underperforming* athlete woke up at five thirty for. This can't be happening. "Underperforming" is repeated in varying levels of decibels and anger around the tables. Vigorously sprinkled with question marks.

"I demand an audience with the school board." Brie flips her hair off her shoulder, and the gold threads of the captain's C sparkle under the unnaturally bright lights of the cafeteria. "My parents will demand an audience with the school board."

"The school board gives us a budget. Sometimes it's just not enough to cover our expenses." Principal Belmont articulates slowly, as if Brie is a child who doesn't understand budgets, one who's always had a credit card with a generous allowance. This treatment is probably warranted. "We go through it line by line and determine where we can apply cuts —"

"Why are we just learning about this now?" one of the swimmers asks. "We didn't get any input."

"And what can we do?" I ask. "Can we raise money for our programs?"

"I'm sorry. It's a decision that has already been made. I know this is a difficult way for you to start the school year. A letter has been mailed to your parents explaining this development."

Because we're too dumb to tell them ourselves?

I can actually see Brie calculating the worth of her SUV. "How much do we need?"

"What?"

"How much money?"

"This is not about putting a Band-Aid on the issue. This is a long-term decision made for the betterment of the school."

I stand, even though I'm not sure my legs will hold me. "We're a team," I say. "We don't have anywhere else to play. There is no other hockey program for teen girls in this town. If you take our team, we can't play hockey." My voice quavers. I wish I could aim fury at him, like Brie's I'm-going-to-stab-you-with-my-skate stare. But all I can think of is the A in my pocket and the pride I felt when Coach handed it to me and told me I earned it. I did earn it. I biked to the weight room in August when I could have slept till noon. I did homework by the light of my cell phone, bouncing up and down on a freezing cold school bus, to play games all across the Upper Peninsula. I skated until I puked. Four times.

I'm happiest when I have skates on my feet, a stick in my hands and teammates by my side. "Please …" My voice cracks and the rest of my plea sticks in my throat. Jeannie rubs my back, which makes my eyes flood even more.

"Please tell us what we can do," someone finishes for me. It's Jack Ray, and I'm so grateful to have thirty eyes suddenly on him instead of my tear-threatened face.

"You can go to school," the principal says, his expression never straying toward sympathetic. "You can find another club to join. This is a public school, people. We aren't obligated to provide extracurricular activities. They are a privilege, not a right."

"But we didn't do anything wrong," Kara says.

He holds his hands up. "It's not personal. It's simply numbers. Ladies, you are an expensive endeavor. Travel, equipment, ice time."

"But the guys' team —" Brie begins.

"Traditionally has a larger, more competitive roster and a higher win percentage. You don't even fill your roster, and there's just not enough demand for your team. You only have one goalie, for heaven's sake. What would you do if she got injured?"

I don't point out that she played with bronchitis last year, that we've all played sick before. We sacrifice like the boys never have to. Yes, this school could scrape up only sixteen girls to play hockey. But we do just fine with our short bench.

"What about us?" Jack asks.

"Title IX regulations require us to offer a proportionate number of opportunities for males and females, so we have to cut an equal number from each gender." He flinches nervously. "We, uh, have come up with an alternative option for the girls' swim team at the Rec Center. Financially, we cannot support our pool facility any longer. The natatorium will be torn down and that space will be used for a much-needed parking lot."

There's a unified gasp from the boys' table. They're tearing out the pool? My eyes lock on Jack Ray's face as his jaw clenches. I've been to the pool on several occasions. The wall behind the starting blocks is lined with pennants for league titles and team records. Jack's impressive swim history is recorded on that wall.

"When?" he asks.

"The pool is closed," Belmont says. "It's already undergoing demolition."

That's the point when the former Owl River High School boys' swim team walks out.

2

I'll never eat Ben & Jerry's again. We should have binged on kale chips or something else I'd never miss.

We could rebuild the natatorium with the empty ice-cream cartons littering the floor of Brie's bedroom — and by bedroom, I mean her palatial chamber where all sixteen of us are comfortably sprawled on the plush carpet. I took down an entire pint of Americone Dream myself. Ironically. By the time my spoon scrapes the bottom of the container, my face is streaked with tears and snot and my mouth is numb and thickly coated in cream. I'm not sure if my headache is sugar induced, brain freeze or from too much crying. Or D: all of the above.

Brie passes me her half-used tissue. We're running low and rationing essentials at this point. She's still in the anger phase of the grief paradigm. Self-diagnosis; her mom is a psychiatrist.

"Since you guys won't help me slash Belmont's tires, my newest idea is going to be solitary sabotage. I can get access to his coffee mug, and I'm going to spike it."

Hanna swallows nervously. "Like, with … poison? Or just something to make him sick?"

Brie shrugs. "Depends on how pissed I still am."

I shake my head at Hanna. Sophomore hasn't learned yet how to ride out a Brie mood.

"Screw the school," I say. "Let's go out on our own. We can register with USA Hockey and play —"

"Who?" Brie asks. "No offense, Mich, but Assmont was actually right about there being no teams for us to play. None of the high school teams will be allowed to play us if we're not in the league. And where are we going to get the money to field a team?"

I gulp.

"And no, my dad won't sponsor us. Not that much money."

OK, I'll admit I'd been thinking it. But she's right, hockey's steep. Ice time for an hour is like $150. Travel, with massive amounts of gear, in the middle of winter, adds up fast. Coaching stipend, officials for home games, insurance, registration. Gear and supplies. I almost can't blame the school. Almost.

"At least my idea is more productive than coffee spiking," I mumble.

"I got it," Brie says, her face suddenly shining. "Oh, I got it. This is a good one, ladies."

This is the part where we're supposed to let Brie's theatrics build before she tells us. Emma rolls her eyes at me, but I lean in, waiting for our new captain to save the day.

"I'm going to tryouts," she says. Insert dramatic pause. "For the boys' team."

Even I didn't see that coming. We're all silent. I don't even bother to come up with a Supportive Friend Response because it's Brie and she's going to provide her own.

And she does. "You know I can skate faster than almost all those boys. And I can take a check. We'll flood their tryouts and when all the boys are pissed that they can't even make their own team, Assmont will have to give us ours back."

Cherrie, cradling her goalie helmet like a security blanket, shakes her head sadly. "Avery and Eddie are the best players on that team. I won't make it."

"Coach Henson picks the team," I say. "None of us will make it."

"If we're faster and better than the boys, he'll have to take us," Brie says. "That man likes to win." He has to, or the boosters will toss him like they did his predecessor. Coach Henson has been here three years and he's still trying to whip those boys into shape. My guess is he's getting nervous watching his game clock tick down. He can't afford to take a chance on us.

I scan the room, mentally placing bets on our odds. I have no doubt Brie could hang. She was the only girl on her teams growing up. She'd never played with girls until she moved to Owl River and joined our team freshman year.

Cherrie is right. The coach will keep his two stellar goalies, no need for a third. Laura splits time between swimming and hockey, and while our coach had allowed it, most wouldn't. Delia is tiny, which won't work so well for playing defense against bigger guys. Jordan just doesn't have the speed and skill.

I don't know where I fall. Coach always said I have the best shot on the team. I'm pretty fast. For a girl. But I've never thrown a real hit. Not on a guy, most of whom are twice my size.

Out of sixteen girls, I figure only Brie is a sure bet. And that's because I know she can bully her way into a spot. Not only does she have an unfiltered mouth and Daddy's credit card, but she did date the captain of the boys' team last year. None of the rest of us have that kind of leverage. I'm reaching for my phone to google "how to spike coffee" when Brie's parents poke their heads through her doorway.

Dr. Hampton's eyes go straight to the pile of oozing ice-cream containers in the middle of Brie's ice-colored carpet. I hastily scrub a licked finger across a drop of chocolate on the floor next to my foot. Unsuccessful.

Mr. Hampton's gaze focuses immediately on his daughter, purposely avoiding the other fifteen girls in the room. For an attorney with a killer reputation, it's funny how terrified he is of teenaged girls. As soon as Brie hit dating age, he started blood pressure meds. If you play Lady Gaga near him or talk about tattoos, you can actually see the migraine forming. It's kind of a game for us, usually resulting in a later curfew and extra money for our evening out.

But tonight he looks triumphant, like he won a big case.

"Good news, Brie," her mom says, hooking a plastic grocery bag over one hand and shuttling ice-cream pints into it with the other.

I jump up and begin collecting trash to add to her bag.

"Did you find a way to keep the team?" Brie asks. Hope rises quickly in the room, pulling the girls up to fully seated positions.

"No." Dr. Hampton eyes the rest of us. It suddenly feels like we shouldn't all be here.

"We were able to secure a position for Brie," Mr. Hampton says. "At the Wiltshire Academy, in Chicago."

A pink plastic spoon, dripping with caramel, slips out of my hand and glues itself to Brie's pale blue comforter. *Chicago.* Her big-time lawyer dad didn't even try to save the team. Around the room, girls slump back to their pillows, reaching for the nearest half-empty carton before Dr. Hampton can snag it.

"It was the last spot on the roster," Mr. Hampton adds, his eyes on the floor, lest he glimpse a bra strap or tampon wrapper. "But if Wiltshire still had a spot available, that means there are other schools with roster spots left. Start calling around, girls, or have your parents do it."

"Boarding school tuition? It would have been cheaper to sponsor us," Emma whispers to me. Not as quiet as she thought she had.

"There is still school tomorrow," Dr. Hampton says. "For the rest of you. Brie, even though it's no longer a school night for you, we have a lot of details to attend to before you leave for Chicago."

"When?" I croak. My eyes lock with Brie's. Her hands reach out and grip mine.

"We'll move you in this weekend. Classes start on Monday."

Brie is silent.

And there it is. The first sign of the apocalypse.

*

The second comes the next morning.

"Silver Lake's goalie had shoulder surgery this summer! They don't have a backup!" Cherrie squeals. She nearly runs into my locker door as I open it.

"Sucks for them." I contemplate options for my wet raincoat. Drip all over my locker or wear it to class until it dries? "Wait, why do we care about Silver Lake's goaltending situation?"

Cherrie's excited expression ebbs into one of guilt.

I freeze, immune to the raindrops sploshing from my coat onto my shoes. "Cherrie. You didn't."

She holds her hands up. "Don't be mad. Their coach offered me the backup. What else are we supposed to do?"

I shove my wet raincoat into the bottom of my locker. Who cares if it won't dry, I'm going to get soaked walking home anyway. "Congrats, I guess."

Cherrie grips my biceps. "Listen, Mich. Their coach agreed to get approval for us to play with them, but he won't cut his own players. So there are only three roster spots left. He'll take anyone who's willing to drive."

My heart rate quickens. We're not dead yet. But it's only three spots. How will we choose who gets them? And what about the rest of the team? The words "willing to drive" knock against my skull. Over an hour to Silver Lake. And an hour back. If the roads are good. Five nights a week. And that's just for practice.

"I don't have a car," I remind Cherrie.

"So carpool with us."

"Wait, who's 'us'?"

"I'm going to ask Di and Hanna."

Obviously, our two best players, besides Brie and me. This all seems wrong, though. Shouldn't there be some kind of a team discussion? A tryout? Who's running this team if Cherrie's suddenly in charge of doling out roster spots like a hockey Santa?

She crosses her arms and pouts at me. Rainy walk to school and a cranky goalie. Great start to my day.

"Do you want to play this season or not?"

I do want it. I am craving ice time. Which is stupid because it's September. We wouldn't be practicing yet anyway. But knowing I have nowhere to play this season makes me want it even more. I stuck my nose into my hockey bag last night, just to get a whiff of that stale-sweat hockey smell.

And then I'd started crying again for the thirty-eighth time.

I don't think Coach would have given me that A if she'd known this was how I'd lead her team. But what if walking away from them is the only way I'll get to play this season? I need time to figure out another solution before Cherrie starts selling the team for parts like a car thief.

"Let me check with my parents," I say, digging my phone out of my backpack.

*

"Yes or no?" Cherrie asks, setting her brown bag next to mine at our usual lunch table.

"Nothing yet." I'm pretty sure I know what Mom will say about driving to Silver Lake every day. So I texted Dad. But when he's out on patrol he doesn't answer unless it's an emergency. Literally. Didn't think I should go through the 911 operator for this one.

Di and Hanna squeeze in next to Cherrie, as if they're already their own team. Traitors stick together, I guess.

"So who's coming with us?" Di asks Cherrie.

Cherrie nods at me. "Hopefully Mich. She's working on it."

Across from me, Jordan inclines her head. I meet her eyes reluctantly. "Cherrie found a couple of spots on Silver Lake's roster."

"You're leaving us?" Whit turns on Cherrie, sitting across from her.

Jordan's glare slips from Cherrie to Di to Hanna. "Snap up the best players we got left and get the hell outta Dodge?"

Cherrie shrugs and primly picks onions out of her tuna wrap, dropping the purple squares onto her napkin.

"Do you have a better idea, Jordan?" Di asks, her eyes narrowed and voice sharp.

Instead of answering, Jordan sticks two fingers in her mouth and whistles loudly. She aims her perma-glare behind me. I pivot on my seat to see Laura, Delia and Emma pass by, carrying their own bagged lunches.

"Uh, hello?" I gesture to the same table where the girls' hockey team has always eaten lunch, at least for the last two years.

"Oh," Laura says. She fiddles nervously with the tab on her pop. "I'm introducing Delia and Emma to the other swimmers today."

Delia nods. "Laura convinced us to go out for swimming with her. Since the team is …" She shrugs. "I'm pretty good on backstroke. And Emma lifeguarded for the coaches this summer."

"It'll actually be much easier for me this year, only balancing one sport," Laura says defensively.

"But we're still upset about the team," Emma adds. "And we'll still sit with you whenever we can." They wave and hurry off. Run away while they still can. Or swim away.

Plague, pests, swimming. And the four horsemen galloping off toward Silver Lake. I growl into my yogurt.

"So, Cherrie," Jordan says, her voice thick with Cheetos and poison. "Thanks for inviting the rest of us to play on your shiny new team."

Cherrie's cheeks match her name as she stares down at her lunch. There's a reason Jordo's always been our team enforcer. And that goes for verbal fights, too.

"There's no way to save our team," Di says. "It's over. And Brie's leaving."

"And our goalie," Jordan says. "So even if we did figure out a way to keep the team, we're screwed."

"Well, I'm still waiting to hear your great idea," Di says.

The entire table looks to me. And I don't have a single answer. I left the A Coach gave me in my dresser drawer this morning, but I still feel it burning against my left shoulder.

"What's the point?" Jordan asks, tearing into a packet of Oreos. She crams a whole one in her mouth, still staring down Cherrie. Jordo's like a Chow dog; once she gets her jaws around someone, she won't let go. Cherrie's lucky the Oreo is taking the beating. So far.

Hanna nudges Di, who reaches over to scoop up the remains of Cherrie's picked-apart lunch. "I so don't feel like getting into a Jordo fight today. Let's go raid the donuts at the Gas 'n' Snack." Cherrie scrambles out of her seat and the Silver Lake trio stalks off.

I sigh at Jordan, but really I'm angry at myself for sitting like a pylon on the ice instead of stepping up to lead what's left of this team. "So what now?" I ask the sparse table.

"Sorry, Mich," Jordan says. "It's not like I expected them to ask me. I'm not good enough to play anywhere else. Don't know why Coach kept me as long as she did."

I'd argue, but it'd be a short debate. Jordo's never been in great shape. She has too many bad habits: greasy food, cheap beer, purposely throwing body checks when she wants to rest for two minutes. Instead, I ask, "Kendall?"

Kendall's shoulders droop. "My parents said I need to concentrate on grades anyway. So I guess I'm done. Retired at the ripe old age of seventeen."

"But don't you want to skate?" I ask the whole table, but I'm looking at Kendall especially. She and I have been on every team together since we were nine. I don't know what a hockey bench would smell like without her rotating seasonal perfume collection. Don't want to know.

Whit holds her palm up to Jordan. "Beer league, baby. Eighteen's old enough to play pickup on Sunday nights."

Jordan doesn't look too upset about that concept. She high-fives Whit. "Finally. I can combine the two things I love best. Senior year's not looking so bad."

"I'm starting a skate club at my church, if you want to join," Jeannie says to me. For some reason, her Yooper accent gets even thicker when she talks about church. She really puts the "eh" in "amen."

"It sounds like toe picks might be involved."

"Oh, you can skate in your Vapors. It'll mostly be me teaching the kids how to stop or do two-foot spins."

"Plus the added benefit of going to heaven," Jordan says.

"Mich." Kendall slides into Cherrie's empty seat next to me.

"You should go to Silver Lake with them. We won't be mad. We understand."

Jordo just nods, her mouth full of cookie again.

"You're too good to retire to Sunday beer league," Whit agrees.

Not to mention too young. I know I still have goals left in my stick. Silver Lake is my last chance.

Mom and Dad, please say yes.

3

"No."

Mom drops two aromatic bags of Louie's takeout on the kitchen table and scowls at the pile of mail at her spot. She kicks off her scuffed pumps while doling out the food. Dad slides his newspaper over to make room for a condensation-filled plastic box of pasta. Trent charges into the room and crashes into his seat, simultaneously flipping open the lid of his pasta and the tab on his pop. He stabs a piece of sausage and is chewing before I've even finished my sentence.

"Dad?" I plead.

The man carries a gun for a living but he still exchanges a look with Mom before he answers. "Sorry, kiddo."

"Why?" I stick my hands on my hips and stare them down. "This is my only chance to play hockey this season."

"That would suck," Trent says through his mouthful.

"It already sucks," I say. "What about college, Dad?"

"You don't need hockey to go to college," Mom says. Not

that she knows anything about real college. Or hockey.

"It sure would be nice."

Dad sets down his fork and gives me his full attention. This is the man who put me in my first pair of pink Bauers when I was two years old. I let my eyes well with tears, which have been on standby all day anyway. "Mich, I know that's what you want," he says. "And I want — we want — that for you, too. But college hockey is a long shot. This team in Silver Lake, they're an OK team. They're nothing special. We're talking full days of school, a long drive, practice, another long drive and then homework. Late nights with not enough sleep. Are you willing to live like that, just to play hockey? Spending your evenings in the car, your weekends in the car, no social life."

"That would be my social life. Hockey is my social life. Those are my friends."

"You'd only be with three of your friends," Mom reminds me. Wounds from Brie's impending departure reopen in my chest.

"I'm used to traveling a lot. I can handle it. And we'll do homework in the car."

Mom snorts. "You won't do homework in the car. Does that Di even do homework? You know she'll be driving fast with the music loud. You won't get anything done. You'll put your life in danger every day just to practice with a mediocre team." She plops into her seat, her chicken-topped salad and the TV remote on the plastic placemat in front of her. I know what she's doing, playing the dangerous-teen-driver card for my state trooper dad. I up the ante with the ace of grades.

"I'll maintain all A's. Promise. If I slip, you can make me quit."

"No," Mom says, already scrolling through the TV guide.

But Dad makes a humph-sigh sound. I turn on my weakening prey.

"Dad, I'll take on extra chores around the house when I'm home. To offset gas money."

"No," Mom says.

"Sleep on it?" I plead. "Please? You know how important this is to me, right?"

Dad jumps in before Mom can. "We'll sleep on it."

"All I'm asking." I pick at my dinner to avoid Mom's frown.

*

I text Cherrie while I should be keeping my end of that all-A's promise I made. Still maybe. Keep your fingers crossed for me.

It kind of sounded like you were a no.

Well, they said no. But then Dad agreed to sleep on it.

The thing is, at first you said they said no.

Wait. Does this mean ...???

Kara's parents said yes. We thought you were a no.

I type: Kara? She barely scored a point all last season.

And then I delete it. This is not the time for our team to fall apart.

What team? I toss my phone onto my desk without replying to Cherrie. Two days ago, I had a team and a coach and a best friend who lived less than a mile from me. I had a shiny new A for my jersey, an off-season conditioning program and a lot to look forward to.

There's a knock from my open door. Trent leans on the door-frame, because apparently eighth-grade boys need something to hold them upright at all times.

"Coach Norman said to call him." Trent holds out his phone. News travels fast in a town where the biggest building is the ice rink.

"What for?" I realize I'm wiping my eyes yet again. They'll be permanently raw.

He smirks. "We need a backup goalie and you look like you could pass for a thirteen-year-old boy."

"Ha ha." I could *not* pass for a thirteen-year-old boy. I shower too often.

"Just call him. It won't fix anything but it'll make you feel better."

I could use a Coach Norman pep talk. He coached me when I was Trent's age. He's the best coach I've ever had. His practices are actually fun and he treats his players like they're real humans, not just hockey players or kids. Or girls.

He's also really hot and young (-er than my parents at least). I still have a major crush on him. Sadly, Coach Norman has a gorgeous girlfriend his own age and gives me noogies through my helmet.

I take Trent's phone, with Coach Norman's number on the screen.

"Hey, I need that," he says. "Use your own phone."

"You gave it to me."

"Yeah, to get his number."

I tighten my grip on the phone. "Get out. I'll give your phone back when I'm done."

Instead he flops onto my bed and rubs his sock feet on my pillow.

I push the number to dial from Trent's phone. "I'm telling

Coach to give you sprints at practice. Russian circles. Backwards. I know you loooooove those."

"Like you loooooove Coach." But he lifts his feet from my pillow and sits like a normal human being at the foot of my bed.

Coach answers. "Manning, what's up?"

"Hey, Coach."

"Did I not kick your butt around the rink enough at practice?"

"Um, it's not Trent."

"Mich! Make sure you tell your brother he sounds just like you."

I look over at my brother, who scowls. He'll be talking like Vader for the next week. I do feel a tiny bit better already.

"Well, this sucks, doesn't it?" Coach says. "What's your plan?"

"I'm thinking of taking up knitting."

"I could use a sweater."

"I might only be up to scarves by Christmas."

"So I guess this means you're hanging up the skates."

The framed team picture on my desk catches my eye. I can barely stand to look at Brie next to me in the back row, both of us proudly wearing our green-and-gold jerseys. We would have been at the center of the team, in the place of honor, at this year's team picture. And the next year's. Two years of my life have been taken from me.

I sigh. "I don't have much of a choice."

"Well, what are your choices?" Coach asks.

"I wasn't kidding. I have no options. Principal pulled my team out from under me. Closest school team is an hour away, and four of my teammates took their last roster spots because my parents said no. Don't have the money for tuition at a fancy private school like Brie, unless you want to spot me fifty grand. And that's it. I'm out."

I feel his empathy through the phone. "I'm sorry, Mich."

"Want a forward? I'm quick on the draw and I cycle fast."

"Absolutely. You're hired. Just drop three years from your age."

"So, hang a half-naked Selena Gomez poster in my room and obsessively check my chin for hair growth in the mirror?"

Coach laughs again. "You been stalking me, Michigan?"

Well, hell, I do need a new hobby.

"How about a consolation prize?" he says.

"What's that?"

"I can take one more assistant coach on my bench. Come coach with me."

With my finger, I trace an X over Brie on our team picture. Over the swimmers. The Silver Lake girls. The early retirees. My own photo is the only one left, hanging on to nothing, all by myself.

Or I could spend my afternoons yelling at eighth-grade boys. "I'm in."

*

"You're my new coach?!" Trent uses his hip to block me from the bathroom sink. Our nightly ritual. Morning ritual. Anytime-either-of-us-needs-something-from-the-bathroom ritual.

I manage to get my fingertips on the toothpaste and slide it across the blue tile. "Ha!"

Trent digs in to his stance, angling his body between me and my toothbrush. "How 'bout I'll actually listen to you at practice if you let me have the bathroom first?"

I plant my bare feet firmly on the linoleum and sink my weight into my lower body. "How 'bout I won't make you do extra push-ups if you let me get my toothbrush?"

"Only way you're getting that toothbrush is if you push me out of the way."

So I do. It takes longer than I'd like to admit and we're both panting and red-faced, but I win. For once this week.

*

Saturday morning. Departure day for Brie. It's a seven-hour drive to get to Chicago, six if Mr. Hampton lets Brie drive. She'll stay at a hotel with her parents tonight and they'll move her into her dorm room tomorrow morning. She's going to have a roommate and a new team and a bathroom she won't have to check her way into when she needs to pee.

It's a brutal goodbye. There's crying and Kleenex and croaked promises. And yet, somehow, there's excitement. On Brie's part. Me, I've got nothing. Except a long trek home by my car-less self.

As I walk past the high school, I'm drawn to the closed-off pool. It's not an area I go by often. It's attached to the farthest edge of the school, an afterthought by the building committee back in the days when education regularly included things besides math and language arts. I took swim lessons there when I was younger, but I've spent more time in pads than swimsuits in the last eight years.

I wonder if the pool looks as empty and lonely as I feel.

A ragged chain-link fence runs the perimeter of the building, with yellow construction tape hanging from it in uneven swags. One whole wall is missing, offering a glimpse inside the natatorium. The pool is empty of water but filled with construction debris. Black lane lines jut up through piles of drywall and cinder blocks, all covered with a thick layer of dust. Straight across from the hole is the wall I'd remembered, painted green with large gold varsity letters proclaiming it the home of the Owl River Muskrats. The gold threads no longer sparkle under the construction dust, and wires dangle in front of the pennants. The list of titles won spans the years back to 1968, but the longest stretch of pennants is at the most recent end of the wall. They almost all belong to Jack Ray.

It is exactly as empty as I feel.

But not as lonely. The chain-link fence dips forward as hands grip it next to mine. Jack Ray leans over the metal rail, his eyes on the wreckage.

It doesn't matter that we've never been introduced. That we've never spoken. He's an ally. "They didn't even take your pennants down," I say.

He shrugs. "They're just pieces of cloth."

"Where do you swim now?"

"I'm lucky," he says. "I've been with a regional club for years. I train with a private coach over at the university or the Rec Center. I just swam here because I liked the guys. It gets lonely training by yourself."

"You *are* lucky."

"So that was all true about you guys having nowhere to play?" He looks at me, and I feel concern coming from this stranger.

Concern that I wish my parents had shown. Or Brie's parents. Even Brie.

I nod. "Yep."

He turns back to the empty pool. "If I didn't have a team or a pool, I'd still have to swim. I'd jump in a lake if I had to. Guess it doesn't work that way with hockey."

"I like skating outside. But you can't play a real game without a team."

"True. It wouldn't be as fun if I never got to race."

"What was — is — your event?"

"Mostly freestyle sprints."

I nod; I do know what that means.

"One hundred and two hundred fly. Two hundred IM occasionally. Free relay and medley relay whenever I can."

"OK, now you lost me." But that explains the plethora of pennants on the wall.

"I hear Laura's recruiting former hockey players for the girls' swim team." I don't miss the hint of bitterness in his tone. It's how I feel when I see the male hockey players wearing their team jackets in the school hallway.

"Yeah, but she was smart enough not to invite me."

He squints at me, his face relaxing almost to a smile. "You can swim, right?"

"Well enough to tread water until a lifeguard gets to me. You can skate, right?"

"Well enough to … aw, who am I kidding. But I'm not afraid to fall."

Oh, dear Lord, that smile. Please tell me that was flirting because I am swooning hard. I always knew Jack was crush-worthy, with his dark hair and matching eyes and what could be assumed, from his swimming statistics, to be a solid swimmer's body under that hoodie. Added benefit: I've never seen him act like a buffoon in the school hallways.

But mostly this conversation is the first time all week I've felt like someone was on my side. Even my own team doesn't seem to understand what I'm going through. What we're supposed to be going through together.

"Brie — Gabrielle Hampton, my best friend, from hockey —"

"I know who she is."

"Yeah, she's kind of hard to miss."

He does this eyebrow-lift head-nod thing that conveys I've got that right.

I sigh. "She left this morning. Like thirty minutes ago. To play for a private school in Chicago." My throat tightens again.

His head droops. "I'm sorry, Michigan."

And he knows my name. My inner cheerleader does a few high kicks and shakes her pompoms. The roller coaster of emotions over Brie leaving and Jack arriving has me so dizzy I'll never walk straight again.

"Are you thinking of going, too?" he asks.

I snort. "At twenty-five grand a year? Who has that kind of money?"

"Geez, that's worse than most colleges."

"Yeah. If her dad thinks fifty grand is going to finally buy Brie an A, he's mistaken —" I swallow the end of my sentence. Trashing my best friend and she's barely out of town. *Well done, Mich.* "Anyway, no private schools for me. I'm going to help coach my brother's bantam team instead."

"If you're good enough to coach boys, why don't you go out for the guys' team here?"

"Oh! No. I mean, we all joked about it the other day. But no, it's a different game. Girls don't check."

"But you're wearing all that padding, right? So you must be used to some kind of hitting."

"Oh, yeah. There's plenty of physical contact. And we hit the ice hard sometimes. Checking is more of a strategic thing."

"So learn."

"I doubt they'd let me play."

"You don't know unless you ask."

"I'm sure they'd say no if I asked."

Jack flashes a full smile that paralyzes me. "Then don't ask."

4

Walking into the rink is bittersweet. Walking into the rink next to my brother, pubescent stink wafting off his hockey bag, well, that part just sucks ass.

At least I still have my home rink. At least it's not a pile of rubble like Jack's pool.

Although an outsider might not agree with me. The Owl River Community Ice ain't The Joe. A handful of the low-hanging lights burned out sometime in my youth and haven't been replaced yet, leaving a couple of dim spots on the ice. It smells musty in here, too, especially on the damper days in springtime. And the locker rooms are fricking freezing.

But it's the same faded green carpet and yellowed bleachers that my friends and I played tag on while Dad's P.D. buddies played against the fire department. The familiar buzz of the old scoreboard, the Say No to Chew poster in the locker room hallway, permanently flecked with — of course — chew stains. The spot on the home bench where Brie's sophomore-year boyfriend Daniel etched his initials. When they broke up, she and I sneaked a bottle of purple nail polish onto the bench and painted over them.

This will always be home. Even though home is currently overrun with belching bantams.

Today is only tryouts for the season. The boys will get split into two teams, AAA and AA. They'll start real practices next week. Coach Norman wants me in half-pads so I can demonstrate drills safely, which is the most on-ice action I'm going to see this season. I push into the women's restroom with my bag.

"Oh!" I start to back out of the one-seater bathroom. There's a half-dressed girl sitting on the floor, taping up her shin pads. "Sorry. Didn't realize anyone was in here."

She shrugs her blond hair over one shoulder and unwinds a roll of pink tape around her pad. "No worries. I'll be done in a minute."

"OK if I throw some pads on?"

"Of course. I don't care if you see my sports bra."

"Ditto." I'm used to sharing not only a locker room but also a shower room with my entire team. Modesty left us back in junior high. I know exactly who has the biggest boobs, who has the paunchiest tummy and who I'll never share a razor with because I know where it's been.

I pull down my warm-ups to shove shin pads into my pant legs. My mind is on Coach Norman's practice agenda, on how good it feels to breathe the cold damp air of the rink again. I'm admiring my shiny new whistle when something occurs to me. "Wait. Are you trying out for bantams?"

The girl looks at me like I'm a moron. "Well, I'm not here for figure skating practice."

I grin. "No, you are not. I don't remember seeing a girl on Trent's team before."

"I'm new to town."

"You're not going out for the U14 girls' team?"

"I checked out their practice. They're kind of a lot younger than me." She shrugs. "It's OK. I've always played with guys."

That's the non-ego way of saying *I'm too good.* I'm curious to see how she fares out there. Best of luck to her. If she doesn't gag on their stench, she'll be fine.

We don't even get through warm-ups before the first idiot makes a comment to me. While leading team stretches, I instruct the boys — and one ballsy girl — on a frog stretch.

"Ooh, Mich," Trent's best friend moans. "Just like that. That feels so good!"

I get to my feet, stride over to him and look down. "Start pushing."

"I'm kidding! It's a compliment, Mich."

"Ten push-ups. Now. Or it goes up to fifteen. And that's Coach Manning to you." So cool. I've always wanted to say that.

As the kid drops to his gloves, the team counts aloud, giggling into their facemasks. Coach Norman nods approvingly in my direction.

The girl is good. I realize I wanted her to be. I wanted her to come out and rise above their crap and outskate them and out-skill them and she does it. She completely kills tryouts.

"Do you think we'll get to share a locker room with Megan?" Trent asks, as I drive us home in Mom's car. Making a note to hang an extra tree off the rearview mirror because one is not going to cut it for Trent's bag this season.

"Definitely not."

"Do you think she'll smash us if we hit on her?"

"Definitely yes."

Coach Norman didn't even hesitate to put Megan on the AAA team. The guys are thrilled she's there. Whether that has to do with her gorgeous blond hair or her gorgeous wrist shot, I don't know.

*

I'm antsy this evening and a long list of math problems is not holding my attention.

My mind keeps returning to the ice. I wasn't even playing tonight, just demonstrating drills. But I desperately craved the opportunity to demonstrate one more drill so I could take another shot, dish another pass, let my heart race against my feet on another sprint. I'm like a dog who gets a whiff of barbecue from the neighbor's yard and paces the fence hoping for another whiff, even though there's no chance someone'll drop a burger on my side.

My phone is maddeningly silent. Nothing from Brie for two days now. I texted her about tryouts earlier, but I guess her fancy new boarding school is more interesting than eighth-grade boys. Shocker.

A run is what I need, although it's not like I have anything to train for. My mom will give me hell about homework if she sees me slip out, but by this time she's usually zoned out in front of the Lifetime channel, dulling the pain of another day in a job she hates, in a town she hates even more. I bang around in the laundry room a bit, pretending to look for something, before sneaking out the back door.

The sky is turning dusky; the sun is gone, but its remnants are enough to run by. I didn't bring music because nothing fit my mood: post-practice adrenaline plus post-team depression. Instead I listen to my breath, faster than it should be because I haven't been training properly in the last few weeks. And my solitary footprints, not as fast as they should be because I haven't been training properly in the last few weeks.

I wonder if Brie's running right now with her new team. If the Silver Lake defectors are running with their new team. Or lifting weights or even having a captain's practice. I wonder if Laura and the other swimmers are training right now, although I don't think swimmers do much running.

I'm not used to training on my own. I need to know that somewhere, someone else is running. Matching my pace, pushing me forward. Spotting me from a distance.

Of course they are running. They all have a season to prepare for, whether it's on frozen or chlorinated water. I'm the only one with no destination at the end of this run.

Swimmers make me think of Jack, and before I realize it, my feet have led me to the empty pool again. The open building gapes like a cavernous mouth in the twilight. I stop at the fence and replay our conversation.

Pathetic. I'm so pathetic, running at night by myself, swooning over a boy I barely know. I never would have done this before losing my team.

OK, I still would have swooned over a boy I barely know. But at least I'd be running with my best friend.

They didn't even take his pennants down. If they tore the rink down, I'd like to think someone would remove the ancient team trophies in the glass cases lining the lobby, tarnished and dusty as they are. Even if it's first place for the local beer league — a cheesy plastic skate glued to the front of a stein — someone worked for that trophy. I climb the fence, carefully lifting myself over the pokey metal fringe at the top. I drop to the ground and tiptoe through the pockmarked, debris-strewn site.

I make my way to the pennant wall, my sneakers crunching concrete pebbles into the tiled pool deck. I can just barely make out which pennants are Jack's. They're only cloth, he told me. They don't matter to him. Assmont can tear the building down, but he can't take away what Jack has already achieved.

There are no ladders or benches, but eventually I find a large cinder block — by stubbing my toe on it. I drag it, scraping loudly across the floor, to the base of the pennant wall. Stretching up from my tiptoes, I snag the only pennant I can reach. It pulls off easily. I step down, holding it away from my face to shake the dust off it.

Jack Ray, Michigan High School Athletic Association, 2017 U.P. Finals, 100 Freestyle, 42.68

Jack stood alone on a starting block, dived into the water and relied on no one but himself to push across the finish line before the other seven swimmers. He accomplished that.

Megan moved to town. She needed a hockey team. She tied her skates like a big girl, sitting on the floor of the women's bathroom without whining about it. She beat out at least half of those boys and earned her spot on the AAA team.

Cherrie was desperate to play. So she found a team. Di, Kara and Hanna were desperate to play. They jumped at the chance.

Brie … It hurts, but Brie got in that car and went. For the first time, she went without me. I've been part of a team for so long that maybe I've forgotten how to do something by myself.

I roll the pennant up and carry it home, jogging like a track athlete with a baton. At home, I open my hockey bag and slide the rolled pennant into my skate.

There's one high school hockey team left in this town. Tryouts are in two days. I'll be there.

5

What the fuck was I thinking?

Sign-ups should be the easiest part of getting on a school sports team. All we have to do is fill out a packet of paperwork. They even provide pens. The Athletics secretary hovers nearby, ready to help anyone who can't sign their own names or spell "hockey." Which, believe me, is a possibility with some of these guys.

But I am in the hallway, like a big huge wuss, peeking through the ajar doorway. The Athletic Office is crammed full of guys in team jackets. Talking smack to each other, inflating their stats and their skills. Strutting and posturing and turning their Yooper accents on thick like they do on the bench. It's stupid — I played with a couple of these guys all the way up to bantams. This is just what they do. No one actually believes that Carson Reilly had four points in a single game last year.

I did. But that was girls' hockey and everyone here would laugh me off the ice if I brought it up.

So I wait until they've all turned in their paperwork and sauntered out of the Athletic Office. I dart in, grab a packet from the secretary's desk and hide in the nearest bathroom. I fill out my paperwork on the laminate counter, smearing the corners of the pages in the soapy puddles of water around the sink.

I abbreviate my name on the forms. M. Manning. It's a small school and I assume Coach Henson knows most of the girls from my team, at least by the names on the backs of our jerseys. But there's no reason to draw attention to myself.

Right. I'll show up at tryouts, make the team and then — ta-da! — pull off my helmet, and my long brown hair will cascade forth and no one will care. I don't even know if it's legal for me to play on the boys' team. If it's against league rules or school rules or Assmont rules.

Then don't ask, Jack had said. Excellent advice.

When the coast is clear, I slip my paperwork into the middle of the stack in the office and run like hell.

*

For tryouts, I wear a plain black jersey and plain white hockey socks nabbed from Dad's hockey bag instead of my green-and-gold-striped team socks or my team practice jersey. I scrub my face clean of makeup and spend forty-five minutes on a complicated braid that will fit completely under my helmet. Actually have to refit my helmet to get it on.

Also, if I ever get asked to prom, I'm definitely doing the same hairstyle. Too bad it'll be wasted under a helmet tonight.

Since I'm the only girl here, the rink manager wouldn't let

me use a full locker room. And someone's mom was hogging the women's restroom. But the manager did unlock a broom closet for me to change in. I counted three spiders.

So here I sit, my cute braids smashed under my helmet, listening to the faint sounds of male laughter drifting through the walls from the guys' locker rooms on either side of me. They get two locker rooms to accommodate the full tryout roster while I dodge spiders and try not to notice what's floating in the dirty water of the mop bucket.

I've been playing hockey since I was six. I have now coached three bantam practices and have zero problem showing up those boys when necessary. Which is frequently.

Pre-game butterflies are normal for me, but today there are dragons brawling in my gut. I have no idea what to expect out here. I can't order these guys to do push-ups if they make a rude comment. If I get laughed off the ice ... well, I guess it's a good thing I didn't tell anyone I'm here. Not Brie, who has only texted three lousy lines in the last week. Not my former teammates, who are busy with their new activities. Not Jack, who's given me seven adorably sexy smiles in the hallway at school. Not my parents, who would definitely flip if they found out about this.

I peek out the door. The Zamboni machine is still circling the ice. I'll wait until everyone's out there and then sneak onto the ice before anything gets started. Blend in, lie low.

"Coach?" asks a girl's voice. There's another girl here? My head whips around.

It's Megan. Standing in the hallway, shifting a pile of clipboards, with a bucket of pucks at her feet.

"You recognized me?" Not *Hi, Megan!* Not *What are you doing here?* But *Oh, shit, I'm recognizable.*

"I'd recognize your stick anywhere." She gestures to the butt end, which is wrapped in neon pink tape. Wow. I'm sure all the guys have Barbie-pink tape on their stick handles. *Way to blend in, Manning.*

"It's so great that you're trying out," she says.

"Yeah," I snort. "That remains to be seen."

She reshuffles the clipboards. "No, no. You've got this. I've seen you skate at my practices and that was only half speed. I've watched a lot of tape on these guys, and believe me, they're not as skilled as you."

"You've watched their tape? Are you a manager or something?"

"Unofficially. My stepdad's the coach."

No. Way. "So you really think I can keep up?"

She cocks her head and a blond curl tips out from behind her ear. "Haven't you ever seen them play?"

"Of course. I go to all their home games if we're not playing."

Duh. I mentally smack myself on the helmet. I do know how these guys play. Not only did I play with some of them as a kid, but I've watched them. Sat in the bleachers with my girls and pointed out every mistake they made, as if we'd do better ourselves.

And I can. They're a dump-and-chase-and-collide kind of offense and I'm a cycle-until-you-have-a-chance kind of forward. There's a good possibility I do have better hands, better eyes than most of them.

The problem is that I'm used to playing with teammates who skated the puck well and passed a lot. I know I'm not going to be able to rely on these guys. I'll have to do it myself.

"They'll have size, strength and stride length on you," Megan says, as if she's been following my mental path.

"So I'll have to be quick." Quick feet, quick on the draw, quick on the turnover.

"And smart."

I nod. Look for the open ice. Pick my opportunities. Don't barrel in.

Behind us, the rink manager scrapes the last bit of snow off the ice. Boys will be pouring out of the locker rooms any second now. I step back toward my broom closet. "I'm just gonna —"

"Uh-uh," Megan says, with an awfully knowing smirk for a thirteen-year-old. She points to the rink. "First on the ice."

I can't shrink back now. This kid skated confidently onto this same sheet of ice only a week ago, one girl in a sea of eighth-grade boys. Lead weights attach to my skates, but I force them forward to the rink door. First one on the ice.

It's the same smooth white sheet I've known all my life. The same blue face-off dot at center ice. The same scratched red goal-posts and nets patched with bits of skate lace. This is my home ice. I've won a helluva lot of battles here.

I'll do it again.

*

There are whispers up and down the goal line that some freshman puked in the locker room while getting dressed. I think I might have gotten a whiff from the kid next to me, but I don't dare look at him to see if he's nervous or pale. I keep my facemask pointed at the ice as we skate through the warm-up.

If he is the puker, it works for him. He's the only one who beats me back to the line.

"Nice, dude," he says, knocking my glove with his.

I make the mistake of looking up.

"Whoa," he says. "You're not a dude." He sounds impressed, but he still backs away. On the next whistle, he returns to the line three players down from me, whispering to his buddies. Ugh, at least attempt subtlety, boys.

By the time warm-ups are finished, there's so much empty ice around me that I could swing my stick in a circle and not hit anyone. Even though I'd like to. Hope Puke Breath is making you all gag.

I'm here to make the team, not make friends. I focus on skating, on digging hard into each stride. On battling for every puck and every piece of real estate in front of the net. If I'd played like this on my old team, I would have had to kick my own ass for being a puck hog. But it seems to be the norm here in Boy Land. And when in Rome, right? Besides, if they're all going to stare at me, might as well give them something to see. Hopefully, Coach Henson sees me, too.

When Coach calls us in for a water break, there's a four-foot radius around me, like I'm contagious. The only one who breaks it is Megan, who brings me a fresh water bottle when I drain mine. I'm trying hard not to look at the cluster at the opposite end of the bench. Sucks that I'm the odd woman out, but if I make the team, they'll get used to me.

Megan gives me a reassuring tap on my helmet and takes a water bottle to her stepdad. I hear her say, quite loudly, "Did you see Manning on that back-check?"

"Nice wheels," he replies. My heart soars.

I have to admit, it's the best I've ever played. I'm so high I don't know if my skates will ever hit ice again.

The real test is still to come. Our first tryout was a ninety-minute practice ending at nine. Round two is at 5:00 tomorrow morning.

After practice, I attempt a Superman-fast change of clothes in my phone-booth-slash-broom-closet. I plan on being the first one out of the rink so I don't have to face any more of the glares I got on the ice.

I know, I know. I skated like the bomb tonight. I should hold my head up and walk out of here like I own the place. But when you're The Girl, one good skate doesn't earn you balls.

When I hustle out of my broom closet, Megan is leaning against the concrete wall. She pushes herself off and hands me a Gatorade. "Hydrate," she says. "Straight to bed."

"Yes, Coach." I open the Gatorade and chug half of it while Megan grins with pride. "So," I say, shouldering my bag, "any strategy for the morning?"

"It's going to hurt," she says. "Just survive it."

Sounds like a good plan.

6

I tiptoe in the back door, through the laundry room, to avoid questions about where I've been and if I remembered to put gas in Mom's car after borrowing it. It's well before curfew, so as long as I make enough noise upstairs to alert my parents to my presence, there's no reason for them to leave their *Twin Peaks* reruns to check for me.

After easing the squeaky back door shut, I race up the stairs and into a hot shower. Wolf down a peanut-butter-and-banana sandwich. Guzzle enough water to pee lemonade-yellow … but not so much that I'll have to do so in the middle of the night. Into bed by ten.

Up at four. The alarm on my phone is painful enough, and I haven't even hit the ice yet.

Hot chocolate and another peanut butter sandwich for breakfast on the way to the rink. Five-minute jog around the pitch-black parking lot to burn off the lactic acid in my quads. Fortunately, don't get eaten by a moose. Then I push the wheely mop bucket and the janitor's cart against the wall of my closet so I have room to stretch my legs before getting dressed. I laid my gear out before bed, so at least it's dry. There is nothing worse than cold, clammy gear at five in the morning. I'd rather get eaten by the moose.

Last item on my to-do list: AC/DC's "Thunderstruck" at full blast in my earbuds. Now I'm awake.

The small windows over the bleachers are pitch-black. Not even a thin line of light breaking the eastern horizon. Puffs of steam leak from my facemask as I skate to the bench to see what torture Coach has planned for this morning.

Megan huddles in a puffy coat and knit hat behind Coach, leaning her chin on his jacketed shoulder. I think she's trying to prove she's hardcore hockey by being here, but her sleepy eyes droop as she follows the drill Coach is drawing out on the posi board. When he sets his travel coffee mug on the bench, she clutches it in her mittened hands. She sniffs it warily, then takes a gulp. Her eyes go big and she squeaks. Coach laughs, hands her a Gatorade bottle and nudges her shoulder until she laughs, too. Feeling intrusive, I coast to the far end of the bench and set my water bottle on the boards. Pretend to stretch out until Coach's whistle brings us to center ice.

Coach gives the patented speech that all head coaches buy off the internet and practice in front of their mirrors. "This is where we separate the men from the boys. If you want to make this team, you will give me 110 percent for the next ninety minutes. It is third period of a tied game, men. Can you dig deep when it hurts? Can you rise above the pain?"

Can you not be a sports cliché?

Minute 1: I'm feeling good. Ready to go.

Minute 15: OK, yeah, I skated hard yesterday. I feel that now.

Minute 30: There it is — tired.

Minute 45: Halfway. Halfway there.

Minute 60: Quads screaming. Feet aching. Mind numb. But I wasn't the first puker. I swallowed it down and kept my feet under me.

Minute 75: Keep your feet moving. Keep your feet moving. Fall. Polish the ice with my ass. Get up. Keep your feet moving.

Minute 80: Coach is a sadistic, fucking asshole.

Minute 85: There's no way that clock is working properly.

Minute 90: It doesn't stop.

That's right. He keeps going. You can feel the air whoosh out of the rink when thirty-two skaters realize that practice is not ending when he said it would.

We keep skating. I consider screaming that my name is Mike Eruzione and I play for the United States of America to see if that will make it stop. But I don't have enough breath.

We're running a forecheck and everyone's sluggish and tired. Including me. No one's skating the puck, they're dishing ugly passes or dumping the puck in hopes of an opportunity to skate backwards for a change. Clearing the zone with long shots that would never fly in a game. Coach has used every four-letter word in the book to express his displeasure. The defense are passing back and forth behind the net, arguing about who has to start the breakout, when I get sick of their crap.

On my girls' team, Coach taught us, when you're tired, when you're beat, you touch a teammate. God only knows what these guys would make of that. But it always worked. You may not have breath, but you all don't have breath together. A tap of the stick on a shin guard, a gloved fist bump. It gives you that extra push to keep going. Brie and I used to tap our helmets together when we were too gassed to tell each other "good shift."

I have no intention of touching any one of these guys. But I look to the bench and I see Megan. She's holding her stepdad's clipboard and leaning one foot against the boards, her elbows on her knees. Her eyes are on me, waiting for me to live up to her expectations, to follow the trail she blazed.

I wonder what Jack thinks about when he's swimming, when he's surrounded by water and his own thoughts.

He thinks about his sport. He focuses on his stroke, his pace. He wills his muscles to stay in rhythm, to push through the numb feeling.

My legs are weak, but when I tell my knees to lift, they wobble into obedience. I accelerate and charge the defenseman with the puck. He hesitates, not expecting me to challenge their breakout attempt. But I'm done waiting on him. Waiting on any of these boys. They may be able to afford complacency, but I am fully aware that The Girl will never get a day off. Not if I want to make this team.

I have to make this team. Unlike these guys, I have no other options.

I swoop behind the net. The D fumbles his sweep up the boards and I beat him to it because I am the only person on this rink whose feet are still in motion. Guarding the puck with my body, I curl back toward the goal. My shot tips off the goalie's blocker and into the crease. I rebound my own shot and freeze for a split second with the puck at the tip of my blade. Because you always have more time than you think you do. My hesitation pays off, and the goalie's sideways momentum carries him an inch too far. I flip the puck at the empty space where his left shoulder was a split second before.

I'm pushed to the ice by a defenseman, but it's too late to be anything but a gesture. My puck already sits on the ice, well behind the goal line.

"You were supposed to pressure the puck." The captain, Daniel, stands over me.

I have too much adrenaline from scoring to check my mouth. "You were supposed to play defense," I answer. Yeah, maybe it was a dick move to push that far with not only a shot but a rebound. But it's not my fault the D get lazy when they're tired.

I'm off balance, still getting to my feet, when he cross-checks my shoulder again. My feet skitter and my stick flails but I don't fall. He cross-checks my shoulder a third time, despite the short blast from the assistant coach's whistle.

From behind his plexiglass facemask, Daniel aims a glare that would wither anyone who didn't just score off her own rebound. I outskated him and he knows it. I set my face and stare him down, willing my tired legs to hold strong if he pressures me again.

Coach Henson blows his whistle. "Leave it, Manning."

I don't unclench — I'd bet my roster spot Daniel's still looking to knock me on my ass. It's bullshit that Coach doesn't call him out. But there's no use arguing my case against the veteran captain of the team. I can't look like a troublemaker. With a strong C-cut, I push back from Daniel.

"To the goal line, boys. We'll finish up with a little skate," Coach hollers. I hustle to the goal line. The boys around me groan as they coast to a stop. This is going to hurt. We all know it. Coach knows it. This is the separate-the-men-from-the-boys part.

Lucky for me, I'm all girl.

The whistle sends us skating, over and over again. Sweat gushes out of me, dripping into my eyes. I blink it away and pretend I'm in a swimming pool, submerged in the water. I block out the sounds and the motions around me. Concentrate on the muscle contractions that will push me forward. Remind myself not to get sloppy because I'm tired. Knees low. Don't swing your arms to the side. Extend your stride. Flick your ankle. I think I'd be a good swimmer after all.

I don't pay attention to the other skaters until I realize I've crossed the finish line before almost all of them.

Coach circles us at center ice. "Thank you for coming out, gentlemen. I will post the varsity roster on my office door Monday morning, fifteen minutes before the first bell. If you make varsity, you will attend team meeting Monday afternoon and start practice the following evening. Freshmen and sophomores, if you do not make varsity, check Coach Winters's classroom door for the JV roster and practice schedule. Dismissed."

My legs barely get me off the ice and into my broom closet. As soon as the door slams shut behind me, I collapse on the dirty rubber floor.

And that's when I finally puke.

7

Maybe it's the rebellion of trying out for the boys' team behind my parents' backs. Maybe it's the proximity to apes, both at bantams and at tryouts, that makes me desperate to speak to an evolved male.

Maybe it's the braids. I did a modified version of my new hockey 'do this morning because I couldn't sleep wondering about the roster. I texted Brie a picture and she told me to F off because I woke her up. But she agreed they're cute.

Anyway, when I see Jack in the school parking lot, hopping out of the world's oldest Jeep Wagoneer, I don't slow my gait in hopes that he'll catch up to me. I don't converse loudly with the nearest acquaintance so that he'll notice me.

Obviously, what I do is pat my braids to make sure I don't have any tufts sticking out.

And then I walk right up to him. At which point it occurs to me that I have no clue if Jack has a girlfriend. Even if he does, I'm perfectly within my rights to say hello to a classmate.

Talking is fine. I just can't throw myself onto his lips. Bummer.

I'm nearly to his car when I realize I don't have a conversation starter. I am seconds away from standing like a statue in front of Jack Ray. Unless I blurt out something about the weather or comment that his beat-up old Wagoneer looks nice. Which would kill any chance of coming off as clever or interesting. But if I turn around and he sees me walking away, he'll wonder why I was ten feet from his car and didn't say hi. Or — worse — he'll realize that I turned around because I have a crush on him and I'm a big huge wuss.

If I'm brave enough to take a hit from Daniel Maclane, I'm brave enough to initiate a conversation with Jack Ray.

Right?

He looks up and sees me.

"Hi, Jack," I say. And that's as far as I get. Because those deep, dark eyes paralyze my larynx. And because it turns out he's on the phone.

He smiles and holds up a finger to me. "OK, Mom. I got it. I'll call you then. OK. OK, I gotta go." He ducks his chin to the side and lowers his voice. "I love you, too, Mom. Bye."

Oh, my God, he just got cuter.

His cheeks are pink and I doubt it's from the unseasonably warm morning sun. "Hey, Mich. Sorry about that. It's impossible to get off the phone with her."

I can't help smiling at him.

"What's your first class?" he asks. "I'll walk you."

"World history. But I'm not headed there yet. I actually have to ..." I shift my backpack and check out the color of the parking lot asphalt. Dirty gray with stringy blue bubblegum. "Um ...

I tried out. For the guys' team. This weekend. And Coach is posting the roster on his door this morning." I peek at Jack's face to see if his judgment matches that of the guys at tryouts.

Jack's eyes light up. "Superwoman!" He slams his car door shut and holds his hand up for a high five. I answer with a tap, but instead of dropping his hand, he grabs mine and heads in the direction of the school. "How can you stand waiting? Let's go!"

I laugh and let him tug on my hand. Because I like it. A lot. I curl my fingers around his. "The thing is, I'm not sure I want you to see me puke if I make it or cry if I don't."

He squeezes harder and pulls me toward the school entrance. "I'm washable, I swear. Feel free to puke."

HE DOESN'T LET GO OF MY HAND. All the way to Coach's office. I feel him look at me twice but I don't know what to do if I look back at him, so instead I picture the roster hanging on Coach's door. I'll never know exactly which it is that's making my stomach do flips this morning.

It's almost first bell by the time we arrive. There's a sheet of white paper taped to the middle of Coach's door, and there are already three guys standing around it. I shrink back. There's no way I will do this in front of my competition.

"Come on," Jack urges.

One of the boys rears back and punches the wall next to Coach's door. It's that indestructible concrete-type material, so it doesn't give, but he continues to emit a low growl as he charges down the hallway. One of his friends follows, his head hanging low.

Jack's arm is flung out in front of me, holding me back. Like I was going to breeze on up to the door while the kid's fist was still clenched. I raise my eyebrows at Jack and he grins sheepishly as he lowers his arm.

"Just in case the hockey girl needs backup from a swimmer," he says. "We're tougher than we look."

Just. Adorable. How does he do it?

The last boy remains at Coach's door, scanning the list until a slow smile spreads over his face. After sneaking a peek at his retreating friends, he runs off in the opposite direction.

"All clear now?" Jack asks.

I nod. "That had to hurt like hell. I can't believe he didn't break something."

"Maybe he did. My X-ray vision isn't working this morning."

I roll my eyes at him. "Thank goodness."

He gives me a new grin, and this one sends tingles from the crown of my braids all the way through my toes. Then he nudges me toward the list, staying back about ten feet himself.

I walk up to the door, holding my breath. The list is in alphabetical order. My eyes slide through the last names. *B, C, G, G, J . . .*

The door opens. Coach Henson aims a grumpy look at me. "In my office, Manning."

Like he knew I was there. Apparently, his X-ray vision works just fine.

Oh, gross.

I glance over at Jack and we share a shrug. "Yes?" he mouths.

"Wait a sec, Coach," I say. "I didn't get a chance to look."

His index finger jabs the middle of the roster. *Manning, Michigan, F.*

I manage to swallow my laugh but I can't hide my grin. I did it. I got my hockey season back.

"Hustle, Manning." Coach disappears into his office, leaving the door open.

As I follow him inside, I aim a quick thumbs-up at Jack. His split-second fist-pump victory dance is the best thing I've ever seen.

Coach plops into his swivel chair and it bounces, thumping several times. "I can't not take you, Manning. You were easily in the top five at tryouts. You earned your spot. But I'm not happy about it."

"Uh, I'm sorry? Or, I mean, I ..." ... have no clue how to respond to that. *Thanks for feeling like you had to put me on your team even though you don't want me?*

There's a picture of Megan on his desk, standing in front of a woman who has to be her mom. She's Megan in twenty-five years. She has her arms around Megan and they're both laughing for the camera. I wonder if Coach was "not happy" when we put Megan on our team.

"You will change in a separate restroom."

"Of course." Ew. Seriously? He even thought ...???

"You'll sit in the front seat of the bus."

"OK." Will probably smell better there.

"You will not" — he waves a hand in the air — "date, or get involved with, whatever. No inappropriate interactions with any of the members of my team."

Excuse me? I am a member of his team. And what does he think I am, some puck-muff?

"I tried out for the team because I want to play hockey. Not date hockey players." I try to channel Brie's my-daddy-the-lawyer attitude. "I'm sure my parents will feel better knowing that the *entire* team will be held to such high standards."

He frowns. The first bell rings. He waves a hand toward the door.

"I set high academic standards as well. Get to class. I'll see you at team meeting this afternoon."

High academic standards, my butt. Cherrie tutored half the guys last year in remedial math. But he's got one thing right. I'll be at team meeting this afternoon.

I have a team.

8

I'm the first one at team meeting. Partly because I'm never late anywhere. And partly because the pressure is on to be the Perfect Rookie. Something tells me Henson would jump at any excuse to chop me.

Meeting is in a small classroom, lined with four long tables facing a wall taken up entirely by a huge whiteboard. I choose the table at the front of the "bus," just to be safe. But in the interest of not getting teased, I leave my note-taking implements in my backpack. For now.

They slump in. My new teammates.

"Uh, we got a meeting in here," one of the guys says.

I turn in my seat. His hat is on backward, barely controlling clumps of wavy brown hair. He's got like three layers of shirts on, and yet I can still see his boxer waistband peeking out.

Yeah, I think I'll be able to follow Coach's "no dating" rule just fine.

"I know," I say.

"Team manager," his friend hisses. I don't know how they could mistake my long, straight brown hair for Megan's blond waves. But whatever. When I knock his butt into next week at practice, he'll remember me.

Slowly, the room fills up. Except for my table. I stay facing forward, listening to the scraping of chairs and the rustle of clothes behind me.

"Dude, the chick made it," someone whispers.

"I can't wait to tell Max he got cut for a girl," another whispers back.

I jump as a short, skinny kid plops into the chair next to me. It's the starting goalie. He's a junior, too, a Canadian transplant who solidly backed the team after he moved here last fall. He pulls his black knit beanie off and strands of choppy sandy hair zing straight up with static electricity.

"Avery Gardiner," he says, holding his hand out to me.

"Michigan Manning."

"So you must be from California."

"Ha ha."

"Gardiner." We both look up. Daniel Maclane stands in front of Avery, his arms crossed. Again, I wonder how Coach could ever think I'd be tempted to have "inappropriate interactions" with his team. Daniel's dirt-brown hair could use a cut, his stubbly chin could use a shave and his T-shirt could use an iron. I'll give Brie this: Daniel Maclane looked a lot sharper when he lived by her standards.

He makes eye contact with Avery and points to the back of the room. "Move. Go sit next to Breaker."

"Aw, man, he smells bad." But Avery gets up and moves

anyway. "Nice to meet you, Michigan," he calls over his shoulder.

Daniel shoots me a quick frown before following his goalie to the tables behind me. *Sure, pretend you didn't date my best friend for three months last year. Pretend we didn't double-date like half a dozen times. Pretend we didn't play mites and squirts together.* What kind of captain acts like that?

What kind of captain moves six hours away and leaves her best friend to sit alone at the front of the room?

Stop that, Michigan. You earned that A. Act like it.

Coach strides to the whiteboard. His presence in the room has the same effect as pushing a mute button. "Gentlemen! Congratulations on making my varsity team, men." He hesitates a split second as his eyes land on me but doesn't amend his word choice. He hands a cardboard box to Daniel. "Phones. Toss 'em in." Daniel walks the aisles, collecting each player's phone. He stops in front of me last. I set my phone in the box. The sequined Red Wings case looks especially garish on top of a pile of black, blue and even camo-colored phones.

Coach hands Daniel a heavy ring of keys. "Put that in my office. You'll get 'em back after the meeting, boys. For the next two hours, I own every cell of your brain."

When Daniel returns, his new job is to pass out a billion sheets of paper to each guy. Game schedule, practice schedule, team fees, at least five sheets for our parents to sign to acknowledge that hockey is not chess and there will be checking involved.

And a long list of team rules.

"Each member of the team will dress appropriately for home games," Coach says. "We do not show up to the rink looking like hobos. Hair combed. No hat. Long-sleeved collared shirt with buttons. Slacks without wrinkles. And a tie. Every single" — he fixes me with a glare — "member of this team will wear a tie to the rink for home games."

Oh, for heaven's sake. Whatever. I'll bum one from Trent. Like Coach's poor fashion sense is going to chase me off.

"There is no drinking in season. Do I need to repeat that? There is no drinking in season. If I find out that you have been drinking — and yes, I do know how to use Instagram — you'll be benched. Even cut, if I think that's warranted. Same goes for drug use of any kind."

He points at me. "Stand up, Manning."

My muscles stall, hoping he'll change his mind. Coach glares at me, daring me to disobey and be The Girl who got cut six hours after making the team.

I stand.

"Turn and face the room."

I confront my new team. Every single one of them is smart enough to hold a poker face.

"This is a girl. She's on the team this year. There will be no relations with her. I don't care who you crush on at this school. Who you make out with in the library or give your letter jacket to. But it will not be this girl. Any questions?"

One of the seniors, a known man-whore, raises his hand. "What if I accidentally fall and catch myself on her boo —"

"I'm not joking, Breaker. Do not test me on this, boys."

I'll knee your balls into your throat is what will happen. My face is burning with embarrassment but I still aim a glare in his direction.

Without looking at me, Coach says, "Sit, Manning."

Happily.

"Good puppy," Daniel hisses somewhere behind me. The entire room stifles laughs. Coach ignores them, flipping to the page that details his "high academic standards."

Thus concludes the single most humiliating moment of my life.

*

The meeting runs over two hours between Coach's rules and a long chalk talk to get us ready for tomorrow's practice. I'm starving and I've got loads of homework that has to get done tonight because I'll be juggling bantam practice with my own tomorrow night. And for the next four months.

Of course, Daniel gives my phone back last so I have to wait around while he empties the rest of the box. The other guys slump or strut or stumble out of the room and I get that deliberate don't-look-at-the-chick feeling from every one of them. Fine, so they need to go gossip among themselves. I'm sure after one or two practices, it'll stop being a big deal that the person next to them on the bench is wearing a sports bra.

Daniel hands my phone back with a smirk. I snatch it and run out of the room, expecting a million "where have you been" texts from Mom. I'll call her while I jog home.

But instead of a list of Mom texts, there is a topless, string-bikinied Playboy-type model on my screen. My new wallpaper has an airbrushed bikini region, a fake tan, and wow — with an endowment like that, it's no wonder she can't find a bra that fits.

Classy, Daniel. What a born leader and a role model for all young men. If he really wanted to scare me off the team he'd have sent a picture of Coach in that — ew. I shake the image out of my head. Just, no.

The house smells like pizza. My stomach rumbles as I step inside.

"Where have you been?" Mom demands. "I've been calling you for hours."

"I'm sorry, my phone is all messed up." *Please do not ask to see it.*

"And it didn't occur to you to let me know?"

"I'm sorry, I would have called if I thought you were worried."

"Set the table, please."

I pass around the plastic placemats and paper napkins. Pull a handful of forks from the drawer for the iceberg lettuce that the pizza joint calls a salad.

"Get your brother, please."

"Trenton!" I holler.

Mom frowns. "I could have done that."

But she didn't.

Trent slides into home plate. "Dibs on meat-lovers'!"

"You don't get it all." I block his path to the box with my hip. He digs in. I dig in harder. Dad swipes the box up over our heads.

"I got some stuff you guys have to sign," I say, reaching for a slice of plain cheese. I like it better than meat-lovers'; I just fight with Trent because I can.

"What'd you do?" Mom whips her head up from her phone, ready to throw down some grounding.

"Geez, nothing. It's for hockey."

Dad swallows fast and leans forward eagerly. "They reinstate your team?"

"No. I, uh" — I sneak a glance at Trent — "I made the guys' team instead."

"Whoa!" Trent drops his pizza back on the plate. "Seriously? That's awesome." He holds a greasy hand up for a high five.

Braver, I smile and slap his hand. "It *is* awesome. Thanks."

"Mich! Wow! Good job!" Dad says, using more exclamation points than in the rest of his life combined. "Any of the other girls make it?"

"No. I was the only one who tried out."

"How's the rest of the team look? When do you start practices? You'll have to get me a copy of the game schedule so I can arrange my shifts around it. This is great, kid."

"Thanks, Dad. I've got the schedule in my bag."

Mom's mouth is puckered to one side. "You should have talked to us about this."

"Isn't that what we're doing now?"

"You know exactly what I mean. I don't like this."

"Why?"

"Because you are five foot six. One hundred twenty-five pounds. They're going to knock you down and run you over."

"I was one of the fastest skaters at tryouts. But thanks for the vote of confidence."

Dad humphs with a mouthful of pizza. Translation: *I'm supposed to reprimand you for sassing your mom.*

"Well, someone's eventually going to catch you," Mom persists. "And it's going to hurt."

"Mich isn't that easy to push around, Mom," Trent says. "I've got her trained up right."

"You're thirteen. She'll have eighteen-year-old boys hitting her. And what are you going to do about locker rooms? I will not have you traveling all night on a bus with twenty boys."

"And three coaches," I remind her. "Oh, my God, Mom. I'm not going to share showers with those guys. Geez." I retrieve my backpack from the hallway and bring my stack of papers to the table.

"Here's the schedule. I need you guys to sign these."

Mom won't take the stack. She stares at it like I rubbed it around the inside of Trent's hockey bag. I hand it to Dad, who leafs through. "Got a pen?"

I get him one from the junk drawer. He signs the permission forms. Mom doesn't say another word.

*

My fingers have barely managed to curl around my toothbrush when Trent bursts into the bathroom.

"Mine!" he hollers.

"Only if you fight me for it."

He takes two steps from the doorway of the bathroom and slams into me. I grip the pedestal sink as my knees buckle under me. "Asswipe!"

"You knew I was coming."

"So? I didn't think you were going to slam into me."

He backs up to the doorway again. "Warning, Mich. I'm going to slam into you."

"What? Get out, you twerp!"

"Bend your knees and drop your weight because I'm going to slam into you."

I barely have time to obey, clenching tight, before he throws his body into mine again. I fly into the sink but at least this time I'm not under it.

"Absorb the hit," Trent says, backing up into the doorway again. "You know I'm coming. Meet me."

There's no time to argue — he's charging me again. I drop my weight and instinctively lead with my shoulder. We collide, shoulder to shoulder.

"Now keep your feet moving," Trent grits out. We both use our feet to push against the other.

"OK, release," he pants.

We stumble back and regain our balance, breathing hard.

"You'll survive," he says. "But you are gonna hurt this time tomorrow night."

*

French worksheet is due Wednesday. I think I can dash it off between practices tomorrow night. I can skim my chemistry reading at lunch tomorrow. But I have to finish my world history essay tonight because it's due first thing Wednesday morning. So of course it's the one subject my mind refuses to focus on.

A creak from my bedroom doorway startles me. Mom leans against the frame, her arms crossed. She's in her comfy clothes: long, open gray sweater over a plain white T-shirt and drawstring sweats. She's taken off her work makeup, which always makes her look more tired than the clock says. Tonight she's looking like midnight.

"Your grades will not drop," she says.

I nod but say, "No."

"You made a commitment to Trent's team."

"I'm keeping it. I'll miss it when practices or games overlap, but otherwise I'm still coaching."

She nods and then comes into the room, sitting on the end of my bed. "I don't understand why you're doing this."

Suddenly, world history seems like the lesser of two evils. "And I don't understand why you can't understand. I love hockey. I miss it. All my friends are off doing new things, and hockey is all I have."

"No, it's not. You could make new friends. Join new clubs, learn new things. Get a job."

"Make new friends. Like it doesn't matter that my old ones have changed. Just get new ones."

"I'm not saying that. Maybe you show up and support your old friends at their new games."

"Maybe they show up to my games."

"So what, then you win? You picked the biggest new thing? It's not a competition, Michigan."

"Why is being competitive so bad?" I cross my arms over my chest.

"I just don't understand it. Just be happy. Get good grades, find something you enjoy, do it."

"I am. I did. Be happy yourself." And now she looks like two a.m. Like an all-nighter spent cramming for an exam she'll never ace.

She pushes grades because she slacked in high school. She thought she was big shit, leaving the U.P. for community college. But she couldn't hack it. She ended up back here, working long hours as a secretary for the local court system. She knows — and I know — that if she'd buckled down and done better in school, shot higher with her goals, that she could have had a chance at more.

But I think that's what I'm doing. And she thinks that's what I'm missing.

I hold up my world history textbook. "I still have work to do."

It's the ace. She won't mess with homework. "OK. I love you, honey. Get to bed at a reasonable hour."

"Yep. Love you, too, Mom."

She stands and leaves my room and I throw myself into ancient Chinese inventions.

9

"Hey, Wayne Gretzky!" Jack leans his shoulder against the locker next to mine. The faint scent of chlorine tickles my nose.

I narrow my eyes at him. "Do you see the resemblance?"

"OK. How 'bout: Hey, Kendall Coyne. What's up, Amanda Kessel? How are the Lamoureux twins today? OK ... that last one did not come out right. I meant that in a strictly hockey sense."

A giggle escapes my throat. "Are you for real?"

"I studied up. Don't want to be a hockey dunce when I come to your first game."

I shut my locker and lean against it, facing him. "Thank you."

He tilts his chin. "Thank me for what?"

"For being the only person who seems truly psyched for me."

His demeanor changes instantly, his shoulders softening. "Seriously? I mean, hockey's your thing. Who wouldn't be psyched for you?"

I think he actually wants to know. "My mom's not too happy with me. And my dad thinks it's cool but since my mom is being weird, he's toned down his excitement. And Brie." I exhale. "Brie has barely spoken two words to me since she left. When I texted her that I made the team, her response was that she couldn't believe I tried out without telling her first."

"Aw, she's just mad that you made the team and she didn't get a chance to prove she could make it, too."

I cock my head. "Do you know Brie? I mean, have you guys ever spoken?"

"Not really. Had a class or two with her."

"Because you pretty much nailed her." Which is not a nice thing for a best friend to admit.

"They weren't that kind of class." He grins and elbows me until I laugh with him.

"Speaking of class. I should probably go to mine," I say. I'm pretty sure there's less distance between us than there was when I first shut my locker and leaned against it. In fact, there seems to be less distance between us than there was only a moment ago. My weight is on the front of my toes, as if the earth is tilting toward Jack.

"Yeah. Me, too."

Neither one of us moves. Unless you count my racing heart, my tumbling stomach and my spinning brain.

"World history?" he asks.

I nod. "You?"

"Don't laugh."

A smile tugs at my lips even as I nod.

"Freshman English."

"What?!"

"It turns out I forgot to take it freshman year. It didn't fit in my schedule. And when I met with my adviser to make sure I had all my grad requirements for this year, she realized I'd slipped through the cracks. I took all the upper-level English requirements but they won't let me graduate without it."

"Oh, my gosh. So you're the only senior in a roomful of fifteen-year-olds?"

"Yep."

"Oh, that's so painful."

The first bell rings, interrupting what could have been a nice day.

I push off from the row of lockers.

"Hey, Hilary Knight?"

I grin. Knighter's my favorite. "Wow. You have been studying."

He holds out his arms. "Hilary Knight. Gold medalist, Olympian three times over, has played pro with both the National Women's Hockey League and the Canadian Women's Hockey League. And" — he points at me — "she started out on a boys' team."

She did. And she survived. I will, too.

The warning bell sounds.

"Not bad, Michael Phelps."

He shakes his head. "Too easy."

"Ian Thorpe?"

"Partial credit."

"Nathan Adrian."

I relish the stunned look on his face. I shrug. "I always watch the swimming. They have nice arms."

"Oh, do they?" He grins. My knees contemplate buckling.

The hall is nearly empty now. I back away toward the Social Sciences wing, preparing to sprint to beat the tardy bell.

"Michigan?"

I lock eyes with him.

"Have lunch with me."

YES. TODAY AND EVERY DAY. But then my heart slumps as I remember my new in-season schedule. "I have to study over lunch."

"I chew really quietly. I promise."

"Deal."

*

Enough of tryouts and chalk talks. Hockey season starts tonight, at my first practice with the Owl River High School varsity hockey team.

I drop my gear in the broom closet and strip off my warm-up jacket before heading outside for conditioning with the team. I used to wear my spandex for off-ice conditioning; my whole team did. Then we'd just throw our gear on over it for practice. But even though I'll be miserably hot, I keep my baggy sweats and hoodie on. I'm assuming spandex goes against Coach's Rules for The Girl.

Daniel leads us on a short jog around the park next to the rink. At least a third of the guys are huffing and puffing. I'm breathing easily. Score one for The Girl.

Back in the rink lobby, we stretch out, following Daniel's lead through standard hamstring, quad, glute and lower-back stretches. He takes us through an ab series, but it's nothing impressive. Just crunch variations that inspire several poorly made claims about the six-packs the boys think they'll get out of it.

I realize the rest of the team, including the other rookies, are all in matching team T-shirts. I'm the only one wearing an Owl River High School Girls' Hockey hoodie. Complete with pink cursive lettering, which probably isn't winning me any points right now. In fact, a lot of the guys are also sporting stiff new ball caps with *Owl River Hockey* on the front. I'm kind of disappointed that I got left out of the new swag.

And it seems that's not all I got left out of.

As we crunch, Daniel weaves around our supine bodies. He pauses to tap one of the rookies on the abs with his sneaker. "Winston! There's my *NHL 17* champ. Mad gamer skills last night. Next time, you're on my team."

"Awesome, man. Can't wait."

"Soon. We'll do another team bonding night next week."

As Daniel walks away, the freshman's buddy elbows him. "Nice, dude."

Winston beams like the prom queen asked for his number. I roll my eyes. It hurts a little that I got left out of whatever team thing happened last night, but it's not like I'd risk bonding with this team anyway.

If nothing else, it saves me from having to kiss up to Daniel.

*

The first hit hurts.

The second hurts more.

By the third I'm numb.

And so it goes.

Welcome to the team. The boys are checking on drills that

have nothing to do with hitting. As the assistant coach of a bantam team, I am well aware that a boys' hockey practice does not revolve around hitting one's own teammates repeatedly.

I can't evade them, can't wuss out of the hits, or they'll just make it worse on me. I have to take it like a human punching bag. Once they see that I can handle myself out here, they'll back off. They're testing me, that's all.

I slump against the boards between drills, my ribs and shoulders already sore only halfway through practice. My trembling hands spill water all over my chin. Megan looks up from the penalty box, where a textbook sits open in front of her. She gives me a smile, but her teeth are gritted and her jaw is tight. Trent sits next to her, very obviously not paying attention to his own homework. My parents refused to make separate trips to the rink, so we now live here every evening until both our practices are over. I don't think it's a hardship on Trent. He looked pretty happy when he found out he gets to "study" with Megan during my practice.

"Bounty, baby!" The upperclassmen are all grouped at the other end of the bench for a water break. William Breaker bumps fists with Daniel in my peripheral vision. "I'm at three. Anyone beat that? No? Looks like Daniel's going to be buying my beer this weekend."

That's all it is with these guys. Smack talk and beer.

"No way," Vaughn says. "Watch this. I'm going to nail her twice next shift. I call Pabst, Daniel."

I freeze. Strain my ears in their direction. But after some hooting, they break up and we head to the next small-ice game.

Where Vaughn hits me twice in the first shift.

To be fair, the first one was half-assed, just an elbow graze. But those fuckers have a contest going for who can hit me the most. Cheap beer to the winner.

I take my place in line, fuming as I wait for my next shift. For my next beating.

A small white blur bounces off my facemask. I flick my head, but it's just a balled-up piece of paper that falls to the ice. I pick it up and cock my arm to toss it on the bench when Trent waves his arms at me from the penalty box. I frown at him. He's going to cost me sprints or push-ups if Coach catches him distracting me on the ice.

Trent points at the paper, mouthing, "Open it." I glance around to make sure I'm not being studied. I don't care what these guys think, but I don't want to get called out by a coach. Then I drop to my knee and fiddle with my skate lace while I unfold the paper against my white jersey.

HIT BACK!

I look up at Trent. He opens his arms and gives me an exasperated "duh!"

I've never thrown a hit. I can shoulder a girl to the boards, hold her in place, even bulldoze her out of the crease if need be. But I've never actually lined up and hit another player. And I've played a non-checking game for so long that I don't even see the opportunities to hit out here. My instinct is always for the puck, skating and angling instead.

Coach blows the whistle and it's my turn again. I straighten up. Did I really think I was going to join the boys' team and never have to throw a hit? Might as well learn now, before I get into a game situation.

It's going to have to be a big one. Shock and awe.

I skate to the line, ready to chase the puck into the zone. I'm lined up against Daniel.

"Don't worry, Manning," he says, smirking. "I'll go easy on you."

Perfect. My first target.

Coach dumps the puck and we sprint for it. At the last moment, I hold back, letting Daniel win the puck in the corner. "Not even a challenge," he says, laughing as he turns to look for his winger.

Bounty. I let it all spew forward: the humiliation of Coach's "this is a girl" speech, the anger at Assmont for taking my real team away, the cold shoulders and hot egos of these apes.

Smash. My hit lifts Daniel off his feet. I slam his torso into the boards, and the tall plexiglass panes rattle in their metal stays. Daniel *whoofs* as the air leaves him and his stick clatters to the ice.

As he slithers down the boards, I pick up the puck and lazily slide it up to my waiting winger.

"You're right," I said. "That was easy on me."

It's the last hit thrown all practice.

10

It's our second lunch date. In reality, I'm eating a sandwich I packed at home and we're in the cafeteria, so it's not really a date. But considering the amount of time I spent choosing a T-shirt this morning and contemplating sandwiches — obviously not something smelly like tuna or that will glue my jaws shut like peanut butter; I finally went with apple and cheddar — this *so* counts as a date.

"I'm blown away by how much skinny guys eat," I say, eyeing Jack's lunch.

He looks hurt. "I better not be skinny. I got a lot of season left."

"After all this" — I gesture to the table in front of him — "I think you'll be OK." He has two turkey sandwiches, an apple, two granola bars, a yogurt and a packet of almond butter. Plus a thirty-two-ounce Gatorade.

"Two practices a day," he says. "Total yardage about seventy-five hundred right now."

I'm trying to remember how many yards in a mile. "That sounds like a lot?"

"Season hasn't even started yet. I'll get up to ten thousand before taper in the spring. And I'll lose about thirty pounds before then."

My jaw drops. "You do this every year?"

"Yep. I have two sections in my closet. Clothes that fit during season, clothes I can wear out of season. Although I'm never truly off-season."

I shake my head. "That's beyond dedication — Ack!" Searing hot liquid slides down my neck and back. I jump to my feet and squirm, but it's too late. I'm soaked.

Jack is on his feet as well. "Are you OK?"

"Yeah, just wet." I reach around and pull the hot, dripping cloth of my T-shirt away from my back. The relief is instant.

"Damn, that was my whole coffee."

I spin to see the kid who hit the wall outside Coach's office. He's holding an empty Starbucks Venti cup. "Guess I'll be sleeping through bio today," he says. I'd like to punch that smirk off his face. He starts to walk away but Jack's hand snags the back of his hoodie.

"That's all you got?" Jack demands.

"Oh. Oops, I tripped."

Jack shakes the kid by the hoodie, and suddenly two other kids materialize behind him like scrawny bodyguards. One is a sophomore on my new team, and I don't recognize the other. Clearly, Jack and I are supposed to feel outnumbered. Not that I care; my hands automatically curl into fists.

Something soft pats against my back. I jump and turn around.

But it's only one of the lunch ladies with a towel. Coming up behind her is a custodian, pushing a mop bucket like the one in my broom closet at the rink.

"Oh, dear," the lunch lady moans. "There's no way that won't stain. Maybe a little bleach, in a hot-water wash. Hope your mama's a miracle worker."

Jack gives the kid a shove as he lets him go. The boy runs out of the cafeteria after his friends, the bastards laughing as they leave. The lunch lady mops up the ends of my hair and dabs the back of my shirt with her towel while I apologize profusely for the mess. Coffee has soaked the butt of my jeans — there's a look that definitely won't get me teased — and my underwear sticks to my skin, forcing me into an unattractive squirmy dance.

"Your skin's all red," Jack says, as the lunch lady scrunches my T-shirt in her towel, revealing my bare back. "Did he burn you?" He grazes the warm skin with his cool fingers, frowning at my back. I'm disconcerted that he's not disconcerted by my bare skin, until I remember — swimmer. Modesty isn't a thing with them.

"No," I stutter. "I mean, it was hot, but it doesn't hurt." I quickly pull the wet fabric from the towel, sure that my cheeks now match the pink bra strap visible to the entire lunch room. "Geez, this is going to be an uncomfortable afternoon."

"Do you have any gym clothes?"

"No. Varsity athlete — I don't have to take a gym class."

"Oh, right. I've got extra clothes in my locker." He gives me a grin. "A pair of taper shorts might actually stay up on you."

Even drenched in coffee, I've still got a smile for Jack Ray. Especially if I get to spend the afternoon wearing his clothes.

I follow him to his locker and he hands me a pair of long mesh shorts and a USA Swimming hoodie.

I hold up the hoodie. "Exactly how good a swimmer are you?"

He shrugs. "That was from some development stuff. Junior level."

Sure, no big deal. He waits outside the women's restroom while I peel my formerly white T-shirt, the one I spent way too much time deciding on this morning, off my back. I dry what skin I can reach with the rough paper towels. Jack's shorts sit low on my hips, even with the waist rolled, but they'll work. His hoodie dwarfs me. Jack doesn't look huge, he just looks athletic, but I'm guessing there are some decent-sized muscles under the baggy clothes he wears.

It smells like chlorine, a smell that's growing on me.

His smile is shy when I exit the bathroom. "Looks good on you."

My answer comes out something like "gwerp" and my skin tingles to remind me that Jack has worn these clothes. I roll my ruined shirt in my jeans and tuck them into a plastic bag Jack got from the janitor. "Thanks for these," I say.

"No problem. Least I could do. Do you know that guy? He was a complete dick about it."

"I don't know him but he tried out and didn't make the team. Remember the kid who hit the wall?"

"Ahh. That's him?"

I nod. "I kind of think that wasn't an accident."

Jack frowns. "What do you want to do about it?"

I don't feel out for blood. I mean, it sucks, but I'm not hurt. Lost a favorite shirt. What am I going to do, go to Principal

Belmont, who I'm sure is my biggest fan already, and say that maybe it was an accident or maybe the kid is pissed that I took what he thinks is his spot on the team?

"Nothing." I sigh. "It's not worth it."

Jack slides an arm around my shoulders. "OK. But if it happens again ..."

"I'll make him take me shopping for a new shirt."

"Oof. Yes, clothes shopping is the most severe punishment I can think of."

"Whatever. Apparently you shop at USA Swimming's gift shop."

He chuckles. "Website. Then I can't get roped into trying anything on."

*

"Mich! Want a ride?" Jordan's retired Crown Vic screeches to a stop next to me. Kendall leans over from the passenger's seat, looking up from her phone long enough to wave hello. "Are you heading home?"

"Yeah. Ride would be great." The after-school rush in the parking lot is terrifying to navigate on foot. Plus, I have to save my energy for practice. I open the back door. Whitney and Jeannie scoot over to give me and my backpack enough room to squish in.

"Where have you been?!" Whitney demands. "We never see you anymore."

"I know, I practically live at the rink."

"And eat lunch with Jack Ray," Kendall sings from the front seat. "What. Is. Up?"

I feel everyone's gaze hit my sweatshirt — Jack's sweatshirt. My armpits grow damp. I really don't want to sweat in his shirt — it'll totally ruin the chlorine smell.

"Uh, nothing. We've eaten lunch a few times."

"And you come out of it wearing his clothes?" Kendall asks. "Nice. I should find a lunch buddy."

I swat her shoulder. "Stop. Some idiot threw coffee on me. Jack lent me his shirt."

"Please tell me he slowly peeled it off his hot swimmer's body."

The image makes me break out in fever. I giggle. "I wish."

Jordan speeds through my neighborhood. Squirrels and small children fling themselves out of the way. "You need to hang out more often," Jeannie says. "We miss you."

"I miss you, too," I say, as Jordan swings into my driveway and stops with millimeters to spare between her bumper and the garage door. "We have our first game next week. Saturday night. Will you guys come?"

"Dude, it's Saturday night," Jordan says.

"You used to spend every Saturday night at the rink."

They exchange looks. "Well …" Jordan says. "Not anymore. Now we do real shit. Like go shopping in Marquette, see a band at the underage club, hang out at the U."

"Seriously?" I ask. I have never known them to be into clubs. Especially Jeannie, who is the stereotypical pastor's kid. The sweater sets and cross necklace stereotype, not the *Footloose* stereotype.

"Yeah. I mean, we have all this free time now and it's so awesome to go *do* stuff, you know?"

"Yeah, totally." No, not at all. I have zero free time and I like what I do with my not-free time. I'd much rather fill my days with hockey than go shopping or clubbing. I just miss the girls.

"But good luck!" chirps Kendall. "We want to hear how it goes!"

"OK, of course. Thanks."

As I get out of the car, I hear Jordan ask, "Where are we getting caffeine today?" Then the car swings into reverse and revs down the driveway, narrowly missing the hedges.

I have forty-five minutes to eat a healthy snack, memorize a sheet of French verbs and get to the rink.

*

My mom better invest in laundry detergent.

I don't know what it is about these guys and beverages. When I get back to my broom closet from conditioning, someone has poured orange Gatorade in my hockey bag. All over everything. They even got it in my skates — I have no idea how to wash those. Not that there's time to clean it up now. We get five minutes to dress after conditioning.

At least it smells citrusy sweet. God knows it could have been worse.

Gatorade squelches in my skates as I clomp to the ice. Icy drips roll into my sports bra from my chest protector. Strands of hair, adhered to the padding of my helmet with dextrose and sucrose, rip from my scalp every time I move my head.

"What is that gorgeous perfume, Manning?" Daniel asks, sliding up next to me at water break. "Not that I'm hitting on you. I just want to know how I can smell as fresh as an orange for practice."

I consider dumping my water bottle over his head but he skates away. Instead, I hand it back to Megan. Her nose wrinkles. "You do smell like oranges."

"They dumped Gatorade in my bag while I was at conditioning," I say. "I'm all sticky."

She gets a sympathetic look on her face but break is over and I have to sprint to the next drill.

After practice, Trent meets me at my closet door. He's sweaty and red-faced, like he's the one who just finished getting his ass kicked all over the rink by vengeful teammates and a cranky coach. Trent hands me a shiny silver key.

"What's this for?" I ask.

He points at the door. "Try it."

I push on the handle, which the rink manager normally keeps unlocked for me.

"No, try the key," Trent says.

It fits. I lock and unlock the door gleefully.

"You can lock up your gear now," Trent says.

"Aw, yes! The rink manager agreed to let me have a key?"

"No." Trent grins. "Megan distracted the rink manager while I stole his key, ran to Ace and made a copy of it. So don't tell anybody."

"I'd hug you —"

"— but I don't want to smell like your sweaty Gatorade," he says, stepping back and running for the rink door. He hollers over his shoulder, "Meet you outside when you're done."

"You're the best, Trent," I holler back. I turn to my newly lockable door.

"Hey, Manning!"

I look up toward the voice, coming from the guys' locker room at the end of the hall. It's Breaker, a tall, stocky senior. And he's completely nude, unless you count the soapsuds all over his body. He does a jerky dance to a chorus of laughter behind him.

I hit the doorknob and throw my body against the door but the fucking door is stuck. I fumble with the key again — I must have locked it when it was already unlocked. I keep my eyes trained on the gray metal door, but the movement in my peripheral vision tells me he's still there, waving and dancing. Finally, the door gives and I stumble inside, my retinas burning and my brain permanently scarred.

I hate boys.

11

"Whaaaaat's up?????!!!!!"

I hold the phone away from my ear and groan. "Not me." My tongue is thick at one thirty in the morning, my words slurring almost as much as Brie's are.

"We just finished team initiation," she shouts, "and it was AWE-SOME! We did a scavenger hunt around campus but it was totally cool and the boys' a cappella group serenaded us — I know that sounds lame but they're all hot and I was totally swooning. And then one of the girls' parents reserved a private room at this swank hotel restaurant and we got all these fancy desserts and we're camped out in a suite here and we have so much champagne and I love bubbles! Bubbles, bubbles, bubbles!"

Did she make a hockey team or rush a sorority? She should be here, sharing the broom closet with me, rolling her eyes at Daniel, bad-mouthing the idiots at our end of the bench during water breaks.

I go from sleepy to mad, zero to sixty. I've bottled all my anger from the last few weeks, because now that I'm on a guys' team, I have to pay my dues to be accepted. I'm supposed to laugh off the Gatorade and Breaker's flashing. Can't act like I'm too weak to take it or that it bothers me. But fuck if I'm going to squeal over Brie's perfect life when she should be bashing on these guys with me.

I sit up and spew like a volcano. "I've spent the last three weeks busting my ass for a team that hates my guts. Studying my brains out. Friendless with no social life. And you call me in the middle of the night — the night before my first game — to tell me that your life is one big party at a swank hotel? It is one thirty in the morning, Brie. What the hell are you doing drinking champagne at some hotel?"

"Oh, my God, did I dial Michigan's number or Mrs. Manning's?"

"Brie, you barely have time to text me. Why are you calling in the middle of the night if it's not to rub it in how great your life is? So, OK. Your life is fabulous. Mine is not. I gotta go. I need sleep."

I hang up, drop my phone on my nightstand and re-curl up under my comforter. But I'm waiting for it … 10, 9, 8, 7, 6, 5 … *ping*! Yep, there it is.

You totally suck

Miss you too, bitch.

Now I can go back to sleep.

*

I am the queen of pre-game. Most hockey players have pre-game planned down to the second. From breakfast in the morning all the way to puck drop in the evening. It is a science. It is an art.

It is wizardry.

Of course, adjustments must be made this season. But the basics are in place. I wore my old, holey MTU T-shirt, although I had to wear it under a buttoned collared shirt with a tie, Coach's orders. I was going to raid Trent's closet for a tie, but Megan surprised me with a green clip-on bedazzled with gold sequins that reads ORHS. It looks kind of Vegas but it's not like I was trying to win any awards for my cross-dressing ability.

Pre-game snack: banana with peanut butter and honey. Pre-game music: Katy Perry and Lady Gaga. Of course, instead of blasting it in the locker room I'm listening to it through earbuds in my broom closet.

But my stick-taping ritual has not changed. Neon pink with three twists on the butt end. White tape and grape Sex Wax on my blade. And I've still got my lucky jersey. At Owl River High School, you have to buy your own game jersey but you get to keep it. Since the boys' and girls' teams wear the same jerseys, my parents refused to buy a new one. Which is fine by me. I've slept in my jersey, that's how tight we are. I'm glad we're going into battle together.

Of course, it was supposed to be sporting an A this season. But I force myself to move past that sad fact.

I've added one other detail to my pre-game this season. I slide Jack's pennant out of my skate and unroll it. After the Gatorade soaking, I was worried it wouldn't make it. But I hand-washed it in the bathroom sink and laid it out to dry and it actually looks better than it did before taking a beating in the pool demolition. I lay it on top of my bag and smooth it out.

Jack swims twice a day, trains so hard that he loses thirty pounds a season and considers weight lifting a day off. He loves swimming and he doesn't expect it to come easily. Not that hockey's been easy for me. But now that I've made this team … I never knew I could work this hard. Maybe this means hockey really can be a bigger part of my future. I have to push my body as hard as I can. I will rise above my teammates' crap. I can take a hit. I can even dish one out if I need to.

Yes. I can do this.

Time to get dressed. There is an exact process to this on Game Day. Spandex, sports bra, tank top, garter. Right sock, left sock. Right shin guard, left shin guard. Right hockey sock, left hockey sock. Attach them to my garter. Breezers and belt. Now I braid my hair. No, I cannot do it at home before I get to the rink. Right skate. Left skate. Tape shin guards from bottom to top. Right first, obviously.

What happens if I accidentally put my left skate on before my right? Neptune rockets through space and crashes into Earth, instantly ending the solar system as we know it. You don't mess with this stuff.

Once the lower half of my body is completely padded, I put on chapstick. Blistex. Mint.

Chest protector. Elbow pads. Lucky jersey.

My chest protector pokes through two circular holes in my jersey, cut approximately where my boobs would be. I stare down at my chest, heaving with panicked breaths.

Take a deep breath. Steel my diaphragm. Tuck my face into my chest pads.

And scream "FUUUUUUUUCK" until my head hurts.

There are boob holes in my lucky jersey. The jersey my parents bought me two years ago when I made the team. The jersey I scored thirty-three goals in. The jersey that has been baptized by my sweat, blood, snot and tears. The jersey that used to have my name on the back, but now, as I pull it back over my head, I realize has tape over the "ng" to read "Mannish."

They sabotaged my jersey. Before my first game.

I can't bear to look at it. I ball it up and stick it in my bag.

My knees bounce. My hands shake. I can't do this alone. I am not meant to be an individual athlete. I need teammates. Brie is MIA. My old teammates are either clubbing, swimming or playing with their new team. Jack — can I really bug out on the guy I like this early on? Should I find Coach? Will he care? Doubtful. Megan will totally sympathize with me. But I'm her coach, I don't actually want her to see me cry ... Oh, God, am I going to cry?

It sounds like someone's running laps in my closet and I realize it's me. My breathing is fast and shallow and out of control. And I'm sweating like a — no, those are tears on my face. I'm crying before a game. I've cried after plenty, but never before. I stand and pace the room in my skates, my arms on top of my head. Slow breaths. Breathe in. Breathe out. Repeat. Repeat slower. Hope the stars in front of my eyes return to the heavens.

Those fucking bastards. I want blood. I want it dripping off my skates. I want them to hurt.

So make them hurt. Take their fucking manhoods and chop them right off. That's what they care about, right? Their soapy manhoods, shaking in the hallway at me.

I will make them look like squirts. I will take their starting positions, their spots on the power play. They want to scare me off this team?

Never. I will die first.

I wipe my face. I hold my cold water bottle to my eyes until I'm sure they're not red anymore. Then I poke my head out the door.

"Megan!" I call. She's standing in the hallway with an armload of clipboards and a bucket of pucks. "I need a blood jersey. And change my number on the roster."

"What happened?" she asks.

I shake my head. "Just get me a jersey. Please."

"OK. Be right back."

Twenty seconds later, she appears with an un-holey jersey from the blood bag. "I'll change you to number sixteen on the scoresheet," she says.

"Thank you." I pull the new jersey over my head, followed by my helmet and gloves. Lock my closet. Fix my eyes forward on the ice. I am so ready to play.

I don't care who's wearing away jerseys tonight. I have a new opponent. My own team.

*

I kill it.

Five shots on net, two goals and four hits (by me, not on me) later, I have won the first game of the season. I am permitted to stand in the doorway of the real locker room while Coach puffs his chest out and gloats over his win — "a real team effort, boys" — before I'm banned to my closet. From behind my metal door, I can hear the guys' celebration. There's a ton of hooting and laughing and obnoxious explicit rap.

I drop my gloves into my bag, followed by my helmet. Plop my padded butt onto the cheap plastic folding chair. Say hey to the spiders.

The second goal — that was the beauty. I close my eyes to picture it. I skated in from the far neutral zone on that one. Picked up a loose puck and just went with it, skirting two opponents, ignoring the call from Daniel to pass to him as he chased after me into the offensive zone. I never slowed my stride as I charged the goal and neatly flicked the puck between the goalie's leg pad and blocker.

I'd love to relive it all night, or at least until my leg muscles find the energy to push me out of this seat, but I have to get out of here. Knowing they still found a way to get to my gear gives my insides an icky feeling. Especially since I can't lock my closet from the inside. I quickly strip my pads off and jam them in my bag. I throw my Coach-mandated slacks and shirt over my sweat-soaked underwear and sports bra, tucking the tie in my pocket. I look like a freaking waitress but I'll be home in ten minutes. I shoulder my bag and keep my head down as I push through the crowd in the lobby.

Everyone here is clad in Owl River green and gold, but I don't get any slaps on the back. No congrats on my two-goal game. The decibels drop noticeably when I enter the overheated lobby. I push past my teammates' parents, my ears straining to eavesdrop. I feel eyes on me, fathers sizing up my puny muscles and wondering how I beat out their freshman sons for a spot. Mothers clucking at my sorry excuse for an outfit, pitying my mother for getting stuck with such a butch daughter. My teammates' girlfriends smirking at my sweaty, tangled hair. Younger brothers staring at my black sports bra soaking through my white button-up shirt.

Two hands grip my biceps. I freeze and look up into dark eyes and the only friendly smile in the room.

"Damn, you're good," Jack says.

I'm suddenly alive, the sad, soaked wick of my insides lit with a quickly growing flame. "I can't believe you stayed the whole game." I know he's got a meet early tomorrow morning, in Houghton.

"I couldn't leave. It was too good."

We're pressed close by the crowd, which seems to be moving and humming again; the girlfriends on their phones and the moms with their green stadium blankets and padded seat cushions and the younger siblings running around with hockey sticks too long for them, clipping knees and shoulders without stopping to apologize.

"I'm smelly," I falter. "I don't have a shower. I change in the broom closet."

He grins, his hands still gripping my arms. "I don't care."

"I, uh, have a confession."

He cocks his head.

"I took one of your pennants. From the pool wall, when they were tearing it down. I keep it in my hockey bag." I don't have a clue why I'm blurting this out. I'm such a stalker.

Jack kisses me. Despite the jostling crowd, his lips graze mine gently.

The red goal light flips on. The whistle blows. The ref signals. I pump my fist.

Our kiss lasts just long enough to elicit a few throat clearings from nearby parents — thankfully, mine are not in sight. When Jack pulls away, his hand slides to mine and he leads me through the lobby. I refrain — barely — from excessive celebration over my most recent goal.

"I like your number — sixteen," Jack says. "That's my lucky number."

My old number was six. "Really?" I ask. "Why?"

"My best fly ever was sixteen strokes on the first length of a long course one hundred."

I have no clue what that means, but I think sixteen might be my lucky number, too.

12

Before we board the bus for Houghton, I catch Coach in his office. I don't know if this is OK — my old coach always wanted us to come to her with issues or concerns. I've been trying not to cause any trouble for Coach Henson, but this is really weighing on me. I need his intervention.

"Coach?" I ask. "May I have a quick word?"

He doesn't stop typing on his phone. "Quick one, sure."

My warm-up pants rustle as I step inside his office. If the guys knew I was here, they'd throw me under the team bus. I glance at the door, but Coach has kept it open the few times I've been in his office and he's sure not looking like he's going to get out of his chair now. Or even make eye contact with me.

"What's the problem, Manning?" he grunts.

To be honest, there's a long list, but only one I'd consider addressing here.

"I would like to know what I can do to earn a spot at center." I practiced that. I didn't want to get in here and stammer.

"You're staying at wing."

"And I've enjoyed playing wing, but I think I could win face-offs for you. And I'm strong on the back-check."

"My centers already win face-offs. And they're strong on the back-check, too." We both know that's a lie. Even his D aren't strong on the back-check.

"It's a goal I'd like to work toward. Is there anything I can do?"

He finally sets his phone down. "It's not happening, Manning. That's my final word."

"Why not?"

"Because it's easier to hide you on the wing. Keeps you out of the corner action, at least on one end of the ice. And let's be honest, you don't have the size to cover the net."

I take a deep breath so I can stick to my script with an even voice. "I don't need to hide. I can handle the corners." Sure, he's got a point about my size. It just means I need to be smarter and faster, and I'm willing to work on that.

"I'm not going looking for trouble, Manning. Besides, why do you care? You scored two last week playing wing. Looks like you're getting plenty of chances for points." He sounds bitter, like I was a puck hog who should have been setting up plays for his boys.

"I've just always been a two-way player, I've always played center. I like the way the ice looks from there."

"Answer's no. You ready for the bus?"

Dismissed. I sigh. I know I can't afford to push the issue. I miss playing center but I should be happy I'm playing any position.

In the hallway, I shoulder my bag, pick up my sticks and take the first seat on the bus. I bury my nose in my phone, trying to ignore my teammates as they board the bus.

"Stay away from the chick, guys!" Daniel hoots, hip-checking Avery into my lap.

"Sorry." Avery grins at me. Since he's the only guy who congratulated me on my goals last week, I give him a grin back as I shove him to his feet.

"Move along," Coach barks, mounting the stairs. The loud chaos instantly changes to quiet, orderly seat-finding. Avery slides into the seat behind mine.

"Avery, move back," Coach says. "I want an empty row between Manning and you boys."

From the back, someone whispers loudly, "Watch out, Avery. Vagina is catching."

I cringe and sink lower into my seat, curling around my phone.

Coach stops in front of my seat and holds up his hands. "And … distraction," he says to me. As if it's my fault his "boys" are actually Neanderthals.

I don't respond. I put my attention back on my phone, because I'm the one who needs distraction from this team. Catching up on the news around the hockey world, I find out that the Silver Lake girls won their first game last night. Cherrie didn't get to play but Di had an assist. Brie's team is playing their first game right now and they're up 1–0 at the end of the second period.

I text Jack to see how his meet is going. He replies immediately.

Just waiting on the relays. Made finals in 100 free, 100 fly and 200 free.

Congrats!

On your way to Houghton?

Yep. In my special front seat of the bus. At least it doesn't smell like boy up here.

Should I take offense at that?

God, no. You're the cleanest boy I know. You always smell like pool.

Should I take offense at THAT???

I giggle and scooch lower in my seat, losing myself in a world that's much nicer than a school bus full of misogynists.

*

"Off the ice, Manning! Get a change!" Coach's voice barely reaches me through the booing. All the orange-clad fans in Dee Stadium are on their feet, shouting unflattering descriptions of the ref's mother at the official signaling a slashing call.

I knew it. I knew Coach wouldn't let me stay on the ice for the power play. I just got off the bench, too. But no, the PP is an honor that I'll never earn because I have, as my teammate so eloquently put it on the bus, a vagina.

I turn from the face-off lineup toward the bench. Scott Sanders sprints from the door to take my place.

An angry blast from the referee's whistle stops me. "Too late, Sixteen." He waves Scott back to the bench.

"Ref! You're screwing up my power play!" screams Coach.

"Then watch my hand next time. I gave you the line change. You didn't take it."

"First chance you get, Manning!" Coach means first chance I get, I'm supposed to get off the ice.

But the first chance I get isn't for a line change. It's to skate the puck in after a pretty poke check by Winston. All five of us storm the zone. There's no way I'm wasting PP time with a change. It's scoreless at the top of the third; we need this man advantage. I slide the puck back to my point. He lets us get down low, buying time with a lateral pass to his D partner. We're closing in on the net, keeping the penalty kill busy, when Breaker takes the long shot. I slip around the D covering me — easy enough to do because he's lumberjack sized and I'm not. The goalie butterflies and blocks the shot, but loses the puck in the chaos. I pick it up and flip it over his shoulder, into the net.

The guys all surround Breaker, congratulating him. I make my lonely way to center ice, surrounded only by the ghosts of my former teammates, hugging me and shrieking with glee. The closest thing I get to a congratulation is Avery. In his goal at the far end of the rink, he hoots and whacks his thick goalie stick against the ice.

Almost forgot I was supposed to line change at the first opportunity. Guess that would be now. I skate to the bench and hop over the boards.

I've always been a solid player, toward the top of the stats sheet on points. But three goals in the first two games of the season? Holy shit. Maybe the animosity has forced me to elevate my game. Knowing Coach would love to have a reason to cut me. Or maybe because my team doesn't pass to me — they don't pass much to anyone, they all want the shot themselves. So there's never anyone there to make plays with. When I played with girls, we were all polite to each other — give Brie the shot opportunity off the face-off because she's got a killer slapshot. Di's the fastest, so get her the puck on the breakaway.

Now that I don't fucking care about my teammates, I shoot whenever I damn well please.

Coach doesn't say a word to me. But when the Gremlins tie up the game with two minutes to go in the third, he whacks my shoulder pad with his clipboard. When I turn to face him, he grabs my facemask and shouts into my ear hole to be heard over the cheering crowd. "Switch with Winston!"

I spring to my feet and race to the face-off, relieving the strong-side winger deep in the enemy zone.

Center wins the face-off back to our D, who sends a quick shot into traffic. The puck is kicked around by bodies barreling into the slot, desperate for a chance to score or to clear the zone. I fight to get near it, but a large defenseman crashes into me, driving me back. He's got me on sheer size but I'm still on my feet. I dig in, holding my ground. The puck dangles tantalizingly just behind his feet. I maneuver until I can get my stick on it, then make a one-handed pass to the slot. Daniel slides the puck past the goalie for the game-winning goal.

During time-out, Coach tells me to stay in for the rest of the game. At 1:15 left, it'll be a long shift, but I had a whole time-out to rest. I can handle it.

I know how to kill time, but Coach instructs me like a rookie anyway. "If Sanders wins the draw," Coach says, "get it down low, preferably against the boards. Kick it around a bit but don't freeze it. Keep that clock running. If Sanders loses the draw, hustle back as third D." So he still won't let me take the draw, but once the puck is in play I'm expected to play my ass off on both ends of the ice.

Gladly. I want this win.

Coach wasn't kidding about killing time. Sanders does win the draw to our D, who pushes over the center line before dumping the puck to the corner. I fly after it, crashing into the D who's trying to dig it out. We fumble and kick along the boards. Seconds slowly tick off the clock but I can't afford to check how much time is left. Pushing a two-hundred-pound load is no easy feat, and thirty seconds along the boards will gas even an NHLer. My chest heaves and my legs weaken. The puck is in my feet; I could kick it out if one of my teammates would get close enough to catch it. My head swivels, looking for the pass. Daniel stands outside the blue line.

"Kill time," he calls.

Sanders also stands at the blue — why isn't he dropping down to pick up the puck? Every one of them is standing around waiting for this game to end. Except me. I'm bench-pressing a mammoth while time stands still.

I'm finally saved by the buzzer. Coach hugs Daniel like a homecoming hero, slapping his helmet and yelling happily through his cage. Drops of sweat sting my eyes, and I shake my head so no one will think I'm crying. This isn't my old team, my old coach or even Coach Norman. Of course Coach Henson would never hug me. Doesn't mean he isn't proud or appreciative. It means that he told his players to keep a respectful distance and he's doing the same.

Avery whacks my shins with his stick as we cycle into the handshake line. "Thanks for the win, chica."

"Nice game," I say, tapping his pads back. But then I focus on moving through the line. I don't want to cause trouble for the only guy who's nice to me.

*

My stomach rumbles the whole way home. Peters, the assistant coach, climbed on the bus with a stack of pizzas after the game. He gave the seniors first crack at them, torturing my nose with the sweet, garlicky smell wafting from the back of the bus. The boxes were nothing but greasy cardboard by the time they made it up to me.

It's eleven when we pull into the high school parking lot. I'm relieved that neither of my teams has practice tomorrow. I plan on spending quality time with my pajamas in the morning, until at least noon. My heart breaks thinking of our post-game sleepovers at Brie's house, making a mess of her kitchen while cooking pancakes in the morning.

The bus driver and coaches shuffle down the stairs to drag hockey bags out of the cargo hold and we all dawdle, hoping it'll be done by the time we exit the bus so we don't have to help. This is a rookie job on most teams but the coaches seem to know they'll be here all night if they wait for those boys to untangle their earbuds and find their jackets.

"*NHL 17* at my house!" Daniel shouts as he struts down the aisle of the bus. "Dudes only, no dykes," he amends as he passes my seat.

I'm up without thinking. My hands grab Daniel's throat, pushing him backward. He crashes down into a bench seat, and suddenly I'm in a flurry of fists and knees. Grunts and swears fill my ears. Hot, garlicky breath hits my cheek. Something sharp like an elbow grazes my eye and I lose my knit hat to the floor. Hands wrench my arms behind my back. I fight like a cat in a washing machine until I realize it's the assistant coach. I let him steer me back to my seat. He shoves me roughly and I bounce onto the vinyl bench, breathing hard.

It is dead silent on the bus.

Coach stands in front of me, his body blocking Daniel from my fists. Daniel's panting but his eyes glint, even in the deep shadows of the bus. "Go on, Danny," Coach says, giving Daniel a nudge toward the door. "Everyone off!" he calls to the rest of the team, who have packed the aisle, drooling for some drama.

I grab my backpack. I should give Daniel room to leave, but I am so ready to obey Coach's orders and get the hell out of here. Coach turns an angry eye on me. "Sit, Manning."

Aw, shit.

The team files by. A few deliberately stare straight ahead as they pass. Most smirk. Some even give low snickers, like it's amusing that I'm in trouble.

Not one of those bastards says Daniel was out of line. Not to me, not to Coach. Certainly not to Daniel.

Yeah, OK, I shouldn't have lunged. But Daniel does not get to use that word. Not with me, not with any woman, regardless of her sexuality. Having been on a team full of hockey-playing girls, I am fully aware of the appropriate way to address a non-heterosexual woman and that term is not it. If you're going to use that word, you damn well better own your lesbianism. Daniel does not.

The bus empties. Outside, the parking lot lights shine on clusters of boys filtering into cars, tossing bags in the back of SUVs, threading sticks through the seats.

It's pitch-black on the bus. The driver is still outside, sliding bags out of the storage chutes. Assistant Coach Peters stomps a foot onto the seat behind mine, leaning his elbow on his knee. Coach Henson stands at the front of the bus. He crosses his arms.

"The only reason you made this team," he says, "is because I couldn't justify to Megan why I would cut you."

The dark makes me brave. I stand and face him. "I would never allow a player on her team to call her a dyke."

"Good for you," he says patronizingly. "She is a thirteen-year-old girl. *You* are sixteen. What did you think would happen when you joined a boys' team? Did you think you'd get a free pass for being female? Luckily, it was only Daniel, instead of you costing us a penalty for charging someone in a game. Did it occur to you, Manning, that when you're out on the ice with teenaged boys, someone might call you a mean name?" He uses a condescending tone for "mean name" and this pisses me off most of all. I've taken a lot from these guys already. Talk to me like a fucking adult. "Did it not occur to you that you have to toughen up if you're going to play boys' hockey? You think all these guys do is call names?"

No. I know they also know how to use scissors and are so uncoordinated with beverages that they should have to use sippy cups.

But I keep my mouth shut. It doesn't sound like I'm getting cut. Yet. *Keep mouth shut. Keep mouth shut.*

Coach leans forward and the shadows of the bus darken his features even more. "How about the first time you go into the corner and some guy pulls your feet out from under you? Whacks you in the back of the head because he doesn't like girls on his ice? How about if he grabs your butt or your chest or pulls that cute braid of yours?"

Is he talking about opponents or my own teammates? Mouth. Still. Shut.

"Did you have any clue what you signed up for?" Coach growls.

No.

I swallow. "I just want to play hockey. I can take care of myself on the ice."

"No, you can't." He sits back, resting against the front of the bus. "You can't even keep your shit together around your own teammates."

The bus driver slams the luggage doors closed. *Thud. Thud. Thud.* I think Coach is waiting for me to apologize. But I won't.

I wait to be cut.

Coach sighs. "However."

Air whooshes back into my lungs. Coach stabs a finger in my direction. "You scored three goals for me this week. If you hadn't, I would be crossing your name off my roster this minute."

Interesting. I raise my chin and stare through the darkness at him. "I want to play center next game."

There's a sharp intake of breath from Peters behind me. Yes, The Girl has balls.

Time ticks even slower than it did when I wrestled the sumo-sized defenseman in the corner this evening.

"One chance," Coach finally says. "If you deliver, you stay at center. If not, you go back to wing."

"Deal." I swing my backpack over my shoulder and sweep past him. "Night, Coach. Good game."

13

Dad's is the last car in the parking lot. The engine quietly hums and steam puffs out of the exhaust pipe. I can see Trent's silhouette in the backseat. When I drop my bag on the pavement, Dad pops the back of the Explorer and gets out to lift my bag in.

"Great game, kid," he says. I knew he'd follow the live stats online.

"Thanks, Dad. Coach said I get to play center next game."

"Yes!" Dad ruffles my nasty dried-sweat hair.

"Got any food in here?" I ask.

Dad tosses a granola bar at me as I slide into the passenger seat. I grin. "Got any more?"

He tosses the whole box at me. I will probably kill it on the five-minute drive home. Trent's fist appears over the shoulder of my seat. I bump it with my own.

"Not bad, Sixteen," he says.

"Thanks, Six."

He tosses a lump of fabric into my lap. "What's this?" I ask, with half a granola bar crammed into my mouth. But it's obvious what it is from the sleek, heavy mesh. I hold it up. The Owl River Youth Hockey logo is barely visible in the dark car. "Your jersey?"

"Turn it over."

I do, and he shines the flashlight from his phone over my shoulder on the large 16 sewn on the back.

"You changed your number."

He turns the light off and flicks my shoulder. "Yeah. We're sixteen now, right?"

Granola bar clogs my tightening throat. "Yeah." I never thought about why Trent wore number six. If I had, I guess I would have called it a coincidence. "It looks good, dude."

"Got a call from the sports guy at the *Gazette*," Dad says. "He wants to interview you tomorrow. Pretty impressive, huh?"

"Do I have to?" I tear open another granola bar. I'm not a big fan of raisins but I'd eat my seat belt right now.

Dad looks over at me, his brow wrinkling. "You don't want to? I thought you'd be more excited."

The last thing I need is to be singled out, to put an even bigger bull's-eye on my back. In the first two games we played, the only team that seemed pissed to have a girl on the ice was my own. But it's early season. I've got a lot more teams to meet. And starting the season strong doesn't guarantee anything. I don't need any more pressure on me to perform. I already have to "deliver" next game.

"I've got a good start, Dad. I don't want to screw this up. If I finish the season this strong, then maybe I'll talk to the guy."

"Yeah, OK. I get that. No one likes to be seeded number one before they've really been tested."

"Exactly."

"I'll call the guy tomorrow, push him off a bit."

"Thanks." Then I get an idea. "Can you suggest to him that it might be cool to put a spotlight on the teams that got cut? My girls' team and the guys' swim team? Maybe he could start by interviewing some of the other athletes before we talk."

Dad nods, eyes always on the road, of course. "Great idea, Mich. I'll suggest it."

I rip open granola bar number three.

*

So the *Gazette* guy is off my back and now stalking Jack. Although I can't take all the blame for that. It would have happened anyway; November 11 is the signing day for college swimming, and Jack is officially a Cal Berkeley Bear now.

But unfortunately I couldn't keep the school paper from making a big deal over my season openers. When I get to school Monday morning, the cheerleaders have covered my locker in shiny green gift wrapping paper and a large pink 16. They get a varsity letter for this, for gift wrapping, while I have bruises up and down my body. And that's from practicing with my own teammates.

"I'm dating a superstar," Jack says, appearing next to me. He waves a copy of the school newspaper and hands it to me. The front page proclaims, "With Girls' Team Cut, Manning Scores with the Boys." Oh, geez. Don't they have an adviser to edit this stuff?

I choose to focus on Jack's use of the word "dating" instead. Because, swoon.

"Oh, we're dating now?" I tease. "I thought you were just waiting to get your sweatshirt back."

He turns serious. "Actually," he says, "lunch in the cafeteria is a lame excuse for a date. How about, the girl I *want* to date is a superstar?"

"Kind of sounds like a boy-band song."

"So how about it?"

"Can you really sing?"

"No. I mean, I want to —" He falters. "I'm sure you're wondering why I haven't asked you to Winter Homecoming. I want to ask you — to go with you — but I can't. I have a meet, at Michigan Tech, that Saturday night."

"What if … I come to your meet after my game?"

His eyes light up. "You'd come? Really?"

"Yeah. If you want me to."

"I do. You're OK with missing the dance for a boring swim meet?"

I doubt Jack without a shirt is boring. My face grows hot and I hope my blush isn't giving away my thoughts. "I don't want to go to the dance with anyone else. And I'd really like to see you swim."

He slips his hand in mine. "It's a date. I'll come to your game, you come to my meet."

"It's a date."

IT'S A DATE.

*

Are you seriously leading the league in scoring right now or is that a typo on the website?

I'm surprised Brie even cares enough to follow the league news. I hide my phone under the table. The library doesn't frisk you for phones, but it would still be stupid to overtly text. Especially since Brie knows nothing of the zebra mussel invasion of the Great Lakes, which is what I'm supposedly researching.

Under the table, I type: Do you mean, sorry for waking you up the other night and being a brat?

Daniel and those guys must be shitting themselves.

If they did, I'd know because they'd put it in my bag. They're all jerks.

Sorry it's not going well. But great about scoring three goals so far.

And two assists. But who's counting?

It would have been better if there was a sleepover and pancakes after the game. ☹

You do not want Daniel cooking for you, trust me. Or sleeping over.

I'll take your word for it.

Not that Daniel ever slept over at Brie's. There was no sleeping of any kind between them, but even the thought makes me cringe.

It's a tenuous string, but I'll hold on to it. It feels so good to have a teammate to talk with that I can't risk running her off.

*

I'm dead serious about practice this week. As Coach said, I have to "deliver" at next Saturday's game. Once or twice, it's occurred to me that I should quit while I'm ahead. Odds are there's something nasty waiting for me in my hockey bag, someone lurking in the parking lot to jump me. I'm looking over my shoulder so often that I'm eventually going to walk into a wall. There's a 50 percent chance I'm about to jump out of a plane and a 50 percent chance I'm about to get pushed out before I can strap on my parachute.

But I'm playing boys' hockey. And I'm kind of rocking it.

No, I don't have my girls around me. I'm not wearing my A. But I'm a better hockey player than I was two months ago. And there's something about giving everyone the theoretical finger for thinking I couldn't do this.

Jack thinks I'm a superhero. Megan analyzes my stats like I'm on her fantasy team. Trent spent over an hour in the garage with me last night practicing face-offs. People who have never talked to me before congratulate me in the school hallways. Dad stashed a box of granola bars in my hockey bag. The good kind, peanut butter and chocolate chip.

So I will deliver.

I drop my bag in my broom closet before practice. Say hey to the spiders as I strip out of my jeans and T-shirt. Somewhere in my hockey bag is a sports bra and spandex shorts. Hopefully. I begin the excavation process.

I don't hear the door open until it slams shut behind Daniel. I hit the ceiling.

"Shit! Get out! Get. Out." I scrabble in my bag, looking for something to cover Michigan's Secret, which is that I buy my bras and underwear at Target.

He smirks at my chest. "Looks like you fit in better with the boys after all."

"Get. Out." I can't believe that when Brie and I were freshmen, I crushed on this guy. OK, even last year I did, before Brie started dating him and we hung out a couple of times and I realized he's kind of perfect for her, which means completely not my type. I drape my practice jersey over me as best I can, covering my thin tan bra and the tops of my thighs.

Daniel doesn't waste time. "Quit the team, Manning."

"That's what you barged into my dressing room to tell me? Get the fuck out before I tell Coach."

"I'll tell Coach I was looking for a mop to clean up a Gatorade spill in the locker room. Who do you think Coach would rather believe?"

"You touch me and I'll scream bloody murder and knee your balls into your intestines."

"Ooh, you've gotten feisty, haven't you? Don't worry, I have no interest in" — he pointedly scans my legs — "that."

"I'm not quitting the team just because you walked in on me."

"Walking in on you is nothing, Manning. It gets worse. Get out before then."

"I've scored three goals for this team. Dished you a pass in front of the net. You're welcome, by the way. What is your problem with me?"

"Do you think my old man comes to my hockey games to see some girl set up my goals?" Daniel spits the words at me. "Do you think Breaker's parents enjoy sitting through JV games because his little brother didn't make varsity? Because you took his spot?"

"I earned it. And your dad needs to get over it."

"This is my senior year. My last year of hockey. It's supposed to be sweet shit and you're fucking it up. Coach is a bipolar mess with you around. The guys are all uptight, everyone's pissed all the time. I want my old team back."

"So do I. We don't always get what we want, Daniel."

He leans closer. I shrink back as far as I can. The icy cinder-block wall pins me in place. I turn my head away from Daniel's hot breath and clutch my jersey shield.

Daniel doesn't move away, clearly enjoying my discomfort. I'm paralyzed, every part of me but my racing heart. If he touches me, I don't know if I'll have the breath to scream.

He doesn't touch me. He laughs in my face. It scares me even more.

"I always get what I want, Manning."

*

I should be running out of this rink. I should be shaking and cowering. Killing a box of Kleenex while on the phone with my girlfriends. Admitting to my mom that she was right; it's too much. Meeting my dad at the station to file a police report.

I should be telling Coach I quit. They win.

I know this is what I should be doing. I hold my phone in my hand, contemplating my options, until the last minute before practice starts.

But my heart rate has returned to normal. I'm no longer quaking like an aspen. I put on my breezers. My shoulder pads. I am strong in them. I put my skates on. Balanced on a 1/8th-inch blade of steel, I am steady, stable.

Daniel will not win. Hell, no.

I come out raring to go. I kill practice. The boys are huffing and tired by the end but I could keep skating.

There might actually be something wrong with me.

14

Saturday. Winter Homecoming game. Playing center. Delivery Day.

FIRST OFFICIAL DATE WITH JACK RAY.

Our Homecoming game is against Calumet High School, our biggest rival. The entire school is busy on Homecoming; every sport has a game before the formal dance tonight. I'll catch the girls' basketball game in the late morning, then race to my game, then stop at home to shower and spend much time and effort on my hair, then to MTU for Jack's meet. My mom even agreed to lend me her car for the night. She almost never lets me use her car at night. Unless I've got a late practice or game that she doesn't want to have to pick me up from. Or if she sends me out to pick my brother up. Or to pick up dinner. But never for social stuff.

Like my FIRST OFFICIAL DATE WITH JACK RAY.

Puck drop is at three o'clock, so most students are home for a pre-dance nap or spending ridiculous money on pedicures and updos. The cheerleaders are beat after cheering the boys' basketball team to a loss, and all their hard work gift wrapping lockers. So the stands consist of parents, younger siblings and whichever unlucky girls said yes to my idiot teammates for the dance tonight and now have to show up here instead of getting their hair and nails done.

No one has sabotaged my broom closet or my gear, so it's gonna be a good day. I can't lock the door from the inside, but Megan is sitting outside and we agreed on a knock-and-delay strategy if someone tries to come in. I'm not worried about putting Megan in a dangerous situation. As Coach's stepdaughter, she's safe. These boys are stupid, not suicidal.

I'm getting used to my solitude before games. I listen to whatever music I want. I use the quiet to visualize plays. I've even given myself a few pep talks. Out loud. 'Cause why not?

"Keep your feet moving in the corners," I tell the spiders. "Wide, low stance on the draw," I remind the mop bucket.

I'm back at center. Right where I want to be. I never imagined I'd be playing so well that I could call the shots. I was always a good hockey player, for a girl. But I'm starting to think ... maybe I'm just a good hockey player.

I have to keep playing this well. I have to deliver. Like a pizza. Like FedEx. Like an obstetrician. Ick.

Other than taking a shot in the middle of the back from Vaughn during warm-ups, presumably for taking his spot at center and relegating him to winger, the team is chill today. Most likely focusing today's brain cell allotment on how to get into their dates' strapless bras at the dance tonight.

I catch a glimpse of Jack in the stands. He'll have to leave in the third period, but he's going straight to the pool from here so he can see as much of my game as possible. He sits in a crowd of random people: Laura, Delia and Emma, a couple of boy swimmers, a guy I recognize from my world history class and the exchange student from Finland. Jack is on the outskirts of the crowd but he looks comfortable there. Wherever he is, he's just Jack.

I think about his pennant and how I channel my isolation, like a swimmer. Except I'm a center now. Isolation can't be my MO anymore. I'll be drawing the puck to a teammate, I'll be covering with them getting back on D.

Or I'll just be doing it all on my own now. Yes, I draw the puck back to a teammate. Yes, I call some plays. But we're no team, me and these guys.

During a stoppage of play, while the ref gives Avery a minute to fix a strap on his leg pad, the opposing center across the face-off dot makes conversation. "Not bad, Sixteen," he says. "You've beat me three-oh so far. I'm taking a beating on the bench."

"Isn't that why you wear all that padding?" I ask.

He laughs. "If I finally win this one, can I get your number?"

"Sure," I say. "It's sixteen."

He laughs again. From behind me, on D, Daniel grunts. "Manning!"

I turn.

He glares at me. "Shut the F up."

Both the ref and the other team's center sputter in disbelief. I shrug them off. A mere comment from Daniel isn't going to take me off my game anymore. The linesman standing next to Avery waves at the ref, who gives a short blast on his whistle and gestures for us to take our places. We crouch into our stance.

"How 'bout if I hit your captain?" the center asks across the dot. "Can I have your number then?"

I grin and sweep the puck back. Four-oh.

I'm guessing "deliver" means I better come out of this game with at least one goal. And with the game tied late in the third, I'm starting to sweat. Even more than typical hockey-game sweating. I've had at least eight missed shots and haven't even scuffed the goalie's leg pads. Or his confidence. But that's hockey. You can skate your butt off but you're not guaranteed anything. The only control I have is over my own body, so I keep my legs moving, my stick ready, my eyes sharp. My patience pays off. With four minutes left in the third, I squeak in the game-winning goal, a redirect off a long shot from Daniel at the point. We win Homecoming, 2–1.

After the handshake line, I skate directly up to Coach. "Did I deliver?"

He can't wipe the smile off his face. Winning Winter Homecoming against Calumet, in front of a bunch of alums and parents and administrators. We both know he's got a lot of backslapping and handshaking in his near future.

"You got your center spot" is all he says.

*

My broom closet is definitely a Superman phone booth today. I enter it a victorious hockey player but when I leave I'll be a girl on a first date with a gorgeous swimmer boy. My tummy flips happily. I change like my room is on fire, haphazardly tossing gear into my bag.

I lock up my closet while reviewing clothing options. Purple sleeveless top vs. off-white lace T-shirt. It'll be humid in the natatorium — will the lace get scratchy? Is lace too much for a swim meet? The purple is a good color for me, but it doesn't work quite as well with my denim skirt. I miss Brie terribly in this moment. I'll text her my options when I get home. She'll choose neither, of course, and berate me for not attending the dance.

My sticks wrench from my hand.

"Team meeting," Daniel says. "Follow us." Standing behind him in the hallway are Vaughn, Breaker and Carson, the assistant captain and a junior like me. I played with Carson from age five through thirteen, but he hasn't spoken a word to me since I joined the team. He won't look at me now.

My oh-shit-o-meter flashes red. "Coach didn't say anything to me."

"Captain's orders."

"I have a thing —"

"It'll be short."

Breaker takes my bag off my shoulder and Daniel carries my sticks. These are no gentlemen; my gear has been taken hostage. Against all survival instincts, I follow them, skirting the rink. My fingers curl around my phone in my pocket. But there's no one to call.

Daniel leads us around the Zamboni machine to the back of the garage. I've never been back here before — I'm sure it's strictly off-limits to the public. It's a messy dumping ground for dulled resurfacing blades and extra sections of boards. Scratched and cracked panes of plexiglass lean against the concrete walls. It smells like grease and gas and it's so cold that I can see my breath. The rink compressors hum loudly.

Breaker drops my bag on the concrete floor. In an icy puddle. Daniel holds my sticks, leaning on the butt ends. The rest of the team is MIA.

Shit.

"Team tradition, Manning. You took Vaughn's spot. You owe him something in return."

"Yeah, OK. I'll bake you cookies, Vaughn. That make you feel better?" I try to keep my voice light, but I'm scouting the exits. From the heavy diesel smell permeating the air and the deafening vibrations, I can tell the rink manager is still edging the ice. There's no one to accidentally walk in on us back here. I finally let go of my phone and hold my hands lightly at my sides. Ready to … what? Take on four guys, all much larger than me?

"Cookies," Daniel snorts. "Cute, Manning. Vaughn gets one punch."

"You punch your teammates for changing positions?"

A sadistic grin twists Vaughn's heavily blemished complexion. "If you can't take a hit, offer me an alternative." He rocks his pelvis back and forth. My stomach tightens and nausea creeps up my throat.

The other guys cackle. "If she's any good, she can have my spot, too," Breaker says.

My muscles are contracted, ready to fight. I will not go down easily. The obvious available weapon would be my sticks, but Daniel's still leaning on them. I scan the walls. Those long steel blades would do damage but they're so heavy. If I could heave one at them, maybe it would distract them long enough. I've only got to make it a few yards and then I'll be in screaming distance of the rink.

"A punch," Daniel's firm voice interrupts. "You want a spot on this team, you play by our rules."

"You're fucking crazy."

"Then you're off the team."

"Does Coach know about this?"

He shrugs. "Doesn't matter."

I mentally reason whether I've scored enough points, won enough games, to persuade Coach to keep me over whatever story Daniel will concoct.

That's some fucking insane "reasoning."

"Dude, I got dinner reservations with my date," Carson says. "Can we wrap this up?"

"Yeah, me, too," Breaker says. He comes at me and I stumble backward, bumping into a workbench. Breaker grabs my right wrist just as I pull it back into a fist. Carson grabs my left and they drag me forward. I struggle for everything I'm worth, trying to twist my arms free, digging my heels into the floor.

Daniel throws my sticks down and grips my jaw. "Take it like a fucking man," he snarls, shoving my face away. "Drop her hands. If she runs, she's done."

Breaker and Carson let go but don't move away.

"Fine," I say. I hold my arms out, leaving my midsection vulnerable. "Take your punch. Be a fucking man yourself."

"No problem," Vaughn says.

"Not on the face," Daniel instructs.

Vaughn stares me down, pounding his fist into his palm. I will myself not to flinch. Absorb, like a hit on the ice. Above all, do not cry in front of them.

It is sudden. I barely see it coming, but I sure as hell feel it. A momentary curtain of darkness falls over my eyes, replaced with stars. I gasp for breath. Cold concrete on my knees lets me know I've hit the ground. I stay down.

But I survived.

There's laughing above me.

"And now I'm ready for some dinner," Carson says.

"Beer first," Vaughn says. "I need me a beer first."

"More like six beers."

"Twelve."

Wait it out, I tell myself. *Breathe through the pain and they'll go away.*

Footsteps pass by my head. I'm seconds from freedom when pain erupts in my side again. And again. And again. I curl and swing my arms at the retreating boot but my kicker slips away. Running footsteps fade through the garage.

My side screams and I press my hands to it, squeezing against the pain. I force my head up to check my surroundings. I'm alone. They're gone. I crumple, curling inward, pressing my forehead to the cold concrete floor. I'm done. I can't do this anymore. I won't. This is sick and wrong. Illegal.

The pain morphs from sharp stabs to dull throbbing, my muscles cranked tight. I prod the area. The punch knocked the wind out of me, but it's the kicks that are going to hurt for a long time. I don't know how to tell if I'm really hurt, but people get punched every day and are just fine, right?

It's not my side that's nauseating me.

I lurch to my feet and hug the dusty wall for support. My biology teacher last year told us that starry vision and head rushes are your body's way of telling you it needs oxygen. He also told us that fainting is the body's way of telling you it wants you to lie down. I can already tell my body's going to win this argument.

I ease myself back down to the hard floor and breathe deeply, inhaling fully even though my abdomen screams with each breath. Mr. Blakely was right. The stars recede. My body decides to let me stay conscious. I'm allowed to stand. Unable to lift my bag, I drag it through the wet garage. Through the now-empty lobby. I stumble out the door and through the parking lot to my borrowed ride.

It's when I slump onto the front seat that the tears start. The silent, hot, fast kind. I don't try to stop them. I don't drive. I don't think about what happened. Staying conscious and breathing through the pain are all I can manage right now.

Eventually, my body and mind settle on numbness. My eyes get the message and dry up. My consciousness stops the astronomy project. I turn the car on and drive home. Sneak up the stairs, letting the sounds of the TV cover my steps. Drop my clothes on the bathroom floor and stand under a hot shower, shielding my new bluish-purple bruise with my hands to keep the water from pelting against the tender skin.

Lace shirt. Definitely the lace shirt. With straightened hair; curls will flop in the humidity. I'm still Superman emerging from the phone booth, even if I'm crawling instead of flying.

No … Superwoman.

15

Jack bounds over to me as soon as I arrive in the pool area. He's wearing blue warm-up pants and a long parka that says Club Wolverine U.P. across the back.

He smiles wide as he approaches. "Heard you won Homecoming."

The bitter taste of blood creeps up the back of my throat. "We did."

"That's a good thing, right?"

His smile wavers and my chin quivers. I clench my jaw and try to curve my lips up. It's my first official date with Jack Ray. We're finally on our first official date and I can no longer muster up the capital letters. "I'm just a little beat up, that's all. Rough game."

"But you survived."

"I did."

"Well, since this is Homecoming." He brings his hand out from behind his back. He's holding a clear plastic box. "I got you a corsage."

My smile finally turns genuine. "You did!"

He opens the box and pulls out a delicate weaving of pink and white flowers.

I gasp. "It's beautiful. I love it."

He slides it over my wrist. I stare at the contrast of fragile flowers over my short nails and callused palms. I have one knuckle that tore open sometime during the game and a cracked thumbnail. "After the day I had, it's nice to feel like a girl."

He leans in and kisses me slowly. Now it's even nicer to feel like a girl.

A sharp whistle echoes off the walls and the announcer calls a race. Jack pulls back and glances at a digital scoreboard with names and numbers I don't understand.

"Do you have to go to that?" I ask.

"Nope. We have three heats to talk." He takes my hand and leads me halfway up the bleachers.

"I usually get at least five heats for a first date," I say, amazed at how normal my voice sounds. We sit and he keeps my hand, the one with the corsage.

"Tell me about your game."

I hesitate. I won't talk about Fight Club, of course. First rule of Owl River Hockey. "Final score was 2–1. Good game, shots pretty even. Avery stood on his head." In fact, the whole team played well, but it's easiest to talk up Avery's performance.

He nods. "I saw the score online. Why don't you tell me about the parts that sucked?"

I sigh.

"I've never seen you so bummed after hockey. Especially a win."

"It's the team. They hate me." I inhale slow and long, to keep my voice from cracking and my rib cage from splitting. Even after my marathon sobfest in the car, I'm still teetering on the brink of another meltdown. I know that if even one tear slips, the whole truth is coming out. Jack is the kind of guy who would call in the armed guard, and I'm not sure I'm ready for that. Right now, I want to breathe and relax in this warm, humid place, with normal, non-abusive sports happening around me and a corsage on my wrist.

Jack squeezes my hand. "So they're insecure because the one girl on their team is carrying them."

"I doubt they'd like me if I was riding the bench either."

"You get that this is all their problem and not yours, right? You're not doing anything wrong."

My side is bright hot, so much pain that it's almost numb. No, this is not all their problem. They've definitely brought me into the picture a bit.

"If I was a guy, even a freshman, they'd be all proud of me. Is this normal for guys? If a girl hopped in the water right now, swimming against you, would you be pissed off if she beat you?"

"Absolutely. But I'd be pissed off if anyone beat me." He rubs his thumb against my palm, taking the edge off my tension. Jack's better than Advil.

"What would you do about it? How do you treat the swimmers that beat you?" I suddenly think of the wall of pennants. "Assuming there are any, that is."

He chuckles. "There are plenty. I like it, actually. It's good to know that somewhere out there — maybe at this meet, maybe not, but somewhere — there's someone faster than me. It gives me something to push for when I'm training. Swimming laps back and forth — it's not like someone's going to knock you off your feet. It's the same thing over and over again. You have to push yourself forward. You have to have a reason to make every stroke count."

"You are a true athlete," I say. "You do it for the right reasons, you do it the right way. It's admirable. I wish I could be more like that."

"You are," he says. "It's what I like about you. You're different from the rest of your team. You skate like you mean it. I can see you pushing yourself. You never sit back and slack."

"I can't afford to. Aw, who am I kidding. I don't like to. And I finally have opponents who really challenge me, and I don't have a team to sit back and rely on. It gives me something to work for —" I stop suddenly.

I'm talking in the present tense.

Less than two hours ago, I lay on the floor of the rink garage telling myself that no one would put up with the literal abuse I was receiving from my team. And now I'm talking like I'll be back at practice on Monday.

I can't go back. That's insane. I should tell Jack that I'm done.

But I don't.

*

Possible internal bleeding aside, it's a pretty great first date. Jack makes the finals in all three of his races, although those won't happen until tomorrow morning. I was kind of freaked out about seeing the guy I'm dating in a Speedo, but it turns out he wears these legging things, so it wasn't creepy at all. Not that Jack's body is creepy. I just don't need too much information about certain parts of it on our first date. Although I was quite happy that there was no shirt component to his racing uniform because, let's just say, damn.

After the meet, we go to dinner at a brewpub near campus. Jack's dark hair is still damp, and even though he's back in a long-sleeved T-shirt and jeans, I can now picture the well-defined muscles underneath that shirt. He holds my hand almost constantly, to the point where neither of us knows how to eat our burgers. Finally, I get up and slide into the booth next to him, pulling my plate across the table. He looks at me questioningly.

"If I don't have use of both hands, I'm going to end up with melted cheese and tomato all over my lap," I explain. "So I'll trade you. My hand back for" — I scooch closer, until our shoulders bump — "a shoulder."

"Shoulder's good. But maybe not quite equal to a hand. Throw in a knee" — he bumps mine with his — "and I'm in."

"Deal." We press close enough that our shoulders and knees — our entire thighs — touch.

"I like real dates," he says. "Better than lunch in the cafeteria. I mean, I like lunch. But I like shoulders and knees better."

"And no one dumping coffee on me."

He frowns. "How accidental are we thinking that was? I mean, after what you told me about your team tonight?"

I shrug. We're so close that my shrug pushes his shoulder up as well. "It's ancient history, either way. And he's not on the team."

"If that guy had dropped hot coffee down your back when you were on the girls' team, what would have happened?"

"Brie would have ripped his, um, manhood off. Jordan would have stuffed it down his throat. Kendall would have tipped off every girl in school so he'd never get a date again. Laura would have talked all of his teachers into extra homework."

"I feel like I should have done something. I feel like the rest of your team should have done something."

I'm sure they did. Bought him a replacement coffee. I shrug it off. "It's not worth it."

"But it's not OK. I wanted to help you."

"You did. You gave me dry clothes."

He drops his crumpled napkin onto one of his plates — he ate two orders by himself. "Will you tell me if anything like that happens again?"

My side throbs as I add guilt to my pain. "Look, I'm perfectly capable of defending myself. And you are helping. You always manage to do the right thing and say the right thing."

He leans in and softly presses his lips to mine. "Like this?"

"See? Exact right thing."

*

I wake up gasping for air. My entire midsection is frozen solid. I can't take a deep breath. I can't roll over in bed. I can't sit up.

Oh, my God, it was internal bleeding and now I'm paralyzed. I pull up the side of my pajama top and check my torso. A deep purple bruise two pucks across greets me. My toes curl in agony. But at least that means I'm not paralyzed. I'm just really freaking sore.

With much grimacing, I'm able to push to my opposite side,

bend my knees and, keeping my torso straight, push myself to sitting.

How the hell am I supposed to skate at practice tomorrow? How am I supposed to coach today?

Keeping my core still, I stretch my fingers until I can reach my phone. In selfie mode I'm finally able to get a good look at the whole bruise. I snap a few pics and type a text to Coach Norman. Got a helluva bruise from the game. Lower ribs/abdomen. What do I do?

But I hesitate to push Send. The guy has been around hockey his whole life. He's seen a few bruises. He's definitely going to call bullshit.

Also, is it sexting if you send a picture of your bare torso to your hot, older coach? I decide to send the text without the pictures.

My phone *pings* right away. He's probably getting ready to leave for our game. Do you need an X-ray?

Probably. But that would require an explanation to my parents, who are not going to buy the story that I fell on someone's boot. Repeatedly. No, just bruised.

Since you're u-21, my normal prescription won't work. Ice, hot showers, light stretches, ibuprofen. Wrap with an Ace. Do you need a break today?

I don't want to let Trent and Megan down. Or Coach Norman. And, of course, there would be Mom questions. Dude, what do I look like — a 13-year-old boy? I'll be there.

The hot shower is geographically closer than the freezer, so I'll start with that. I creak to the bathroom like an old lady. Oh, yes, a hot shower does help. I'm at least able to pretend I'm walking normally when I finally make it down the stairs.

Every hockey family has a comprehensive medicine cabinet. Ours is in the laundry room. I can't bend down to pull the crate from the lower shelf, so I hook a toe through the plastic lattice and drag it forward until an unraveled Ace wrap comes into view. I clench it between my toes and lift until I can reach it. Mom's slippered footsteps shuffle over the kitchen linoleum, so to be safe I duck into the mudroom before lifting my shirt. It's not a pretty job, but I manage to wrap the Ace around my lower ribs. It helps immediately.

I straighten my spine, practice a normal gait and brave the kitchen.

"How was the dance last night?" Mom asks. The coffee carafe in her hand is half-empty, which is the only reason she's this chatty. My family doesn't talk until at least thirty minutes after the coffeemaker beeps in the morning.

"Didn't go." I pour the nearest box of cereal into a bowl.

"I thought that's why you borrowed my car last night." Her tone is already accusatory, like I was out delivering drugs when I was supposed to be having a yearbook-worthy high school experience.

"I went to my date's swim meet instead."

"Oh." It takes a moment and a few more sips of coffee until it sinks in. "Wait. They cut the boys' swim team. Are you dating … did you go to a girl's meet?"

As much as I'm enjoying her reaction to that, I clarify. "He — Jack — swims for a regional team."

"But he goes to your school."

"Yes." If it was such a big deal to vet my date, don't you think she'd have done it before the actual date? "He's a senior."

"He missed his senior Homecoming for a swim meet?"

"Of course. Why would he miss an important meet for a dance?"

And therein lies the essential difference between my mother and me.

Trent saves me by lugging his hockey bag through the kitchen, overpowering the coffee smell with stale sweat. "Ready, Mich?"

I lift my bowl and chug the remaining milk. Put my palms on the table to push myself up to standing. Bowl in the dishwasher. Creak back up to standing position. Pocket the bottle of ibuprofen Mom keeps next to the coffee maker.

"Ready."

*

"Here she is!" Megan says, coming at me with two little girls in her wake. "This is Coach Mich, leading scorer for Owl River High School."

"Hi." I lift a hand in a wave, which is lame but I'm totally caught off guard.

"These are my cousins. They really wanted to meet you," Megan says. "This is Lindsey — she plays squirts. And Betsey is in her first year of mites."

They look like mini-Megans, with blond curls and pink cheeks. And tutus. You gotta love a hockey girl in a sparkly pink tutu. I shake their hands solemnly. "Nice to meet you both."

"Will you sign my puck?" Lindsey asks. She hands me a plain black puck and a purple glitter pen with silver feathers sprouting out the top.

"I'll try," I say, shaking the pen and trying to get ink to stick to the black rubber. It's sloppy, but it'll do. I hand it back to her.

"I drew this for you," Betsey says. She hands me a picture of a girl with black skates and a green-and-gold jersey with the number 16 on her chest. I'm also wearing a gold tutu and a gold bow in my hair. No helmet, which is kind of dangerous in the kind of hockey I play. Artistic license, I suppose.

"'Good luk, Michigan,'" I read. "'Love, Elizabeth Abigail Singer.' Thank you, Betsey, that's beautiful. Should I hang it in my room or keep it in my bag for luck?"

"You should put it in your bedroom. On your closet door or your dresser so when you get dressed for hockey, you'll see it and remember to have good luck."

"That makes sense. I'll do that. Thank you."

"OK, girls," Megan says. "I have to finish getting dressed, so I'm taking you back to Aunt Nancy now. Bye, Coach Michigan!"

"Bye, Coach Michigan," they echo. I wave goodbye.

They stay with me, though. All through Trent's game, I see them across the ice, cheering for Megan. In the lobby, when I leave, they're playing floor hockey with a tennis ball and bright pink hockey sticks. Nostalgia hits hard. Back before pink gear became more common, when Kendall followed her older brothers and joined our team, she pined for gear that matched her color scheme at the time — sparkles, sparkles and more sparkles. Come to think of it, Kendall hasn't changed much in the last seven years. Anyway, four glue sticks and three tubs of glitter later, we had her sparkling under the dim lighting of the rink like a disco ball. She shed glitter all over the ice for the next three months, leaving a fairy trail wherever she skated.

I lean against Mom's car while I wait for Trent, the world's slowest showerer. Now that I'm not standing on the bench, in public, my core muscles have called it quits. Ibuprofen's wearing off. But it's nice to stand outside by myself when I'm not afraid of getting jumped. In fact, it's nice to be at the rink without being afraid of getting jumped, period.

What will happen when Megan gets to high school and she still wants to play hockey? Will the boys turn on her, punch her in the garage, insinuate that she should give them sexual favors for taking their spots? What about Lindsey and Betsey — will there still be no girls' team for them when they get to high school? I want to punch the guys who would consider threatening those girls.

If I'm blazing a trail for them, I'm doing a poor job of it. Some role model, relying on a strict regimen of ice packs and hot showers just to be able to walk. Allowing my team to physically abuse me because I don't know how to get myself out of these situations.

If I blow the whistle on them, I'll be gone. Done with hockey. And then what kind of trailblazer will I be? Generations of girls could skip tryouts because the last girl screwed it up. If I keep my mouth shut and put up with it, then I'm setting a dangerous standard for the girls yet to come.

For a girl on a scoring streak, I'm sure stuck in a no-win situation.

16

It's a rare day at Owl River H.S. The moon aligns just right with a couple of planets, and almost my entire girls' team ends up at the same table at lunch. Jack takes the hint, planting a light kiss on my cheek before going to sit with the soccer team. I swear that guy knows everyone at school.

I sit next to Kendall, who squeals and holds out her arms to hug me. Yep, still sparkly, with glittery nail polish and a rhinestone bracelet on each wrist. I maneuver carefully into her familiar hug, slumping to make sure she doesn't squeeze my lower ribs.

Homecoming is, of course, the topic of the day. I checked out everyone's pictures online last night but now I get all the stories that weren't fit to post on Insta accounts that parents can access.

"Yes, yes," Jordan says, bowing proudly. "I am the puker of this year's Homecoming."

"Ew. That is not a title I am jealous of," Kendall says.

"Oh, but you're proud of the title 'homewrecker'?"

"They had a fight!" she says. "Everyone knows we've always

had chemistry. It was only logical that when Rory finally dumped him, Vaughn would seek solace with his very first girlfriend."

I choke on my quesadilla. "Ew, what? Vaughn? Vaughn Gaines?"

"Yes, remember? We went out in sixth grade."

"That counted?" It was like a week. And sixth grade. The only chemistry involved was grape-flavored lip gloss plus Mentos.

"Well, it counts now. I can't believe how much I missed him. He always was the sweetest guy I've ever dated."

The ghost of Vaughn's fist dents my abdominal cavity. I set my quesadilla down. "Kendall, are you sure this is a good idea?"

"What, are you on Rory's side all of a sudden?"

"No! I'm on yours, of course. I just don't want to see you get hurt."

She tilts her head and sets her hand on my arm. "Sweetie. I won't. But thanks for worrying about me."

I meant actually hurt. A guy who will punch a teammate won't think twice about punching his girlfriend. And what was that crack about twelve beers the other night? Was he serious?

"Please just be careful," I say.

"Why weren't you at the hockey party after Homecoming?" Kendall asks. "I was sure you'd be celebrating with the team."

"Aren't you required to be there?" Delia adds.

I'm not sure if I'm proud or ashamed to admit that my team doesn't invite me to their parties. Since ice was invented, there have been rumors about what goes on at the hockey team's parties, and frankly I'm relieved that Coach's Rules for The Girl have kept me off the invite list. One beating was plenty the other night. Of course, this being Homecoming, with dates and all, it was probably pretty tame. Well, other than puking and home-wrecking.

But I can give the girls what they really want. "I had better things to do."

The entire table leans forward, fixing me with fourteen pairs of curious eyes.

Kendall breathes, "Please say Jack Ray."

I duck my head to study the speckled white plastic table and grin like crazy. "I went to his meet on Saturday, and he brought me a corsage. Then we had dinner at The Library after the meet."

"So it's true?" Cherrie practically shrieks. "You're dating Hot Speedo Boy?!"

Laura thumps her on the shoulder. "If you guys would spend more time in this town, you'd be up on the gossip."

"We're gossip?" I ask. "Why?"

"Because you have accomplished what every straight girl in this school has been trying to do for years."

"Jack's gone out with other girls."

"Not many."

I can't help it — my eyes search out Jack two tables away. He's halfway through a stack of peanut-butter-and-jelly sandwiches, a tall carton of milk on the table in front of him. He's even cute with a milk mustache.

Breaker and Daniel pass through my line of sight and I instinctively curl inward, protecting my midsection. Daniel catches me looking and follows my gaze to Jack. That smirk I've come to hate jumps to Daniel's face. He stumbles and his arms flail, red Gatorade sloshing out of its bottle. Daniel steadies himself by clapping a hand on Jack's shoulder. His bottle of Gatorade, high in the air over Jack's head to counterbalance, tips dangerously but miraculously doesn't spill. Jack is jostled forward into the table, and my breath catches as he turns around. But there's only some good-natured laughing between the two. Jack seems to be waving Daniel off with a "no worries."

I exhale into a growl. That stumble was totally fake. Daniel makes eye contact with me on his way out of the caf, confirming my suspicion with an evil grin.

My stomach turns me away from my lunch. Daniel wouldn't do anything, would he?

Everyone loves Jack. And Jack's a guy. He can take care of himself.

Geez, Mich, sexist much?

My bruise throbs in response.

"I gotta say" — Jordan taps my wrist with her Twizzler — "I was worried about you when we lost the team and Brie left town. But" — she gestures from my head to my feet — "look at you. Leading scorer on the boys' team. Dating Jack Ray. And boys' hockey is definitely doing something for you." She squeezes my bicep.

"You were worried about me?" I ask, stiffening.

"Well, yeah. I know how important the team was to you."

"I've seen you, like, twice in the last month." Awkward silence slithers down the table. "I've barely seen any of you."

"You've been busy," Kendall says pointedly.

"You guys didn't even come to my game last weekend."

"We were getting ready for the dance!"

"And it's not like you've come to any of our games," Cherrie says. "None of you have."

"No offense, but I ain't driving to Bumfuck to watch you guys play," Jordan says.

"Well, I 'ain't' going to Sunday beer league to watch your games either," Di counters.

Cherrie gives me a pleading look. But I lost that A two months ago.

"OK, OK," Emma says. "We've all been busy with new things. We're still friends." Even though, I note, she's been hunched over her phone with Delia and Laura leaning over her shoulders all lunch period. And the Silver Lake girls are clumped together at the other end of the table.

And Brie is MIA. But we're all "still friends." Like what you tell a lame boyfriend when you break up with him.

Loud laughter erupts behind me. I duck my head and hunch my shoulders, steeling myself for the hit, for the hot drip of coffee or the sudden shock of ice cubes down my shirt.

"Dude, what was that about?" Jordan asks me.

The laughter fades as a trio of boys passes by without incident. I sit up straight and run a shaky hand through my hair. "Nothing."

"OK, swimmers, let's go ice our shoulders," Delia says. "I need my medley relay in top condition for next weekend." Emma and Laura wave and follow her.

"But we're still friends," Jordan mimics to their quickly retreating backs.

Teammates. Friends. I used to think it was all the same thing. The guys killed that theory quick. The girls are burying the body.

*

When Coach cancels off-ice conditioning before practice and instructs us to sit in the bleachers, my lungs constrict. I sit on my shaking hands, squishing them onto the cold plastic seat until they're too numb to tremble. I can feel Daniel's glare on my back, but he can't think I'm dumb enough to tell anyone, right? My brain scans through the day. Could anyone have caught me slumping at my desk or popping ibuprofen between classes?

But when Coach stands up in front of us — really, in front of me, as I have the entire first bleacher row all to myself — he doesn't look pissed. He's bouncing on his toes and grinning from ear to ear.

"Boys," he says, looking over me to the rest of the team, "I got a call from the Michigan High School Athletic Association this morning. Our team is ranked second in the division, which means we have been invited to play in the University Showcase this weekend."

He pauses to allow celebration, and whoops erupt behind me. The Showcase is a big deal up here in the U.P., where we don't have a lot of sports teams to get excited about. It takes place mid-season at the U, on their big, gorgeous sheet of ice, in front of four thousand fans. The top four high school teams play a twenty-minute period against each other, so three mini-games. Then they get introduced on the ice before the U game and everyone stays to cheer on the Division I college team.

Behind me, the guys are practically peeing their pants.

"Scouts!" Sanders shrieks. "Are there going to be college scouts there?"

"Of course." Coach says it calmly, but I'm guessing his pelvic floor muscles are working overtime as well. "That's part of the whole reason to have a Showcase. There will be coaches there from junior programs, Division III teams, even DI. Your future is on the line, men."

I'm psyched about the experience, but let's be honest. I'm not going to get picked up by a guys' team for college and there won't be any scouts from women's teams there. There's no reason for them to be at a guys' Showcase. Still, we get to skate on that big U ice, in front of a ton of fans. And we'll get to watch the U game afterward.

The cheers behind me have disintegrated into mumbles. I peek over my shoulder at the hostile-looking horde behind me. My bruise prickles.

"What about playing time, Coach?" asks Carson. He speaks past me, but his cheeks redden, as if he knows what an ass he is. When we were in peewees, Carson and I played floor hockey in the lobby every night waiting for our parents to pick us up. With a wadded-up ball of hockey tape — blue, because Carson wore blue on his shin pads. I always made him be goalie.

Two nights ago, he held my arms down while Vaughn punched me.

"What about playing time?" Coach asks.

"Well, there are some guys here that already know where they're going to school next year. And others" — his eyes shoot to the floor, unable to look at me — "that don't have a chance of making a college team."

"I'm going to put the best team I can out on that ice," Coach says. "This is big for us, boys. Lots of eyes watching. If we come out of this well, it won't go unnoticed."

Daniel takes a couple of nudges from the guys before he stands up. "OK. I'm the captain. I'll say it. Manning's taking a spot that could go to a guy who needs to get seen."

Coach frowns and rocks on his heels. "You come out of this thing the bottom-ranked team, that doesn't look so good. For any of us," he says. "Manning makes this team look better than it is."

I'm feeling a little love for Coach for actually sticking up for me. Although it sounds like he doesn't have much choice. I'm sure the administration is putting pressure on him to win.

"However," he says, looking straight past me. "I'll make you boys a deal. I'm planning on putting my best centers on the ice on Saturday. You show up this week at practice, you look good, and maybe one of you will win Manning's spot."

Oh, how nice. And will I get to punch that bastard in the gut?

17

I may not have a scholarship or roster spot on the line, but I want to play on that big ice at the U. I want my dad and my brother to see me play in front of a huge crowd. And, as much as I'd like the opportunity to punch someone on this roster, I'd really like to maintain my status as leading scorer.

So I'll step it up this week. I've been playing well, so that's a tough concept. But there's always something more you can do. My slapshot is inconsistent. I can work on that. I'm still tentative going into the boards, wondering if I need to brace for a hit. So I'll work on keeping my feet moving and reaching for the puck instead of worrying about the check. I think, in the last week, I've proven I can take a hit.

On Tuesday, Coach hands out a packet to each player before practice — our access pass for this weekend. Plus we each get four tickets for our families, both for the Showcase and the U game after. It's like injecting Red Bull into our veins. I swear, even our slowest skater could get drafted off that practice. The rink manager takes a hint and lets Coach have an extra twenty minutes at the end of practice, and no one complains or slows a stride.

This eats into homework time, which will send Mom's blood pressure up a few ticks. But I don't care. I've already decided French and world history will take a hit this week so I can get some extra sleep. I need to be well rested.

School has turned the Showcase into a popularity contest, of course. All students get free entry to the Showcase, but each player gets only four extra tickets to the U game after. Apparently, it is *the* thing to do this weekend and tickets are in high demand.

I'm jittery waiting for Jack before school on Wednesday and it's only partly due to the extra ticket in my jacket pocket. My back is pressed against the lockers so no one can sneak up on me. I've got the nearest restroom on my radar so I can sprint toward it if I need a safe haven. I've stashed extra clothes in my locker.

I wonder if I should add a first-aid kit.

Jack meets me at my locker, now our regular routine, and kisses me hello. I can still taste his morning toothpaste and smell the chlorine from his morning swim. Now I don't mind being pressed up against my locker.

"So," I say. I hold up my extra ticket. The other three went to Dad, Mom and Trent, of course. "But I have to warn you, you'd be sitting with my family." The thought brings me nearly to hyperventilation. But there's no one else I'd rather have there.

"I thought you'd never ask!" he says.

"If it weren't for the interrogation my mom will spring on you, I would have asked yesterday. Are you sure you want to do this?"

He rolls his eyes at me. "Of course! This is huge!" He takes the ticket and slips it into his backpack before setting his hands on my waist. "You're still holding strong to your spot, right? 'Cause I don't want to show up with number sixteen shaved into the back of my head unless —"

I swat his chest but then pull back. "Wait. You wouldn't, right?"

He sighs. "Sadly, no head shaving until taper."

"This is a sadly? Really?"

"Bee-otch!" The familiar screech stops me as I'm leaning toward Jack's smiling lips.

Between stressing over whatever my mom will do/say to Jack, stressing over the inevitable "I get paid to carry a gun, son" convo with State Trooper Dad, stressing over keeping my spot this week and the small amount of attention I've given my classwork … Yeah, there's a chance I forgot to check in with my friends.

I turn around and there she is: latte in hand (nonfat, sugar-free vanilla), makeup and hair in her took-me-an-hour-to-achieve-a-rolled-out-of-bed-looking-gorgeous look. Brie scans the school hallway with her nose turned up, as if public school is contagious. "I can't believe I had to come all the way to your school to track you down."

"Brie, oh, my gosh!" I let her hug me, but then I push her back. "I can't believe you didn't tell me you were coming."

"Surprise!" She eyes up Jack. "And speaking of surprises. Jack Ray with his arms around my best friend. My, my."

If she texted more often than to brag about the hotties at her school, she'd know this. But she's here now, and we can finally get back to normal. I'm already giddy from Brie's infectious energy and the prospect of girl time. "I'm so glad you're back! But, seriously, what are you doing here?"

"Winter break, duh. I'm home through the weekend and then it's the annual winter cruise with my grandparents." She smirks at Jack. "Maldives, this year."

He shrugs, unimpressed. I love him.

"Thanks for telling me!" I scold Brie. But then I hug her again. I used to hug my teammates, many times each day, and suddenly I feel starved for it. It seems forever since anyone but Jack has hugged me. And while he's an excellent stand-in, it's not the same as affection from my girls.

"So what are the chances you can blow off class and get coffee?" Brie toasts me with her to-go cup, as if she needs to be further caffeinated.

"Zero." I check the clock. About five minutes till first period. "I'm under a microscope, I can't ditch. Come do lunch with us." I gesture at Jack, who seems to be fading back into the hallway.

"Spa day with my mom. I cannot get on a cruise with this pedi." She wiggles her foot at me, although I'm sure there are no calluses under those Tory Burch boots. "How about dinner?"

"Practice and coaching. Homework. Bed."

"Geez, girl, I didn't come all the way up to Nowhere, Michigan, to hang with my parents! What's your weekend like?"

"We made the University Showcase," I say, grinning. "So come to the game, OK?"

"Oh, yes! Definitely! Can you get me a ticket for the U game, too?"

"I'm out. But I'll ask around."

She pouts. "You suck."

"Um, hello, it's not like I knew you were going to be in town."

"Like it matters. Apparently I'm never going to see you while I'm here."

"She can have my ticket," Jack says, holding it out toward Brie. My heart flinches. "I'd love to go, Mich, but if this is your only chance to spend time with Brie while she's in town, then she should sit with you guys."

"Good man." Brie snatches the ticket from his hand.

"Are you sure?" I ask. Only a moment ago I was stressing about Jack sitting with my family. Now I'm bummed that he won't get the chance to undergo their trial by fire.

"I'll still come to the Showcase," he says. "Wouldn't miss it. And I'm sure I can get another ticket to the U game."

The bell buzzes and I frown in the direction of world history.

"Walk you to class?" Brie says, slipping her arm through mine. "Then I'm off to get a massage and pretty nails while you poor schmucks learn boring crap all day."

*

Practice is fast and furious. Between pre-Showcase adrenaline and having Brie back, I'm flying high. So is the rest of the team — even Coach is practically exuberant. I doubt Brie's return has anything to do with them, though.

Every time I'm forced to step up my game, I shock myself by doing it. Today's practice is yet another step up, another sprint up the stadium stairs. Sure, I'm breathing hard and my legs are numb, but I get to the top. It's finally clear how hard I've been working. I've upped my game and I'm in great shape. I can hate my teammates all I want, but they've made me a better hockey player.

But none of them is taking my spot. I want it. God, I want it.

Coach ends Thursday practice with a scrimmage, which is smart. Everyone's got a ton of nervous energy and it needs to be directed into actual playing.

I line up against Vaughn. I've already faced off against him once today and I won it. Coach Peters drops the puck and Vaughn ties up, smashing his stick across my chest.

Focus. Puck.

As the wingers barrel down on us, I kick the puck back to my D. I let Vaughn continue to tie me up so my D gets an extra second to start the breakout. Vaughn takes the opportunity to shove against my chest pads and his top hand flies up into an uppercut.

He mostly hits my chin protector but the butt end of his stick scratches the soft spot under my jaw. Guess he's still pissed about that center thing. "Just for that," I grunt, "I'm telling Kendall to hold out on you this weekend."

He uppercuts again.

"Get a move on, Gaines!" Coach barks.

I cough, my windpipe not happy with this match-up. But Vaughn backs off.

My D got too excited on the breakout and iced the puck, so we're back for another face-off. I stand at the circle, waiting for Vaughn to line up. He strides back to Daniel at left D and they have a few hushed words. Both look over at me. Vaughn nods and comes back to the face-off dot.

Subtle, guys. So Vaughn's planning to win the puck back to

Daniel, who's probably going for the shot on net, which means Vaughn's either planning to tie me up — as usual — or he's planning to sprint to the net for the rebound.

But Vaughn will have to win the face-off. No chance in hell, Gaines.

My knees are bent low, my eyes on the puck in the assistant coach's hand. My weight is forward on my toes, ready to push myself into the puck's space the second it leaves Peters's grip. In slow motion, his clutched hand begins its forward motion and I make my move.

It was option one. Vaughn blocks my forward progress, but as usual he's so intent on the body that he's too slow to get to the puck. I duck around him, but I can't shake Vaughn's grip from my jersey. He forces me back toward the boards, where my D is fumbling with the puck.

"What the hell?" I grunt, trying to push around him toward the net. It would be great if Peters would call this hold.

Vaughn gives me an eerie grin. "Get out of this one," he says, smirking.

WHAM.

I'm out.

18

"Jesus Effing Christ, Daniel! What the hell were you thinking?" Avery's voice comes from directly over me.

My eyes won't open, but I know exactly where I am. The cool, fresh scent of the ice is close to my nose. Besides, I'm always on the ice these days, so it's a safe guess.

"Michigan! Can you hear me?" That's Coach.

"Yes," I say, but it comes out "blem."

"Should I call 911?" asks Peters.

"I think she's waking up," Coach says, tapping my helmet. "Michigan! Can you open your eyes? Can you sit up?"

"Don't move her," Avery says.

"But we still have fifteen minutes of practice left," Coach says.

"With a hit like that, she could have a spinal injury," Avery persists.

My eyes are now open, which I don't remember doing. But I sure as hell hope this is the only time in my life that my first waking sight is Coach's face this close to mine.

"Ow," I moan.

They laugh, the assholes. "Dude, how's next week look?" Vaughn asks.

"Where do you hurt?" Avery asks. "Can you wiggle your toes? Do you remember what happened?"

I know he's trying to be helpful, but all I know is that I can breathe, so that's all I do.

"OK, let's move you off the ice," Coach says. He and Peters each take an armpit and lift me. The rink lurches, but I stay on my feet.

They set me on the bench and head back out to drop the puck again. Still inside the zone, because no penalty was assessed on Daniel for charging me from the top of the circle.

Megan hovers worriedly over me as I sag onto the bench.

"I think I'm fine," I tell her.

"I think you should get checked out," she says. "You actually blacked out for a few seconds."

Other than feeling like I took a butt end of the stick between the shoulder blades, I don't feel too bad.

"Can you follow my finger?" Megan asks, zooming her index finger around in front of my face.

"Should I be able to? You're buzzing around like a bee."

"I don't know. I don't know what I'm doing."

I take stock. "My head doesn't hurt. Maybe a little light-headed but not bad." I tilt my head in a gentle stretch. "Neck feels fine. Legs are fine. I think I'm OK."

Coach doesn't let me back on the ice, though, which seems to excite my team even more.

I stomp to my closet after practice. I feel completely and totally fine. I could have finished the scrimmage.

I toss my gloves and helmet in my bag and start unlacing my skates. There's a knock on the door. That's new. I stand and open it.

"Manning," Coach says, staying in the hallway.

"Hey, Coach."

"How's the head?"

"Totally fine."

"Well, your team sure is worried about you."

"Are they." Yeah, right.

"Daniel feels real bad, says he didn't mean to hit you that hard. He thinks his elbow may have hit the back of your head and that's what knocked you out."

"Oh. Well, it feels fine now."

"Good, good. He wanted me to know in case I thought you should get checked out. We take head injuries real serious these days. You actually have to have a doctor's clearance to play again if you get hit in the head."

"I don't think Daniel hit me in the head. I think he got me between the shoulder blades."

"Well, he said it was head. I asked him several times because I wanted to be sure. Like I said, we take head injuries seriously these days."

"So you're saying I have to go to the doctor?"

He nods. "To be on the safe side. Can't let you back on the ice again until a doctor clears you."

Shit. Shit, shit, shit. "OK. I'll get you a note ASAP." How? Where am I going to get a doctor's note at nine at night? With thirty-six hours to go until the Showcase.

"Good, good. Need that head, kid. Got a lot of school still ahead of you."

Yeah. Wouldn't want to end up like you, Coach.

And Daniel, so concerned about letting Coach know he'd hit my head. He might actually be smarter than I give him credit for.

I change quickly and hustle out to Dad's car. As I jam my bag in the back, I holler up to him. "I gotta go to the doc. One of those idiots says he hit me in the head and knocked me out and Coach won't let me play until I get a doctor's note. Do you think I can get in tomorrow morning? I need to be on the ice tomorrow. If I'm not, I'll miss the Showcase —"

"Whoa, whoa, whoa," Dad says, hopping out of the car. "You got knocked out?"

"Yeah, for like a second."

"Well, are you OK?"

"I'm fine." I shove my sticks in the back of the car and look up. Dad's frozen with a look of panic on his face. I soften. "I feel perfect, Dad. This is just a formality."

"OK. Geez. OK." He exhales loudly and pulls me into a hug. Dad's not a hugger — no one in my family is.

"I'm sweaty," I remind him, speaking into his fleece jacket.

"That's OK," he says. "I can't believe you got knocked out. No one called an ambulance?"

"No. I didn't need it."

"You don't know that." He leads me around to the passenger's seat. "Sit."

He reclines the seat until I'm staring at the ceiling and buckles the seat belt, pulling it tight. Apparently breathing isn't necessary for recovery.

"This is ridiculous, Dad."

He starts the car and turns in the opposite direction of home.

"We're going now?" I ask.

"Yes. You could have a fracture or a head bleed and not even know it."

"Mom's going to be pissed."

He exhales. "Yes."

Dad drives to the ER and makes me wait in the car while he checks me in, with strict orders not to move a muscle. When he comes back to the car, two guys in scrubs are with him. Without even saying hello first, they lock my head into a stiff white neck brace.

"Don't move," one of them says.

"Uh, I can't."

"Good."

It's supremely uncomfortable. I "don't move" while they debate on how to get me out of the car. It seems that they're used to getting their patients prepackaged by the EMTs and they don't have the means to do it themselves. So they make me wait, lying on the front seat of the car with this awful collar, like I'm going to lick my stitches without it, until the ambulance pulls in. Apparently those guys can get me safely out of the car without moving my spine. Never mind that I carried a hockey bag out of the rink and my spine was fine with that.

But there's still more waiting because the guy in the ambulance is actually dying and they have to save him first. This seems to go well but takes a long time.

Finally, the EMTs come out. They make jokes about me smelling like hockey the whole time they hook me into a strait-jacket thing and get me on a backboard. Effing Daniel must be laughing his butt off somewhere. Meanwhile, Dad paces nervously in the background, arguing with Mom over the phone. “Yes, I’m sure she needed to go in tonight. No, I didn’t want to wait and see if Dr. Joe could get her in tomorrow. Because we need to make sure she’s OK now. You can’t let someone sleep without knowing if they have a head injury. Yes, I’m aware that it’s going to cost more …”

Icky feeling in my chest doesn’t ease the discomfort from being strapped to a hard board. They wheel me into the ER.

And then we wait some more.

I’m not allowed to eat dinner, despite burning a gazillion calories at practice. My homework is not getting done. Again. I’m going to be sore as hell tomorrow — not from the hit but from this board. I’d kill for a shower right now. I can practically hear the zits popping up on my sweat-caked forehead.

Hours later — literally, hours — they jam an X-ray plate in the miniscule space between my spine and the board and find out that my spine is whole and unbroken. I am freed from the board.

But I still don’t get to go home.

“Do you have a headache?” the neurologist asks.

“God, yes,” I answer crankily.

“How long after the injury did it start?” he asks.

“As soon as they strapped me to that board,” I say.

“Dizziness?” he asks. “Light-headedness?”

“Of course I’m dizzy and light-headed. I skipped dinner after practice and I’m tired.” It’s nearing midnight by now.

“OK. Well, we’re going to run you through the CT scan and see how your head looks,” he says.

“Um, sir? I feel fine, really.”

"Precaution," he says. "I'm sure it's negative."

"Is it a really expensive precaution?" I ask, not looking at Dad.

"Mich," Dad warns. "Your head's more important than an ER bill."

So they motor me into the machine, one of those space-age-looking tubes. I almost fall asleep, I'm so tired. Except it's nerve-racking and I'm not supposed to move at all. Again. My insides squirm with the pressure of staying still. It would be heaven to curl up on my side.

Luckily, I have the brain of a sixteen-year-old girl. Insert joke here.

Do I finally get to walk out of there? Nope. We wait an hour more for the paperwork that says I'm fine. Even though we are the last people left in the ER — even the almost-died guy is gone — and you'd think with nothing else to do, signing a couple of pieces of paper would take the doc only a few seconds.

I stumble to the car and raid Dad's granola bar stash again before falling asleep in the passenger seat.

*

At five minutes before class in the morning, I slap a piece of paper onto Coach's desk. He lifts the sheet of Community Hospital letterhead.

"Well, that is good news," he says. "You gave us quite a worry."

"See you at practice, Coach."

"Are you sure you're up for it?"

"Oh, yeah. I'm sure."

I'm not, actually. They want me out of the Showcase and they only have one day left to accomplish this goal. I'm terrified, even walking down the school hallways. I wouldn't put it past them to drop a trash can on my head, poison my lunch, cut a trapdoor in the floor that only I will trigger and fall into. I'm sure they've got more coming for me at practice today.

The only thing I've got going for me is speed. I have to outskate them. Keep the plays out of the corner. I need to have eyes in the back of my head and wings on my feet today.

I skate a few laps to warm up, testing my body, trying to work the stiffness from my neck and back. When I look up between stretches, Dad is standing on the bench. He's dressed in full uniform, which I hope doesn't mean something's wrong. He should be at work for another hour at least.

Dad waves at Coach, who skates over to the bench. They have a short talk; it seems fairly friendly. There's a handshake at the end. And then Coach calls Daniel over.

Acid swirls in my stomach. I have stopped skating now. I watch as Dad crosses his arms over his chest. Daniel takes his helmet off and speaks to both Coach and Dad, his head hanging.

"Michigan!" Coach hollers.

Reluctantly, I skate to the bench. "Dad. Hey. What's up?"

"Hey, kiddo. I just wanted to give Coach the specifics from our trip to the ER last night. And see how you look at practice today. Which is great, by the way."

"It's warm-ups, Dad." I give him an embarrassed shrug.

Dad nudges Daniel's shoulder. "Son?"

Daniel clears his throat and looks up at me. With his back to Dad and Coach, hatred radiates from his eyes and his mouth twists into an ugly sneer. But his voice sounds contrite. "Michigan,

I'm sorry about the hit yesterday. Sometimes I forget you're not used to playing with boys. I'm glad you're OK."

I narrow my eyes. "I'm perfectly fine. You didn't hurt me."

"OK, you two," Coach says. "Back to practice."

"Mind if I stay and watch today?" Dad asks Coach.

"Of course not. If it were me, I'd want to make sure my daughter looked healthy out there."

Dad rests his hand on his hip. Right next to his holstered revolver. "And make sure she stayed healthy."

No one comes within three feet of me at practice.

*

Brie comes over Friday night. We watch *Miracle* and she paints my toenails and fingernails green and gold. Just like old times. But as nice as it is to have a social evening, I'm exhausted. After surviving school and practice on only four hours of sleep, I can't stay awake through the big USA vs. Russia game. Luckily, I already know how it turns out.

I jerk awake as Brie's phone buzzes and blares her Taylor Swift ringtone. Brie squeals into her phone and turns the TV off, just as Eruzione beckons to the team to join him on the podium. I growl at Brie, although I would have missed the historic moment even if her phone hadn't woken me up.

"People congregating at the Arthurs'," she says. "Comb your hair and let's go."

I yawn as I stumble to my feet. "Sorry. Big game tomorrow. I'm going to bed."

"You suck."

"Yep. I'm OK with that. As long as I get some sleep."

"Fine. Be boring the entire time I'm in town."

I don't feel a shred of guilt. I push myself off the couch and to the stairs. "I'm sure you'll miss me. G'night."

Brie knows where the door is. She might even manage to open it without chipping her fancy mani.

I thought I was tired but I can't sleep. I toss and turn.

19

It is chaos in the bowels of the arena. But really cool chaos. I'm not sure if it's excitement I'm inhaling or the smell of fried junk food and buttered popcorn, but my stomach skips as I carry my bag through the arena tunnels.

The cavernous hallways surrounding the rink bustle with medical staff, the ice maintenance crew, a slew of reporters and TV cameras and lots of important-looking people in suits talking into radios. Skate sharpeners buzz loudly through the hallways. Steaming water ricochets out of the garage as the ice crew hose down their metal-studded tires. Four different high school bands warm up in four separate corners of the stands, all of them predictably out of tune.

"I am so sorry," the suited lady with a walkie-talkie says to me. "We don't have an extra locker room for you. But the university coaches have offered to let you use their changing room. I put clean towels and fresh soap in there for you. And I'll lock up while you're on the ice. Will that be OK?"

I grin. I get a shower? But then I hesitate. “I don’t want to kick the coaches out. Especially on their game day.”

“Oh, no, they’re happy to do it. They’re not skating today; they don’t need it. It’s your game day, too.”

A real bench to sit on. Hangers for my clothes. Not a spider in sight. Welcome to the big time.

*

All four high school teams are dressed and lined up in the tunnel leading to the rink entrance. The reporters aren’t allowed to interview us before the game, but there are a lot of photographers and they all seem to have their lenses trained on me. I try to shrink back behind Avery. I don’t need this attention, especially before the game. They might as well sew a bull’s-eye on the back of my jersey.

“Hey,” Avery hisses. “Get up here. Quit shirking. You need to look confident right now.”

He’s right. Predator, not prey. I’m no easy meal. “Shirking?” I tease.

“Sounds dirty, right?” He winks. From Avery, it’s just a funny joke, not intended to make me uncomfortable. I lift an earbud out of his ear and jam it into my own.

He holds out his phone. “Your pick.”

“Tragically Hip? What the heck?”

He shrugs. “Canadian.”

I switch it to Ozzy Osbourne. Avery lifts his eyebrows and nods along. “Oh, yeah. Let’s play some hockey today, Manning.”

Each team gets a ten-minute half-ice warm-up. I try to pay

attention to our drills, but I can't help searching the crowd for Jack, for my family. The section of green and gold, usually crammed together on our small bleachers, is swallowed up by the vast arena. It's so big from the ice, the seats stretching toward the high ceilings, that it's hard to remember the ice sheet itself is the same size as Owl River Community Ice.

The national anthem is played by the university band. Then my team skates off the ice, and Houghton plays Hancock Central High School for a twenty-minute period.

Our first game is against our Homecoming rival, Calumet, the team with the flirtatious opposing center. He winks across the face-off dot. But since it's a one-period game, we face off against each other only once.

I win it.

And the period. Halfway through, during a cluster in front of the net, I poke the puck in. As I pump my fist on the way to the bench, my ears strain for Trent's yell, for Jack hooting from way up in the cheap seats. But the crowd is drowned out by Coach's "Attagirl, Michigan!" He happily pounds his clipboard on the plexiglass behind him and high-fives Assistant Coach Peters.

If hell's freezing over, at least I've got skates on my feet.

We win our first mini-game 1–0. We're playing back-to-back, so we get a whole two minutes between periods to celebrate our win. One minute and fifty-five seconds more than I need, since it only takes Avery and me five seconds to exchange stick-whacks to the shins.

Hancock High puts the pressure on early in our second game. Not only are they rested but they're also ranked number one in the league. Hard hits, fast feet. I'm checked off the puck in the first shift, but I kind of like it. They're not treating me any differently from the rest of my team.

At least I stay on my feet when I get hit. Unlike Daniel.

It's going to be tough getting one past this team, or so I think, as a tired center changes on the fly late in the period. I hop over the boards, ready to join my team in our defensive zone. But the puck thunks against my shin pad as my skates hit the ice. I can hear Avery laughing as I chase his long clearing pass into the offensive zone, my fresh legs giving me an advantage over the tired D. I bury the puck five-hole on the surprised goalie. The game ends in a tie.

We have to sit through an ice make and another period before we play again. I pace the rubber matting in the tunnel, hoping to keep my muscles warm as my soaking-wet gear chills. We get only two minutes on the ice before the puck drops on our last mini-game. There's no time to think about how tired I am or how my sweaty gear is going to do some mean chafing this game. I get my skates moving and use those two minutes to spark a much-needed rush of adrenaline.

I can tell the boys are tired, all except Avery, who vowed nothing would get past him this game. The D is starting to sit back, the wingers are creeping up higher. I'm playing both ends of the ice hard, and it's a lot of skating this late in the day. We're both scoreless so far, and I'm desperately looking for any opportunity to put the puck on net. Best I'm going to get is that Sanders has set up camp at the back door of the Houghton net. I hit his tape with a swift pass.

And the dumbass fumbles it. What's the point of sitting at the back door if you're not ready for a pass? He kicks at the puck as I charge the net. The goalie dives into the crease, hoping to cover, and one of his D falls over him. I whack at the puck and the D slams his hand down over it.

Whistle.

Ref makes the call, crossing his arms over his head. *Yes!* I pump my fist. Our fans go apeshit.

"Who's on the shot, Coach?" the ref barks at the bench.

Without hesitating, Coach points at me. "Sixteen."

Holy fuck. I get to take the penalty shot.

I coast to center ice. This is the first time I've ever played this team; I've never faced their goalie before. I know nothing about him. There's no time to go to the bench for instructions.

So I'll play to my strength. Which is that I am a female forward. The goalie will assume that I have a weak and inconsistent slapshot that doesn't see a lot of use.

It's OK that he's assuming correctly.

The ref sets the puck at center ice. I stand behind it, aware of the four thousand pairs of eyes on me. Four thousand pairs of feet stomping the floorboards. Four thousand vocal cords screaming for or against me.

I settle my gaze on the puck and breathe. The only eyes that matter are those of the ref who will make the call when my puck crosses the goal line. The only feet that matter are mine, poised on the inside edges of my skates, tensed for acceleration. The only sounds that matter are the scrape of my skates on the ice, the tap of the puck off my blade.

And the whistle that tells me to go. I pick up the puck and skate in. At the top of the circle I wind up.

And sure enough, the goalie hunkers down, expecting a low, easy shot. I hesitate, my stick cocked over my shoulder. He has to drop soon or I'll get called for losing possession of the puck.

I shift my weight. He drops.

I fake. Instead of slapping the puck, I sweep it down my stick blade and flick my wrist at his receding shoulder. The puck hits the back of the net.

Natural hat trick.

I scrape to a stop in the corner. The crowd — all of it, not just the green-and-gold section — are on their feet. Their noise swells to fill the cavernous arena, their cheers thundering down to the ice. The guy running the scoreboard holds his finger down on the buzzer and Aerosmith's "Dude (Looks Like a Lady)" booms over the speakers.

It begins to rain hats. The first one thunks off my helmet. I pick up the familiar faded-green Owl River Youth Hockey hat from the ice and turn it over to read the Sharpie scribble on the underside of the brim.

Trenton #16

I laugh out loud and point to where I know my family is sitting in the stands. I didn't think it was possible, but the decibels increase with my gesture. I take Trent's hat with me to the bench, skating around the piles of ball caps and knit beanies and band visors and even one striped Cat in the Hat deal.

Oh, and we win that game, too.

20

Endorphins pound my brain like buckshot. I collapse on the bench in my swank changing room. I've watched pro hockey my entire life. Olympic and college hockey, too. I always thought it would be cool to play in the NHL, in that vague way that every kid thinks about it. Big crowds, loud music, glamorous venues.

Fuck yeah. I could do this every weekend and this is only high school Showcase. I can't even imagine what the NHL life would do to me. I'd black out by second period.

The thoughtful event manager has not only left me fresh towels and soap but also a selection of chilled Gatorade bottles and a plate of bananas, orange slices and protein bars. Big. Time.

And a shower. Ahhh. My muscles could get used to hot water after a game. This is so much better than wiping off with damp paper towels and trying to cover up my stanky hockey sweat with fruity body spray.

I rebraid my hair and slip into my team warm-ups. Coach

changed his slacks-and-tie dress code for this weekend. All the teams are in warm-ups so we can proudly represent our schools. I'm so happy that I don't have to look like a magician's assistant at the U game. I help myself to a banana and Gatorade and jam a protein bar in my pocket for later. And then an extra for Trent.

There's a horde waiting outside my door. Literally, a horde.

Coach stands proudly by. "Michigan!" he says. I guess we're on a first-name basis now. "Great game, kid. This is Eric Johnson, the hockey commissioner for the Michigan High School Athletic Association."

Mr. Johnson shakes my hand. "Congratulations on a great Showcase, Michigan."

"Thank you, sir."

"There are a few reporters who would love to speak with you, if you're willing."

"I, uh ..."

"Of course, she'd be happy to," Coach says, narrowing his eyes at me. "What a great opportunity to show school spirit."

"Well, you couldn't ask for a better athlete to represent Owl River," Mr. Johnson says heartily. "Michigan, I'd also like to make sure that when we introduce the teams before the U game, you are up front with your captain. Can you do that for me?"

I want to roll my eyes. Parade the girl out front. Do they want me to wear a dress, too, maybe doll up with some makeup before the game? But Coach's expression reminds me that I am publicly representing my team, my coaches and my school right now. Somewhere in the stands, my bantams are learning from my behavior. Megan and her little cousins are relying on me to prove that a girl is capable of handling this privilege.

"Yes, sir. I can do that." I will put on a sportsmanlike smile and cough up a few sports clichés for the reporters. Lord knows I've learned enough of them from Coach this year.

I make my way through the gauntlet of reporters with a perma-smile. I channel all the ESPN interviews I've ever seen, rehearsing phrases like "It was a team effort" and "The bounces went our way today." But the reporters don't seem to care about that. They want to know why I went out for the boys' team, what my former teammates are doing this season, how it felt the first time I threw a hit. I think of Daniel.

"It felt great," I say, grinning. "Like I'd been missing out all those years."

"Any bruising?" a reporter asks.

"Yes, I've given out a few bruises this season," I say. I'm rewarded with laughs, and the hallway suddenly sparkles with new energy. I feel them leaning toward me, eager for more.

"Will you ever go back to girls' hockey?" one asks.

"No," I say. "But I'd like to play women's hockey."

"Hoo!" one of them says. "I will bet anyone here that you will."

"No one's betting against this girl," another one says. "'Scuse me — woman."

When the noise of the stadium reminds us that a college game is imminent, the reporters thank me, shake my hand and run off. I hurry to join up with my team. They're lined up in the tunnel again, waiting to walk out onto the black carpet that's being unrolled on the ice. I missed the college teams' warm-ups, and they're filing off the ice now, headed to their locker rooms for their coaches' pre-game talks.

And *hello.* Remind me to definitely go to college. Even in

full gear, there are some hotties. Although I guess any guy built tough enough for college hockey would qualify as hot. Especially in those shiny uniforms. I get a wink from one. No offense to Jack, of course, but I don't mind a little flattery.

"Michigan Manning," a voice says behind me. I turn to face the coaching staff of the U. The head coach holds out his hand to shake mine. "That was quite a game. Too bad we can't suit you up to play for us today."

"Thank you," I say. "I'm free next weekend."

They chuckle and wish me luck before walking away. Who the heck is this girl with the public persona and the cheesy smile and the quick replies?

Death rays shoot from Daniel's eyes as I take my place next to him in line. "How is the performing monkey of the high school hockey circuit?" he asks.

"I'm great. It's nice to get hit by real men for a change."

"Even though everyone else here is excited that you've got tits, on this team you're still a rookie. So get to the back of the line."

"Can't. I was specifically told to walk out with you."

Daniel perks up. "Did they say why? Did we make the All-Tournament Team?"

"He didn't say." I just figured they wanted me to smile for their cameras. I did score a hat trick, but I can't be the only one who had a good game. There's a kid on Calumet's team who already has a full scholarship to Michigan State next year, and the hallways are buzzing about his coast-to-coast goal today.

One by one, the teams are called to the ice. The announcer booms out the school's name and town, the coaching staff and the captain's name. We're the last school to enter, and the crowd is chanting by the time we step onto the black carpet. Daniel's ego and grin barely fit through the rink door as his name booms over the ice. It kind of makes me sad for him. I'm enjoying this, but I don't crave this attention like he seems to. I stay close, as instructed, but I'd feel like a douchebag if I paraded myself out here.

The chanting gets clearer now that I'm on the ice.

"Bring us the girl! Bring us the girl!"

Oh, my God. I double-check the teams on either side of me, but as figured, out of all four teams I am the only girl. A few of my opponents actually clap in my direction, as if all this fanfare is for me.

"And now, to announce the All-Tournament Team is the hockey commissioner of the Michigan High School Athletic Association, Mr. Eric Johnson."

Mr. Johnson steps to the front of the carpet, speaking into a microphone.

"What a Showcase! Thank you all for supporting high school hockey in Michigan! We are proud to present the top four teams at the mid-point of the season, and I know that you enjoyed their skills as well. It is my great honor to announce the All-Tournament Team. Starting with our number-one goalie, with a point-nine-six-four save percentage this afternoon. He faced twenty-eight shots and only got unlucky once. From Owl River High, Avery Gardiner!"

My team goes nuts, screaming for Avery. It's a really big deal to be the best goalie in an event like this. Right now a bunch of college coaches are making notes next to his name on their clipboards. Any time a coach looks him up online, this accolade will pop up.

Mr. Johnson gives Avery a handshake and a small trophy and directs him to stand just behind him. "Our defensemen for the All-Tournament Team … from Houghton High School, Chad Stewart and Bobby Oates."

The boys come forward, receive their trophies, shake hands with the commissioner and give each other one of those slappy boy-hugs. Avery shakes their hands as they slide in next to him. I side-eye Daniel and enjoy watching his posture deflate. No All-Tournament Team for him.

"On right wing, from Hancock Central High School, a playmaker with an astounding four assists today, Matt Hinz."

As Hinz takes his place, all the left wingers on my team whisper, "Come on, come on …"

"On left wing, from Calumet High School, with two goals and one assist today, Trevor Wilcox." That's the Michigan State kid.

Wilcox struts to his spot next to Hinz and the chant starts up again. "Bring us the girl! Bring us the girl!"

"And last, I am proud to introduce our All-Tournament center, and our Showcase MVP. With a hat trick this afternoon … from Owl River High School … *Miss* Michigan Manning."

God, I sound like a beauty pageant contestant.

Wait. That's *me.* I am the All-Tournament center. I am the MVP!

Hells, yeah. I let the grin take over my face as I make my way to Mr. Johnson. Avery doesn't even let me get there before charging me. He wraps his arms around me and lifts me up, shaking me. I laugh, and as he brings me back down to the matting, the other

All-Tournament players slap my back and high-five me. I finally end up in front of Mr. Johnson, where I have to figure out how to shake his hand while juggling two trophies.

The crowd is even louder than when I scored that third goal. I expect that Dad and Trent are screaming their lungs out, but I can't believe an entire stadium of strangers actually cares that I had a hat trick. Whether or not I am a girl.

"Lots of people pulling for you," Mr. Johnson says, away from his microphone. He clasps my hands, still clutching the trophies, leaning in to make sure I can hear him over the crowd. "You're doing great things for girls in hockey right now — for girls in all sports. You're a fantastic role model, and we couldn't be prouder of you."

Pride and pressure take equal space in my heart as I turn to face the crowd and wave hello. I blow a kiss to Jeannie, Kendall and Jordo, who are screaming so hard that it looks like Jeannie's going to pass out. Jack is way up in the cheap seats, but he's pumping his fist in the air and yelling. He's got a big yellow 16 made out of duct tape across the front of his green sweatshirt. Swoon.

This is the biggest night of my life. Sure, I'm only sixteen so I haven't had a lot of big nights. My first slumber party. My first date, which was also my first kiss. That's about it.

But this is huge. I'm swamped. I can't walk up the stairs to my seat without people stopping to congratulate me. Coaches come up to ask if I'll speak to their U14 girls' teams or if I want to play midgets instead of high school. Some guy asks if I'd be in print advertisements for his nutritional supplement drink. Which sounds like a creepy way of taking photos of me. Also, his drink sounds nasty. Another guy tries to talk me into training at his really expensive gym. "I can get you ready for college hockey," he says. "If you train with me, you could play Olympic hockey."

"Let's not get ahead of ourselves," I say, cringing away from his hairy, overly muscled handshake.

I'm mobbed by the Silver Lake girls as I near my seat, but Brie is nowhere to be seen. Once I untangle myself from them, I wave to Jack. He was able to get tickets with a couple of his swimmer friends, so he's staying for the U game. I mime that I'll come talk to him after I check in with my family.

Dad gives me a bouncing hug — that's two hugs in less than a week. "Man, I'm proud of you," he says over and over. He doesn't seem to be able to say anything else, but the emotion is so thick in his voice that he doesn't have to. Mom looks uncomfortable. I don't know whether it's being at a hockey game or that she's unsure what to do with a minor celebrity in the household. She's at a loss for words, but she does squeeze my hand and rub a smudge off my MVP trophy with her sweatshirt.

Trent snags his hat from my waistband. "Hey, I got it back!"

"No way!" I snatch it out of his hand. "I'm keeping this. That was my first hat trick. This goes up in my room."

He looks pleased. "Fine, I'll have messy hair." I don't point out that it's never not messy. I hand him the protein bar I snagged for him.

"Sweet. Thanks." He tears it open. "This is the same kind the U team eats, right?"

"I guess so."

"Awesome."

Brie slides into her seat next to me. "Guess what?" she sings.

"Uh, I won MVP?"

"No. I mean, congrats. But I just ran into Kyle Lennox. Do you remember him? Of course you do, he was so hot. Is so hot! He's at school here and his frat is having a party tonight and we are sooooo going! Oh!" She frowns at my warm-up suit. "You brought real clothes, right? Because I am not taking you to a college party looking like that."

I don't even bother asking my parents if I can go. Like any parent is going to say, *Sure, my sweet little sixteen! Go have fun with the I Felta Thigh college boys. Be sure to sample all the beverages!* Geez, Dad would have half the squad cars in the U.P. lined up out front of the frat house.

Besides, what the F? Sure, Brie's been away for months. But, believe me, for the two years before that, it was The Brie Show, 24-7. I've been through pure hell since she left, and she can't even take a break from herself for five seconds to congratulate me?

I stand and slide past her. She's already pulling out her phone to inform everyone she knows that she's *a-maz-ing* because she got invited to drink with a bunch of guys who are trying to jam every pair of boobs in the U.P. into their frat house.

I'm halfway up the stairs when Jack sees me and jumps up. He sprints to me and throws his arms around my waist, even though the puck is in play and people around us are yelling at him to sit down.

"Great game!" he says, leaning in for a kiss.

I spin around, focusing on my parents' seats. Yep, they're watching. Jack follows my gaze and chuckles. "OK, you owe me double hello kisses next time."

He grabs my hand and pulls me into his row. The beer-toting

fans behind us sarcastically call, “Thank you.” We quickly squeeze into Jack’s seat, next to three other Owl River upperclassmen.

“Joey, Tucker, T.C., you know Mich, right?” Jack says.

We all wave and say hi. My kindergarten cubby was next to T.C.’s. I carpooled to mites with Joey’s and Tucker’s parents. Yep, we’re good.

We’re so far up in the ceiling that the puck is microscopic. And my shoes are already glued to the concrete floor with spilled pop. I’m balanced with one-quarter of my quickly-going-numb butt on the seat, my entire side squashed against Jack’s, and our elbows pushed forward awkwardly because he refuses to let go of my hand, even with Officer Dad only yards away.

It’s the best way I can think of to watch a game. Unless I’m playing in it.

21

The first letters arrive on Tuesday and continuc to trickle in throughout the week. College hockey programs. Select teams. Even a few boarding schools on the East Coast.

They all want me. Four months ago I thought my hockey career was over, and now I get handwritten cards from Harvard in the mail. (They haven't heard how much homework I've been skipping for practice.)

"A scholarship sure would be nice after that ER bill," Mom says, dropping three envelopes in front of my place at the dinner table. Dinner's long over but I had late practice, so I just got home. Still stirring my mac and cheese, I peek at the return addresses.

"A scholarship sure would be nice after I've busted my butt for it."

She huffs. Busting my butt for hockey does not count in her book. Hell if I know what does.

"Trent!" I yell. I pour half the pot into my bowl. "I have extra mac and cheese. D'you want?"

"He ate spaghetti an hour ago," Mom says.

Trent bounds into the kitchen. "Mine!"

"OK, but you have to wash the pot," I say.

"Deal. Thanks, Mich." He grabs a fork and shovels in gigantic bites straight from the pot. "More letters? Can I open one?" He scrapes a chair over to sit next to me.

I hand him Boston College while I tear into brochures for Ann Arbor's summer tournament team and Amherst's DIII team. Not bad for today's haul. I'll add them to the pile in my room. I'm not going to think about them yet. I refuse to picture how awesome I'd look in Badger red and white. I'm going to keep my focus on this season. If the second half goes as well as the first, then when I have time to breathe in April, I can actually give these the attention they deserve.

Sports Illustrated put me in Faces in the Crowd, their high school athlete blurbs, after the Showcase. A Detroit newspaper sent a reporter to one of our practices over winter break and the local paper was there today. If we continue to have witnesses with cameras at each practice, I'll never get illegally hit again.

*

Daniel smacks the squat bar with a copy of this week's *Sports Illustrated*. Not cool when my legs are shaking at the end of my set. My poker face holds strong in the mirror. I already lift less weight than my 160-pound, testosterone-jacked teammates. Can't afford to look weak doing it.

"Guess this means you won't be quitting the team," he says.

I make him wait while I finish my last squat and rack the weight. "I never planned on quitting."

"Well, it's good you stayed."

Wait. What?

He continues. "Really. The visibility has been great for the program. The boosters are buying us more swag and Coach has been in an awesome mood. We're sitting pretty for playoffs in a few weeks. You've done good, Mich."

"Um, OK. Thanks, Daniel."

He tries to smile but his grip on the rolled-up magazine is so tight that the tendons in his hand stick up. I glance in the mirror and see that the weight room monitor — a football coach, obviously — is indeed within shouting distance if Daniel clocks me over the head with a plate weight. "I guess that means you've truly earned your spot on this team."

"OK. Great." Not that it was ever for Daniel to judge. I earned my spot at tryouts. Or maybe when I told Coach to put me at center and he knew he had to.

"So you should come for team bonding at my place on Saturday night."

Spend time with these idiots when it's not mandatory? No, thank you. I much prefer making out with my hot swimmer boyfriend. "Thanks, but I have plans already. I have to coach my brother's game and then I'm meeting … friends for dinner."

"It'll be after your brother's game. And you can meet your friends for dinner another time." He puts on a serious face. "This team is preparing for playoffs, Mich. Coach wants us to be tight. And as you're the leading scorer, the guys need to know that you support this team. Coach needs to know you support us."

"Wait — Coach is coming?"

"He might drop by early on. You know, before his bedtime."

Daniel gives me a nudge. Aren't we great teammates, sharing a joke about how old our coach is.

Can't imagine Coach enjoying an evening of video games, which are the only team bonding activities I've caught wind of. But as this is the first time I've ever been invited, what do I know? Our women's coach once dropped off homemade chocolate chip cookies for our movie night, although she didn't stay.

But now I don't know the rules. I'm not supposed to socialize with the boys. But I don't want to be the jerk who isn't a team player either.

"I'll check with Coach to see if he wants me there."

"Why do you think I'm here, Manning? I just came from Coach's office. Look, he's got us under pretty strict rules, so I'm sorry we haven't invited you to any other events. But he's asking now. Playoffs, Manning. After the Showcase, it's obvious we're in it. We can do this."

Inwardly I groan at his cheesy speech, but he does have a point. No, I don't want to be friends with these guys. But I want playoffs. I want hardware. I want to face that growing pile of college letters with a big-ass trophy and badass stats. I need this team to function as one for the next few weeks.

"Fine, I'll come. Just for a little while. I don't think my parents will let me stay out late."

"The guys will be happy you're there, even if it's for a little while."

Really? They haven't been overtly mean to me since the Showcase. But other than Avery, no one's friendly either. They seem to think it's safest to ignore me.

Should I be worried that no one's been overtly mean to me since the Showcase?

22

After Trent's game on Saturday, I drop him and his smelly bag off at home. I don't bother changing out of the jeans and team jacket I wore to the rink. I'm certainly not trying to look good for any of these guys. I wave to Trent, make sure he gets inside OK and start the walk to Daniel's house. Of course it was OK to borrow Mom's car when it meant she didn't have to shuttle Trent back and forth to the rink. But when it comes to walking through town — late at night, in the middle of winter, in Northern Michigan — for what's basically mandatory team bonding, I have to walk.

I pull a pair of knit mittens from my pocket and hunch my chin into the zippered collar of my bantam jacket. My toes are already numb from standing on the bench all game, and I'm regretting not putting on a real winter coat. I'd warm up if I jogged, but frostbite is preferable to arriving any earlier to this thing.

Daniel lives on the other side of the high school from my neighborhood, so the tips of my nose and ears are frozen by the time I get there. I wipe the cold-induced boogers from my nose and push through the chain-link gate.

Daniel does not come from money, one of the many reasons that he and Brie didn't work out. Daddy's little princess expects to be dined and gifted appropriately. I recognize Daniel's beat-up muscle car in the driveway, but I can't tell if the other cars lining the street belong to the team or to his neighbors. I hope Coach is already here.

My plan is to stick close to Avery, make sure Coach sees me being sociable and yet following his rules. I'll sneak out when Coach leaves. I need a passing grade, but I'm not looking for extra credit here.

Through the banged-up storm door, I can hear boys' voices, PlayStation explosions and, suddenly, Tupac loud enough to rattle the fogged-up windows. Coach is letting this slide?

Not surprisingly, no one answers my knock. I push the front door open.

Fuuuuuuuuuck. My ass, Coach is attending this team bonding event. I've just walked into one of the team's legendary parties.

Hazy cigar smoke assaults my nose and I lift my arm to breathe through my sleeve. I'm sure Mom won't freak when I come home smelling like that. There's already the beginning of a beer can pyramid on the windowsill, and let's just say these guys didn't splurge on the good stuff. Half a dozen guys are crammed onto the couch in front of the TV. Two of them hold video game controllers, and the other four act as expert coaches, eagerly waiting their own turns.

Daniel and the other seniors have taken over the cramped

kitchen, surrounding a table overflowing with bar debris. Red plastic cups, crushed beer cans, a melting five-pound bag of ice and a half-empty jug of whiskey.

I've already turned toward the door when Daniel yells, "There she is!" He crosses the room and puts his arm around my shoulders, pulling me into the kitchen. "Get this girl a drink!"

"I don't —" I start, but then I figure it'll be smarter if I keep a cup in my hand. I can pour it down the drain when I sneak off to the bathroom. Which, I'm guessing, judging from what the boys have done to this kitchen, is so disgusting that I'd never use it. Another good reason not to drink. "I can't stay long," I say.

Daniel gives my shoulders a squeeze. "Team bonding, Michigan. Mandatory. Coach's Law."

Right. Coach insisted on a party that'll probably end with Dad's friends from the P.D. showing up.

Vaughn shoves a beer into my hand and clinks it with his own can. They go back to debating whether the kitchen has enough dimensions for a game of beer pong.

I lean against the wall of the TV room, wondering why I'm here. Coach clearly didn't demand it. Daniel — there's no way he's had a change of heart. The rest of the guys still ignore me, focused only on drinking and gaming. So much for team bonding. *Why did they bring me here?*

And are Daniel's parents within shouting distance?

Avery slings his arm around my shoulders. Foamy beer floods over the top of my still-full can. I lift it quickly so it runs all over the carpet instead of my jeans.

"There's my MVP," Avery slurs. "Hey, don't drink this." He pulls the beer from my hand.

"Yeah, you're the poster child for abstinence," I say. But I can't help smiling at him. A drunk, skinny goalie is better backup than nothing.

"I'm Canadian," he says. "I'm supporting my country's economy." A whiff of his red plastic cup tells me he's drinking the same Canadian rye my dad keeps locked away from Trent and me. Avery takes a sip, winces and sways. I grip his biceps.

"Thanks, babe." He points at me with his cup and fixes me with a stare. "No drinking for Michigan."

"No drinking," I echo. "Maybe no more drinking for Avery either?"

"Oh, Avery drinks. Not this crap." He pours my entire can of beer onto the carpet.

"Avery, stop! Not cool." I can't believe he's drunk enough that he did that.

"It's OK. Winston already puked on the carpet over there." He points to the floor next to the couch. My throat tightens and I look away quickly. Did no one think to clean that up?

"Rookies!" Daniel's voice booms from the kitchen. "Get your asses in here."

"Rookies! Rookies!" Breaker and Vaughn chant and punch the air.

"You, too, Manning, you're a rookie," Daniel says.

That icky stomach feeling I've gotten to know so well this season kicks into full gear. I glance at Avery. Even through the drunkenness, he looks worried. He sets his red cup down and follows me into the kitchen.

I could pretend to get sick and run to the bathroom and climb out the window. That's assuming the bathroom has a window. If not, I'll end up spending the night in the same room as the toilet Daniel pees in.

Or I could pretend to get an emergency phone call from my mom. Suddenly remember that I'm supposed to drive my brother somewhere. Both options will earn me a lifetime of grief, but it's not like I care what these guys think of me.

But it's too late. Breaker shoves a new drink at me. Apparently they've already run through their supply of red cups because Daniel is passing around an assortment of mugs and plastic gas station cups filled with strong-smelling liquids.

"We've fixed each of you a very special cocktail, rookies. You know the rules." Around me, the other rookies groan. Looks like I haven't really been missing out on team bonding. "Last one to drink it streaks the perimeter of the house naked. Did I hear it just started snowing?" He chuckles and his minions Breaker and Vaughn hoot along with him. "If you puke it up, you take a dare. If you correctly guess what's in your drink, you get the privilege of giving a dare to an upperclassman of your choosing."

Fuck. Just fuck. I peer into my Michigan Tech Huskies mug. It doesn't look all that bad, actually. Just clear red liquid, like cranberry juice, with a small swirl of sediment on the bottom. It smells sharp, like liquor, but also maybe fruity. Or at least that's what I tell myself. I peek into Samuel's cup next to me. His smells like asparagus pee and there's something chunky floating in it.

I am not taking my clothes off in front of these guys. I am not giving them a chance to dare me into doing anything. I will swallow this mug of whatever in one fell swoop and then I'll keep swallowing to make sure it stays down. And then I'll get the hell out of here.

Avery catches my eye from across the table and shakes his head, frowning. I shrug at him.

"Rookies, on three!" Daniel yells. "One! Two! Three!"

I lift and drink as quickly as I can, slamming my mug down on the kitchen table. The juicy taste of berries is a welcome relief. Yeah, there's a little burn, too. I hope it's not something designed to make me puke, like hydrogen peroxide. Around me, my freshman and sophomore teammates alternately gag and chug.

"Ugh, was that milk and beer?" Ethan asks, reaching for a chaser can.

Next to him, between coughing fits, Ty chokes out, "Lucky bastard." He burps up an actual soap bubble. "Burping's not against the rules! No puke, I swear!"

Sanders is the last to finish, although when he realizes he's the last, he refuses to finish anyway. Without hesitation, he strips off every bit of clothing and jogs to the front door. He throws it open and wiggles his bare butt at us, giving a full bending moon before running out of the house. By the time he gets back, though, he's swearing up a storm. "Effing frostbite on my junk," he yells, sitting bare-assed on Daniel's couch to pick sidewalk salt out of his feet.

Winston responds by puking, which apparently he's been doing at regular intervals for half an hour now, regardless of the cologne-and-whiskey combo they gave him. As soon as he stops puking long enough to wipe his mouth, Breaker points at him and yells, "Dare!"

Daniel appears to think for a moment. "Text a picture of your dick to ..."

"Ooh, that preacher's daughter," Vaughn says. I mouth the name along with him. "Jeannie Nichols."

"No, no, no," I whisper. Jeannie is not planning on seeing a boy's reproductive organ (as she calls it) until her wedding night. She's never even kissed a guy. Not only that, but her parents monitor her phone very closely. She could get in huge trouble for this.

Someone finds her phone number. I'm trying to think of a way to divert attention from this dare, but I can't come up with an idea that won't draw attention to me. In fact, I can't come up with any ideas.

I can't come up with any thoughts, period. I'm suddenly feeling very zoned out.

It's late. It's been a long day. The stress of being here is catching up to me. But this is the perfect time to slip out, while they're all distracted by Winston, who has dropped trou and is trying to focus his phone on his crotch. That makes three penises I've seen on this team and I'd like to leave it at that.

I aim my body at the front door and try to lift my legs, but they're too heavy. In fact, my whole body is heavy, too heavy to stay upright without the support of the living room wall. I've never had liquor before, only beer, and even then not much. Is this what liquor does to you? I had no idea I would be such a cheap date.

"You don't look so good," Daniel says, appearing next to me.

"I'm fine," I say. It sounds like I'm in a tunnel. "Tunnel," I say, and the word stretches out slowly, bouncing off of the walls close around me. Yes, definitely I am in the tunnel in Daniel's living room.

"Door," I say, and the tunnel echoes it back to me. I push myself off the wall and aim for the door again. Why isn't the door getting any closer? I timber like a tree and grab for the nearest support. Daniel's arm. Isn't he helpful.

"I gotcha," he says. "You just need to lie down for a minute. You'll be OK."

"What was in there?" I slur. Mouth will not cooperate with me. "Will it go away fast?"

"It will. It's just a joke, Michigan. You'll be fine. Here, come with me."

Daniel leads me away from the party, down a short hallway and into a closet-sized bedroom. He sits me on the bed and flicks on a small lamp.

"Ish thish yer room?" I speak slowly, trying to enunciate. "Whatchoo give me?" The room spins and the shadows along the wall deepen.

"Just liquor," Daniel says. So smoothly, as if speaking takes no effort whatsoever.

It smells like hockey gear in here, but as soon as Daniel sits close to me it smells like cologne. Too much cologne. Too close. I grip the bedspread, trying to stop the spinning.

"Michigan, I'm real proud of what you've done this year," Daniel says. I think it's Daniel. But that doesn't sound like something Daniel would say. "You're amazing on the ice and you're so smart and you're gorgeous. I know it's weird because I dated Brie but we were never right for each other. You know that."

His voice fades away, swallowed up by the tunnel that I seem to live in now. But I can feel him right next to me, with his hand on my knee and his shoulder pressed against mine.

"Michigan Manning," murmurs the dark-haired boy.

"Shoulder and a knee equals a hand," I say to Jack. But this isn't Jack. Or is it? No, this isn't Jack. Jack smells like chlorine. All I smell is cologne. All I taste is liquor. Jack would never drink liquor, but the boy who is kissing me tastes of liquor.

"Got it, Daniel."

I didn't say that. That's a boy's voice. Is the boy here Daniel? Why am I with Daniel? Daniel hates me. Where did Jack go?

There's a loud crash and yelling. But there's also a blanket. A nice one, even though it's rough and smells like boy. But blankets are good because you can curl up under them and sleep.

23

Mich! Mich, oh, my God.

You fucker! I will fucking kill you!

Mich, honey, can you sit up?

Kendall, help me sit her up.

Mich. My name is Mich. Someone is talking to me. I already forgot what she said. There's also a very angry girl here but I don't think I'm in trouble. It doesn't sound like my mom.

"Mich, we're here. It's going to be OK." It's a soothing, thick Yooper accent.

The voice triggers a memory. "Jeannie, don't let your mom see your phone," I mumble. I sound sleepy. I feel sleepy. Why aren't they letting me sleep?

"Phone, Jeannie," I mumble again. I know this is important. "Phone."

"Shhh," she says. "I got it. It's actually a good thing they did that."

"I want the fucking police here right now!" Jordan bellows.

"What did you do? Answer me, Daniel, you shit. What. Did. You. DO?!" Jordan's voice comes from outside of my room. Or the room I'm in. It doesn't seem like my room. It's dark and it smells like my broom closet. I burp and the acid tastes faintly of berries. My stomach turns.

I clutch Kendall's arm. Her face is blurry in the darkness of the closet. "Why are we in my broom closet?"

She hesitates. "We're in Daniel's bedroom."

Daniel's bedroom. Not good.

Jeannie holds a cup to my lips. "It's water, Mich. Drink some water."

I sit up and the warmth of the blanket slips away.

"Oh, thank you, God, she's still dressed," Jeannie breathes.

"I will tear this house apart and figure out what you drugged her with and I will take it down to the police station and they will throw your sorry ass in jail. No! Get your fucking hands off me."

Thud.

Groan.

"Jordan just smashed Daniel in the balls," Kendall narrates. "Please tell me you're getting this, Whit."

"Oh, I got it. Video is running. If she can just get him to admit to whatever it was they gave Mich …"

"Can you remember what he did to you, Mich?" Kendall asks.

"Kendall! Not now," Jeannie says.

"But it's important," she says. "Otherwise, do we go to the cops or the hospital?"

"No," I gasp. "No! My dad … No! No cops. No hospital." I don't know what my dad will do, but it won't be good. I drank something from a cup that a boy who hates me handed me. Bad Michigan. And hospitals are just as bad as cops because hospitals call dads who are cops.

Suddenly, I answer Kendall's question. "Oh, my God, Kendall. I kissed someone. And it wasn't Jack." I drop my head into my shaking hands. I can't lose Jack. He's the best thing that's ever happened to me and the only guy I know who's not a complete shithole. As soon as my brain alerts my stomach to the memory of Daniel's tongue against mine, I gag. Kendall fumbles for the blanket but nothing comes up.

"Cop car out front!" Male voices from far away start talking over each other, mostly in expletives.

"Time to go, ladies," Kendall says. She and Jeannie slide their arms around me and lift. I push away from the boy-smelling bed. We stumble through the door. The narrow hallway is a chaos of bodies and noise and bright light.

"Get her out. Back door!"

"Come on, Mich, you can do this."

My legs are unsteady but Kendall and Jeannie are basically carrying me. I hang on for dear life as we bang down the narrow hallway and out a door. The world is spinny and black and cold and starry. Suddenly, there are dark steps and we tumble like dominoes. I hit the ground on my hands and knees. The combination of the jarring sensation and the icy, fresh air sharpens my focus. I stand, shakily, and brush fresh snow off my bruised palms.

Blue and red lights flash against the side of the house. I clutch Jeannie's hand and stumble after her to a car. Jordan's car. I collapse on the backseat on my hands and knees, crawling to the center of the seat. Someone jams my rear farther into the car, someone else sits on my hands. Bodies are squished around me and I can't breathe. Voices on either side of me yell, "Go! Go!"

"Quiet!" Jordan yells back. "I got this!"

They shut up immediately. Jordan eases her car away from the curb and down the street, muttering, "Don't see me, don't see me …" Several houses down, she turns on her lights and picks up her pace and we all exhale together.

"Now what?" Jordan asks.

"Windows," I say. That spinning sensation has returned. My panic rises. "Window. Down. I need air."

Windows crank open on both sides of the car and the fresh air slaps my face again. I concentrate on my breathing. Jordan pulls the car over, into the school parking lot.

"How do you want to handle this, Mich?" she asks.

I don't. I want to breathe. And sleep. Until my body is normal again. Until time rewinds and none of this happened.

"Home," I say. "I have to get home. God, I smell …"

"You do." Jeannie nods. "You smell like smoke."

"You look like hell," Avery says.

"Avery!" I peer through the darkness of Jordan's backseat. "What are you doing here?"

Jordan hits the overhead light and I squint at Avery's swollen nose.

"I tried, Mich," he says apologetically. He's still slurring, or maybe my ears are, but he's sobered up enough to sit up straight and flatten down his hair.

"Not hard enough," Jordan snaps.

"Did — did Daniel plan this?" I ask Avery.

"Yeah. They tried to keep me in the dark, but I heard them talking before you got there."

"Who? Daniel and who?"

"The seniors, basically. They gave you some date-rape drug."

I scrub my eyes with my hands. "Ohhh, this is bad. Are they trying to scare me off the team or get me kicked off?"

"Kicked off."

Stupid, stupid Mich. Of course that's the only reason they invited you. You are such an idiot.

"Why would your own team want you out?" Kendall asks. "You're the best player."

"And the best teammate," Jeannie says loyally. "Of course they want you on the team."

"No," I say. "They don't. They never did." I hate the sadness in my voice. I hate that they hurt me. I hate that I let them.

"I want you on the team," Avery says. "I'm sorry, Mich."

"I'm sorry they hit you," I tell him. "Are you OK?"

He reaches over Jeannie to shove my shoulder. Guess that's a yes. "Are you?"

I shake my head and look away.

Jack. I kissed Daniel, not Jack. My parents — they're going to freak. And how can I play with this team now? Everything was going well. My center position. Showcase MVP. College letters. Playoffs in less than a month. Scholarships.

I'm going to lose it all.

"Home," I say again. "I'll confront Daniel tomorrow, when I've got a clear mind." And hopefully a voice that won't wobble and a stomach that won't threaten to eject its contents.

Jeannie holds up her keys. "First, we get you cleaned up," she says.

"Right, Jee," Jordan says. "Because your parents won't flip their shit if we show up at your house like this."

"Not my house," she says. "The church has a shower. And clean T-shirts."

And lightning bolts to smite me. But to the church we go.

24

I get why they call drinks "spiked." Whatever Daniel drugged me with is stabbing my brain with an ice pick. Even the sliver of moon shining into my dark bedroom is too much light for me.

As soon as my headache woke me, other symptoms made themselves known. Cotton mouth and raw, scratchy throat. Stinging eyes. Bruised knees and palms.

Nausea that has nothing to do with what I drank.

But what I'm really feeling this morning? Fury.

I reach for my phone. It's seven thirty. I text Daniel.

If you're not in the school parking lot in 15 minutes, I will call the cops.

I start to pull on my comfiest pair of old sweats and scan my bedroom for a hat.

No. I can't stumble up there looking hungover and weak. A thirty-second shower washes the gunk from around my eyes and opens my lungs after that cigar smoke yesterday. I chase Tylenol with a large glass of water. Gargle mouthwash. Then I put on my team hoodie and a pair of jeans and sweep my hair into a ponytail. I even swipe on a little blush and mascara. Not to look good for the scumbag but to mask my sunken eyes and pale skin.

Although the mental image of Dad clapping cuffs on Daniel is one I'll daydream on replay, I need to keep this quiet. I'm the one on the power play now. I have to use my advantage to score. I sneak out and hustle to the school, thankful for the frigid morning air that wakes me up and adds even more color to my face.

I review my assets to subdue the anger that only wants me to punch Daniel. I have Whit's phone video evidence. I have Avery willing to testify to what he heard.

The school is a five-minute walk from my house. Daniel's house is half the distance, and yet his is the only car in the seniors' lot when I arrive. Dark gray exhaust clouds from the tailpipe pollute my lungs, already in pain from the cold morning air. It probably took him longer to scrape a small window on the ice of his windshield than it would have taken to walk here.

I knock on his window. He rolls it open and turns down the rap music at the same time.

"Get out," I say.

Daniel smirks. "Is this the part where you knee me in the balls to make yourself feel better?"

My fists clench in my mittens. "Get out of your car," I repeat. "Be a fucking man and face me."

He does, although his movements say that he's getting out of the car because he feels like stretching, not because I told him to.

There is a solidly built six-foot-tall eighteen-year-old standing in front of me. And he hates me.

The morning is too quiet, too dark. The nearest house is two football fields away, and I'm sure its occupants are smart enough to still be in bed on a snowy Sunday morning. Sweat freezes in my pores, and panic dampens my armpits inside my jacket. I wish I was wearing hockey gear, carrying a stick.

So what if I'm not? If he's planning to hurt me, I won't go down easy. I'll defend myself — finally. Just because I've kept my fists in my pockets this whole season doesn't mean I don't know how to use them. Dad made sure of that years ago. My muscles flex, ready to fight if Daniel moves in my direction.

Steam puffs from my mouth like an angry dragon. "You will stop it. The stupid pranks, the crass comments, the intentional hits. All of it."

He grunts, a smug smile on his face. "Or what?"

"I'll take the evidence I have that you drugged me and attempted to … have inappropriate relations with me, to the police."

"I didn't drug you."

"Yes, you did."

"Prove it."

"I can. Av — people — heard you talking with the seniors. Whit taped that fight last night. All four of those girls will happily testify in court to what they saw when they walked in."

"What they saw was me trying to help a teammate who drank too much. And you came on to me."

"I did not." I shudder. I would never come on to him.

But I can't actually put my finger on the memory of last night. He kissed me. I know he did — I would never kiss him.

But I thought he was Jack. At some point, I thought Jack was there.

"Did you go to the hospital?" Daniel says. "Because I'm sure it would have shown up on a blood test if you were drugged." He says it so smoothly. If he's that confident, he knows whatever he gave me isn't still in my system. I mentally kick myself. Going to the hospital would have been the strongest evidence in my favor.

He continues studying my face with his smirk. He knows I didn't go to the hospital. Because I have no poker face. And because we wouldn't be standing here if I had gone. I would probably still be in the hospital.

And he would be in jail.

"Listen," I say. "I have witnesses. And one of them took a video."

He leans against his frosty car and folds his arms over his chest. "Oh, yes, Whit's video. What does it show? That you were drinking last night. That you were in my bed. That your friend attacked me. You take your video to the cops and they'll laugh at you. I take Breaker's video to Coach and he'll kick you off the team."

Breaker took a video? Why would they be dumb enough to video a crime?

Because they didn't video their crime. They videotaped mine. I broke every Coach rule, plus a state civil infraction.

No. No no no no no. I was supposed to be the ringer in this game.

Daniel continues. "How's that look for all your college scouts, huh?"

I swallow. We stare each other down.

We are at an impasse. If he goes to Coach, I'm going to the cops. And he knows it. And if I go to the police station first, he's going to make sure I lose everything.

I inch away, stepping carefully on the slick new snow. "Watch your back, Daniel."

"You watch yours, Manning." He lazily plops into the driver's seat and his car roars to life. I hold my head high, even as my legs beg to run. The muscle car slides through half a donut on the powdery parking lot and wobbles before howling past me, the old V8 engine rattling my insides.

My heart rate skitters. My hands shake inside my sweat-soaked mittens. I don't know how I'm still alive.

*

My phone buzzes against the laminate table, vibrating the salt and pepper shakers. The icky feeling in my stomach multiplies, as if the overpowering smell of Da Diner's sausage wasn't doing enough damage to it. It's the second call from Jack since we got to brunch.

Second time I've pushed Ignore.

I force down another sip of coffee. It's bitter and scalded, even though there's more milk and sugar in it than actual coffee. Jordan promised coffee and greasy diner food would fix my headache and upset stomach, so we came to Da Diner as soon as Jeannie got out of church.

"Shouldn't Daniel be in trouble?" Jeannie asks, twisting the cross pendant on her necklace. "The cops came to his house last night."

Kendall shakes her head. "Avery said it was a noise complaint. They were able to keep the cops outside. Just acted all sorry and promised to be quieter."

The hockey team has always had a partying rep and it's not

like the local P.D. wants to bust them in the middle of a good season. For all I know, the cops who showed up could be Owl River hockey alums themselves.

"I still don't understand why they want you off the team," Whit says. "You're their MVP. Leading scorer."

"It's the vagina," Jordan says. "They can't stand having a girl beat them."

"Jordan!" Jeannie says. "I'm still in my church clothes, for heaven's sake."

"Yes. Covering your vagina, you good little girl." She grins evilly at Jeannie, who hides her pink cheeks behind her mug of hot chocolate.

"Is that all it really is?" Kendall asks. "It seems a bit ridiculous to try to" — she looks at the other booths around us and hides her mouth with her hand — "date-rape someone just because a girl is playing better than they are."

"Daniel was just setting me up," I say. "He wouldn't have actually done that."

"You don't know what he would have done," Jordan snaps. "The guy drugged you. He's capable of anything."

"Avery seemed to think —"

"Avery." Jordan snorts. "Sure, he's a nice guy. But he's no hero. Don't you go defending him."

Avery stole Winston's phone, got Jeannie's number from his lewd text and called in my reinforcements. Then he got punched by Breaker when he tried to walk in on Daniel and me. And he did kind of try to warn me. Of course, it would have been more effective if, the second I walked into that party, he'd said, *Go home, they drugged your drink.*

I'm silent, stirring my coffee in slow figure-eight patterns.

"Are we missing something?" Jeannie asks me. "Has anything else happened with you and Daniel? You went to the ER before the Showcase. Did that have anything to do with him?"

My future shines before me like an open net. I've been skating toward it, strong confident strides, and sure, the ice is bumpy like at the end of a long, hard practice. But I can still skate this pond. If I start cracking the ice, however …

"Accidents happen all the time at practice," I say. "Remember that bruise I gave you when I was trying to clear the zone?"

Jeannie rubs her side. "That wasn't just a bruise. You cracked my rib."

"So, see? It's hockey. People get hit at practice all the time." I won't tell them. Not the pranks, the beating in the rink garage, the illegal hit at practice. There's no way they'll let it stay quiet, not after last night. And if it goes to Coach, the administration … *parents* … I'll be yanked from the team so fast that I'll have whiplash. Season will be canceled, no playoffs for us. No senior year of hockey. Not only will I not be able to be scouted but I'll also be labeled a troublemaker. No one will want me.

Jeannie holds my gaze. I pray she can't read my mind.

"Promise me that nothing else will happen to you," she says. "If there is even the slightest chance that you could get hurt, I'm going to my dad right now."

I stare back. "I promise. Daniel knows that if he does anything stupid, we all go to the cops with our suspicions about last night. He won't try anything."

God, I hope I'm right.

*

I can't ignore Jack forever. What kind of girl could ignore Jack for even a second? My finger hesitates over his number on my phone. And then I set the phone back on my desk. Stack my unfinished French worksheets on top of it.

Two missed calls this morning, two unanswered texts this afternoon. He has to know something's wrong. I should have answered the first call, lied my butt off and told him I was hungover. Grounded for missing curfew. Busy with late homework, a surprise practice session, a fucking earthquake, anything.

I should have lied to Jack. I've been lying to him for weeks. Him and everyone else.

My doorway creaks. It's judgment time. I've been expecting this. Reluctantly, I turn around.

"Two-twelve in the morning." She's leaning against the doorframe, arms crossed over her faded Grand Rapids Community College T-shirt.

"I, uh, I'm sorry. I didn't realize it was that late." Or that they'd heard me sneak in last night. I thought I was so quiet, but then again, my brain was severely compromised.

"Yes, you did. But you think you're a big shot now. The hero of Owl River High School. Blowing off curfew." She uncrosses her arms and waves a sheet of paper at me. "Requesting passes and late turn-ins on assignments because you're too busy with hockey for school."

I'm too busy surviving for school.

"You think I'm too old, too stupid, to know what goes on at those hockey parties?" She harrumphs. "I know exactly how the star of the hockey team acts at a party. They're the ones at the center of the drinking games, the ones screwing the most girls." She waves a hand at me. "Guys. Whatever. God, I'd feel better if you were a lesbian. Less chance of getting knocked up."

"Oh, for cryin' …" I start. I had to learn how to use a tampon from Brie but now she wants to give me the sex talk? "I don't have time for this. Keep the lecture on topic, please."

"No more parties. You're grounded from all social events."

"Fine." Safer to stay home anyway.

She waves the paper again. "Mr. Lindstrom sent a friendly reminder that your world history paper is a week late."

I gesture at my desk. "I'm working on it."

My phone buzzes again, at the worst possible moment, of course. I shuffle through my papers to silence it.

"You think I was born yesterday?" She narrows her eyes at the phone in my hand. "Downstairs. You'll finish your paper at the kitchen table. I'll take that phone."

On the plus side, I can put off lying to Jack about kissing Daniel. Oh, and my world history paper might actually get checked off my to-do list.

I dump my notebook, laptop and painfully thick copy of *A Detailed History of the French Revolution* on the kitchen table. Slumped in my seat, I try to rub the five hours of hangover sleep out of my eyes. Try to think about boring crap like guillotine beheadings and not scary crap like hockey parties.

Trent gallops into the kitchen and throws open the fridge. "Mich! Play street hockey with me!"

"There's four inches of new snow."

"OK, play garage hockey with me." He thunks a glass down

in front of me and pours a thick stream of chocolate milk into it before drinking directly from the plastic jug. “Hydrate, champ.”

I can’t look at him. I can barely look at the glass of milk he poured for me. My chin wobbles. Of all the things Daniel could take from me, the worst would be that proud look on Trent’s face.

“Leave your sister alone. She’s got homework to do.” Mom frowns at the vacuum like it’s Hoover’s fault the floor is dirty. She jabs the On button to end our conversation, like the loud hum and constant ramming of the baseboards won’t be distracting to my homework priorities.

Trent isn’t distracted. He leans closer to me. “What was the party like last night? Were the guys totally cool? Did they have beer?”

I flick my eyes toward Mom, hoping he’ll chill. “It was fine.”

“You’re so lucky. I can’t wait for high school.”

My throat tightens. Trent, punched in the gut. Drunk and puking, streaking on frostbit feet. Or would they expect him to be the kid who does the punching?

I clear my throat until my voice works again. “Do me a favor. My phone’s in Mom’s room. Text Jack and tell him I’m stuck doing homework?”

He grins. “Of course. But I refuse to sign x’s and o’s. Finish up fast so we can play, OK?”

I toast him with my milk and a fake smile until he’s out the door.

25

Jack unpacks his lunch with confident movements. An occasional nod to a passing acquaintance. A massive bite of turkey sandwich. I can almost hear his taste buds sighing in satisfaction from here. Here — at the door to the lunchroom. Where I'm trying to gauge his mood.

Normally, Jack doesn't require gauging. He's just Jack, with a sexy smile and an even sexier morning kiss for me. But he wasn't waiting at my locker before school, his first miss since Homecoming. I spent the first four periods of the day trying to think of where he could have heard about the party. I scoured Instagram between classes. There's a bit of swaggering there by the guys, but only about how much they drank or who beat whom at whatever video game. Nothing about hazing or an altercation with the enforcer of the former girls' team.

Nothing about the leading scorer kissing the captain in a drugged haze.

I approach the cafeteria table. Jack's welcoming smile slices through my chest. I slide into the seat next to him, my usually automatic motions feeling foreign to my limbs. He slips his arm around my waist and leans in to press his crumb-coated lips to mine.

Kissing Jack. My heart thuds painfully.

"I am so sorry," he says, breaking away quickly, before the lunch monitor can whistle him down for a PDA penalty. Hockey rules apply here in the cafeteria. Two minutes in the box for kissing. So, modified rules.

"Sorry?" I'm pretty sure that should be my line.

"For this morning," he says. "Tweaked my shoulder at practice and Coach freaked out over me and I ran late to school."

I pull away to look at his shoulders, but they seem to be as muscular as ever, hidden under his usual hoodie. "Are you OK?"

He waves me off. "Totally fine. Maybe did too much benching yesterday."

I sigh. "Swimmers in the weight room."

"Yeah, yeah. Nothing like you tough hockey chicks." He tears into his sandwich — his first sandwich — and I survey my own lunch. Nothing looks appetizing today, not even the string cheese, which I normally love and gobble up first.

"I missed you this weekend." He squeezes my waist, one-handing his sandwich to keep his arm around me. This does not go against lunchroom PDA rules. "Was the party as bad as you expected?"

Worse.

I shrug. "Idiots and beer."

He squeezes again. "I know it sucks. But sometimes being a team player means dumb bonding crap. You have to do it."

My body stiffens away from him. He only said that because he doesn't know. He wouldn't condone any of it — the hazing, the drugging — if he knew. Right?

"Heard the cops showed up," he continues. "Wasn't your dad, was it?"

The extra inch of space between us feels like a mile. I shred my string cheese into tiny threads. "Nah. Local P.D."

"Not that they'd bust the star of the hockey team anyway." He nudges my shoulder with his but I don't laugh like I'm supposed to. "Hey? Everything OK?"

The fake smile jumps to my face quickly, as I've trained it to do this season. "Totally. Just, spending my weekend with dumb hockey boys and my world history paper? Not exactly my ideal."

"Not mine either." His fingers thread through mine. "I had much better ideas for the weekend." His breath is in my ear now, his voice husky. "I missed you."

I close my eyes. "I missed you, too," I whisper.

"Are you really hungry?"

I shake my head.

"Me neither. Let's get out of here."

He sweeps our lunch remains into the trash and I follow him out of the cafeteria and into the hallway, where there are no penalties for making out. Practically running, Jack takes my hand and leads me to the now closed-off corridor that used to lead to the pool. Which means that these days it's completely empty.

His hands are on my back, slipping under my shirt as he presses me against the painted cinder-block wall. He kisses me like only Jack could kiss me. Nothing like Daniel. How could I have not known? How could I have messed this up so badly?

My skin crawls, rejecting Jack's hands. My mouth freezes, unable to kiss him back. There's a tightness in my chest, making my breaths painful, my head swirling from lack of oxygen. I struggle out from under Jack's arms. I can't have his hands on me. I can't stand to smell the chlorine on his hair.

"Mich? Mich, what's wrong?" Jack reaches out to me just as my knees buckle. He cradles my elbows as I sit heavily on the industrial carpet of the hallway.

I press my hands to my head. What's wrong? What *isn't* wrong? The list is a mile long. But it all boils down to me. I'm what's wrong. From the minute I showed up at tryouts by myself I've been screwing up every move. To say I've handled it all poorly is an understatement. I haven't handled it at all. And now I'm in the middle of a gigantic wasps' nest trying to fight a bloodthirsty horde with a flyswatter.

"I'm sorry, Mich. I should have let you finish your lunch," Jack says. He puts his hands on my jaw and searches my eyes. My skin has that cold-sweat feel and he grips the sleeve of his hoodie and wipes it along my forehead. "Just sit for a minute and then we'll go find you some juice or something." He grins. "And when you're feeling better, I'll make a joke about my kiss knocking you out."

It wasn't your *kiss that knocked me out.*

*

I have an audience at practice. But they are not fans or reporters or scouts; they are bodyguards.

Jordan and Kendall sit in the first row of the stands, right on the glass at center ice. Kendall bats her eyelashes at Vaughn and sips her massive Starbucks blended mocha-caramel-whipped whatever. Jordan sits with her elbows on her knees and tracks Daniel's every move with her glare.

"I get why Starbucks Barbie is here, hanging her cleavage out for Vaughn, but what's up with the angry lesbo? She switching sides again?" Breaker's comment earns him a laugh from his hero, Daniel.

I grip my stick tighter and stretch my hammie until it hurts. I will be aiming a puck at the unpadded back of Breaker's knee today, on the first drill.

I almost spilled the beans about Vaughn to Kendall this weekend. Jordan said who knows what Daniel's capable of. I think the same applies to a guy who knew I was being drugged and taken advantage of. But if I spill about Vaughn, everything else will come out and someone's going to slip to a parent and that's that.

Besides, Vaughn won't need to drug Kendall, if history is any indication.

Coach coasts around the circle as we stretch out. "Ending the season strong, boys. You've got your playoff berth. But playing Calumet the last weekend of regular season means you either go into playoffs beating the best team in the league or you go into playoffs wondering just how far a team can make it if you can't beat the best team in the league. Which team do you want to be, men?"

Gee, I don't know. Do we want to be a team who wins our last game of the season or loses? *Tough question, Coach.*

"I want the power play down on the far end of the ice and

everyone else on a half-ice game over here. Avery, with the power play. And Manning, I want you with the PP, too."

I hide my grin. Coach wants me on the PP. The universe is rewarding me for all the shit I've put up with.

We walk through the positions and plays, increasing the speed on our passes while two defensemen without sticks pressure the body. When I see my point wind up, I bust my butt to the crease to screen the goalie and to redirect or rebound if needed. Daniel meets me at the crease with a check to the shoulder. I hold my ground and let him distract himself from the play. It's hard to get my blade on the rebound while the rhino is trying to push my car over, but I manage it, poking the puck through Avery's five-hole while Daniel's got him screened.

Now that the play is over, I allow myself a split second to relax. And that's when Daniel slides my skates out from under me. My breezered butt smacks the ice. A girly sound of surprise slips out before I can stop it, even though I'm not hurt at all. Everyone snickers. I hate myself.

"Daniel!" barks Coach. "You just put your team back on the PK with that stupid move. Run it again. Daniel, switch out with Arik." Arik skates in to take his spot at defense in front of the net, and Daniel hustles out to the neutral zone, now playing on my line.

We start the play again, and I'm straddling the blue line, waiting for the pass from my D to start the offensive attack. Except Daniel doesn't pass it to me; he slides it just far enough out of my reach that I end up off balance and off-side when my left wing catches the puck and tries to save our play.

"Play it, play it," Coach says, meaning to forget about the off-sides. It wastes ice time to run a drill over again just for two inches of blue line. But now I've hesitated and I'm behind the play. The left wing slides the puck back to the point to buy time while I take my assigned spot in the corner. A D-to-D pass and then Daniel winds up and lets loose. His slapshot misses the net by a mile and hits me right above the pads on my upper calf. The very spot I'd planned on beaning Breaker, ironically.

I stutter-step and grunt, my knee reflexively bending to the ice as my calf cramps. Coach whistles the play dead.

"Goddamn it, Daniel!" he shouts. "Get your head out of your ass before you injure our best player."

Daniel doesn't look too concerned. Hell, he put me in the ER only a few weeks ago and didn't earn so much as a push-up from it.

"Sorry, Coach. She skated in front of my shot."

"Your shot was five feet wide of the net! You weren't even supposed to be taking a shot! You were supposed to run the play I called, starting with a decent pass to Manning in the neutral zone. Instead, you put us off-side, which screwed up the whole damn play. And then you panic and take a stupid shot on net that'll never in a million years go in. Now we've lost twenty seconds of power play and risked a turnover. Get off my power play. Go." He waves his glove at the far end of the rink. "Go run drills with the underclassmen. Send me Ross to take your place."

I don't look at Daniel. I am so screwed. There's no way I won't pay for this somehow. I glance at Jordan and Kendall. Kendall's on her phone but Jordan's eyes are narrowed. I press the toe of my stick blade onto a puck and swirl it in a figure eight while I wait for play to resume. Can't let it seem like a big deal. Happens all the time that Coach sends his senior captain off to protect my well-being.

The clock slowly ticks practice away and I watch my back, like Daniel told me to. He's coming for me. I just don't know when.

There's no time for a breath of relief when practice ends. I scamper off the ice like a scared rabbit. Jordan and Kendall squeeze into my broom closet, which was not made for three people and a hockey bag.

"Ew. You smell worse now that you play with the boys," Kendall says.

"Whatever, you're sleeping with one of those boys."

"I always make him shower," she says.

"Speaking of ew," Jordan says.

"Yeah, my stomach says stop talking now," I say, untying my skates.

"Let's see your calf," Jordan says.

I unhook my garter and peel down my long knit hockey sock. We all inhale loudly. The welt is a raised red puck shape now, but my whole calf will be bluish-purple this time tomorrow. Then it will be really impressive.

"Ooh, yeah, that's a nice one," Kendall says.

I palpate the hot skin, marveling at the numb-but-painful feel. "You've had just as bad."

"Not by my own teammate. On purpose," Jordan says.

"Coach reamed him out," I say. "He won't do it again."

"Not in front of Coach," Jordan says.

I continue undressing. "Coach made it clear, he wants me in playing shape for this weekend. I'll be fine."

"I'll drive you home anyway," Jordan says.

"My dad's picking me up," I say.

"Then we'll wait with you until he gets here."

I'll admit I'm relieved. I wasn't looking forward to waiting in the dark parking lot by myself. Encumbered by my hockey bag if I need to run. Fingers hovering over the 911 on my phone. Searching the shadows and jumping at noises while trying to look totally unconcerned.

I shrug. "Cool, thanks." I lock the broom closet and wave to Megan, who's waiting for Coach at the ice end of the hallway. I keep the eye contact short, though. I don't want her to come over and hear any of this conversation. There's no way she'd keep it from her stepdad. I've been avoiding Megan lately and I miss the girl power she exudes. But I can't bear adding "failed role model" to my list of recent accomplishments.

"Have you talked to Brie about this?" Kendall asks. "Maybe she can call off Daniel."

"Hardly. They didn't end well." Jordan takes my sticks from me as I lug my bag through the hallway.

"They didn't even start all that well," I say.

"I always thought he still had feelings for her," Kendall says. "I don't think he wanted them to break up."

"Oh, she drove him nuts," I say. "He didn't want to break up with her boobs but he pretty much ran screaming from the rest of her. Freaking high-maintenance."

Kendall and Jordan exchange a look across me. Yeah, yeah, I'm a shitty best friend. "Well, it's true," I mumble. It's a well-proven fact that Brie is high-maintenance. I shouldn't have said it out loud, though.

"So you didn't tell her about this," Jordan says.

"She's four hundred miles away."

Jordan knocks my sticks together in a hollow rhythm. "If

Avery hadn't called Jeannie, would you have told any of us?"

Kendall finally slows and gives me her full attention. "Would you have told anybody?"

Mom, Dad, I drank what I thought was a mug of liquor and it turned out to be date-rape cocktail.

Jack, I kissed one of my teammates.

Brie, I kissed your ex.

"Nothing to tell," I remind them. Before pushing the rink door open, I stop and turn around. "You guys, I never thanked you for the other night. For dragging your butts out in the middle of the night, in a snowstorm, to drive my loony ass home. And for your discretion in all of this. I know it's awkward, but I'm working through it. It'll all be fine."

"Of course it will," Kendall says, patting my arm. "You're so strong, Mich. If it were me, I'd be ditching school to cry over sappy movies and eat ice cream. But here you are, getting ready for playoffs." She puts her arm around my shoulders and squeezes.

I look at Jordan. Her mouth is clenched. She's not buying my nice speech. I push through the rink doors, forcing them to follow me outside. Icy, damp air hits my sweaty skin. I shiver. My calf throbs, asking for a cold pack and ibuprofen. I need a shower and dinner, but I'm just tired. Always tired. Maybe homework can wait until morning. Again.

I scan for Dad's car, but he's not here yet.

Voices behind us push us farther onto the walkway. As Daniel exits the building, he lets his hockey bag whack Jordan on the shoulder.

"How are your balls, Daniel?" she asks.

"Want to check them for me? Or are you afraid they'll turn you straight?"

"Thinking about your balls is what made me a lesbian."

"Thank you, Daniel's balls," Breaker says, smirking.

Daniel taps the back of my calf with his stick as he walks by. "How's the wheel, Manning?" He lowers his voice as if talking to a baby. "Are you going to be OK to play this weekend? Coach needs his widdle Michigan out there."

I force away the grimace that wants to take over my face. He knows exactly where that puck hit me and the sharp ache from his stick zings all the way to my ankle. "I'm fine."

Jordan steps in front of Daniel. "And you will not touch her again. No hits, checks, shooting pucks, sharing drinks, nothing. You stay the hell away from her."

"That's why you're here? You're Michigan's bodyguard? Boy, Mich, you are in trouble."

"I'm dead serious. You touch her again, I take it all public." She turns her glare on me. "Scouts and stats aside. I'm not going to wait until you get maimed or raped." She points my sticks at Daniel. "Don't fuck with me, Daniel."

"Ooh, Daniel, you hit on Jordo's girl," Breaker hoots. "She's going to kick you in the balls again."

Daniel isn't laughing, though. He sets his bag down and charges up to me. Jordan tenses, brandishing my hockey sticks. Daniel lifts his index finger in her direction but leans into my space.

"We have an agreement," he says. "Don't we? You get your spot on the team, and your precious scholarship offers. I don't get harassed for giving you a drink."

"I haven't d-done anything," I stutter.

"Call her off." He points to Jordan.

"She hasn't done anything either," I say.

"I'll go wherever I want to go," Jordan says.

The rink door slams shut. "Hey, Vaughn," Kendall sings. I'm momentarily distracted by their reunion.

Vaughn drops his bag on the concrete walk and slides an arm around Kendall. She leans into him, all smiley and sparkly. Bile shoots up my esophagus.

"What'd I miss?" Vaughn asks Daniel. "Looks like a par-tay out here in the fucking freezing cold."

As my dad's car pulls up, we get a nausea-inducing demonstration of Vaughn's methods for keeping Kendall warm during a freezing cold par-tay. His mouth covers half of her face and his hands grope her jacket desperately. Jordo makes gagging noises.

Dad gets out of the car and grunts at the group, puffing his chest out to show off his patrol uniform.

"Hey, Mr. Manning," Jordan says. She makes a fist around Kendall's collar and pulls hard. I swear I hear the suction-releasing pop as Kendall steps back. "Time to go."

I take my time loading my bag and sticks into Dad's car, making sure that Jordan and Kendall leave well before us.

26

It bothers me all evening. I shower and make a sandwich to take up to my room for my studying. But all I can think of is that evil Vaughn running his hands all over Kendall. How can she stand it?

Because she doesn't know.

Because I didn't tell her.

Here they are, rearranging their lives to act as my bodyguards, putting themselves in potentially dangerous situations — who knows how long it would have taken Jordan and Daniel to throw down the gloves if Dad hadn't broken up the freezing cold par-tay.

If Kendall shows up to school with a black eye, I'll never be able to live with myself.

I finally shove my world history book off my desk and plop my half-eaten sandwich back on its plate. I reach for my phone and dial. You don't give news this bad over a text.

"Hey!" Kendall is breathless. "Is everything OK?"

"Yeah, I'm fine. Sorry, didn't mean to freak you out by calling.

I just — are you at home? Did I interrupt anything with Vaughn?"

"No, I'm home. Nine o'clock on school nights, remember?" Right. Kendall's parents are pretty lenient on weekends but she has a nine curfew on weeknights. All guests must vacate before then, too. Unless it's a school project, but no one would believe Vaughn was doing a school project at nine at night. Or ever.

"Right. How's everything going with him?"

"I totally love him," she says, but then quickly amends, "Of course, don't tell him that."

"We don't talk much," I say.

She hesitates. "He's not … he's not part of all of this trouble you're having with the team, right?"

I breathe in relief. Thank God I didn't have to bring it up.

"They're all part of the problem. Vaughn and I have had some … difficulties."

"OK. 'Difficulties' isn't really bad, though, right? Like, you don't think he knew about Daniel drugging you?"

"Did he tell you he knew?"

"He swore he didn't."

"I don't know exactly who knew," I admit. "But he is one of Daniel's best friends. They were attached at the hip that night, like always. And Avery heard a group of seniors talking about it. He didn't say who, but there are only three seniors."

She's silent.

"It gets worse," I say. I pull my legs into my desk chair, hugging my knees to my chest. "He — Vaughn — hit me. When I took his center spot. He and Daniel and a couple of the guys took me to the back of the rink and Daniel let him punch me once, in the ribs. For taking his spot."

She's silent but I hear shallow, quick breaths.

"And then, when they walked away, someone kicked me while I was on the ground. I'm pretty sure it was Daniel, though."

"Vaughn wouldn't ..." But I hear the doubt in her voice.

"That's why I told you to be careful when you got back together with him."

"You knew this? Before Homecoming?"

"It was Homecoming night. Right after the game."

She exhales. "What else aren't you telling me?"

"That's all Vaughn did. Well, he kind of set me up on that hit by Daniel. And there are a bunch of other pranks I'm not sure about. I don't know who did those."

She's silent.

"I'm sorry, Kendall. I hate doing this to you, but if something happened ... God, I couldn't live with myself."

"Something did happen. To you."

My breath catches. "Yeah, I guess."

"Do you hear yourself?" she asks. "You're upset telling me about Vaughn before I get hurt, and I'm upset that you didn't tell me about him before you got hurt. We're both upset and he's the asshole here."

"But I know how you feel about him."

She humphs, but I've known her long enough to hear the sob behind it. "Felt. Past tense. Do you know how I feel about you? You and me have been together a lot longer than Vaughn and me."

I nod. "Before the first time you dated him in sixth grade."

"Way before. I'll always have your back. You're my tea —"

She cuts off, the word hanging in the void between us.

"You'll always be my teammate," I say. "Even if we're not on the ice together."

"I still need this team."

"I do, too. God, I miss you guys." I'm finally crying, for the first time since my Homecoming beating. Hot tears slide down my face, and even though her voice stays even, I know Kendall is crying, too.

"I need to call Vaughn," she finally says. "What about you?"

"I don't need to call him, but thanks," I say. It's a lame attempt at a joke and we both know what she really means. "I don't know yet, K."

"I'm scared for you."

"Yeah. Me, too."

"Team meeting," she says, her voicing strengthening again. "Tomorrow at lunch. We'll figure out how to keep you safe the rest of the season. The other girls will know what to do."

Yes, they will. Laura and Jeannie will insist on parents and police and principals getting involved. Jordan and Whit will suggest maiming and sabotage. When she thinks I'm not listening, Cherrie will whisper that this never would have happened if I had played with Silver Lake's team.

"I wasn't waiting for an answer," Kendall says. "That wasn't a question. Team meeting tomorrow at lunch."

"Yeah. OK."

"I'll bring you Starbucks," she says, her voice sweeter now. And she's the one breaking up with a douchebag tonight.

*

Kendall's normally curled hair is swept up in a messy ponytail and she keeps her dark faux designer sunglasses on as she leans up against my locker. Tactfully, I take a large step away from Jack, letting his hand slide off my back.

"Over and done," Kendall says, her chin quivering.

"Oh, honey." I reach for her.

"No, no." She holds up a hand. "Don't make me cry. I barely got eye makeup on as it is this morning." But she did, so I know the world isn't actually ending.

"When you're ready for hugs, let me know," I say. "And ice cream."

"Definitely. And hey, can we keep all of this quiet? Like, it's just a breakup, just didn't work out with us."

"Conscious uncoupling," I say.

"Exactly. Nothing to do with hockey stuff."

"Why would it have to do with hockey?" Jack asks.

"It doesn't," I say. "It's conscious uncoupling."

His nose wrinkles. "Should I know what that means?"

Kendall sighs. "Boys."

I smile at him. "No. Just smile and nod and when I ditch you for girl time, run like hell the other way."

"Got it." He slides his arm around my waist again, pulling me toward him. I resist, trying to subtly gesture at Kendall.

"No, no. Don't stop being cute on my account," she says. Jack finally gets it and drops his hand.

Kendall grabs his wrist and puts his hand back on my waist. "See? Too cute."

"Too awkward," I say, but Jack doesn't drop his hand and I don't want him to.

My Daniel radar goes off, but I don't have to worry about him when I've got witnesses flanking me. He strides down the hallway, directly at me. With an easy grin on his face. My stomach plummets. I should run to class. Or maybe the girls' room. But my brain and feet mix up their communication and I'm still frozen at my locker when he arrives.

"Mich," he purrs, entering my personal space to drop a kiss on my cheek. I cringe, repulsed by his face near mine.

You could hear a pin drop on the industrial carpet of the juniors' locker hall. Jack freezes, his hand gripping my waist. Kendall's jaw falls open and she slides her sunglasses to the top of her head.

Daniel holds his hand out to Jack. "No hard feelings, man."

Jack's face darkens and he steps backward, along the wall of lockers. His eyes skate back and forth between Daniel's smug leer and his arm, snaking around my waist, where Jack's was only seconds earlier. I shake Daniel off. "Ew. What the hell?"

The sleaze continues to gaze at me with a smile. "Well, I've been thinking. I admit I was surprised when I found you in my bed last weekend. But when you kissed me — wow. I've been thinking about it ever since. Let's make this work. I know it's what you want. And, obviously, I just can't say no to you."

So this is how he plans to break our deal. I shove him as hard as I can, but he only laughs as his back rebounds off the wall of lockers.

"Jack, no," I say, righting myself. "He's lying."

But I'm speaking to empty space.

Jack is gone.

*

The news spreads like a rash on a junior hockey team. I don't even make it through second period before Coach pokes his head into Madame Kowalski's room.

"*Bonjour, Monsieur le Coach!*" she chirps from the whiteboard. "*Qu'est-ce que vous désirez?*"

He frowns. "I need to speak with Michigan Manning."

I slowly close my French workbook and stack it on top of my textbook.

"*Oui, oui! Mademoiselle Manning!*" She beams at me because, after all, she's been going easy on me for all my late homework and barely passing quizzes so I could fulfill the MVP title of the team I'm about to be kicked off.

I follow Coach out the door. He shuts it and scans the hallway.

"I gave you one rule, Manning," he says. "Do not date my players. And you broke it."

My players. I busted my ass for his team. I was his golden child, his leading scorer. And now we're back to *his* players.

I changed in a broom closet. With spiders. I let my grades slide. I haven't slept a full night in months.

I was hazed. Insulted. Injured.

Drugged.

"You're off the team," he says. "For coming on to your captain. For drinking. For dragging the reputation of this team through the mud. For being a poor role model for my stepdaughter. Turn in your uniform to my office before school tomorrow." He walks away, smacking the cinder-block wall with his palm.

I lean back against the French classroom door and close my

eyes. Of course this happened. It was bound to. It's what Daniel wanted. And he gets what he wants. He can finish his senior year a hero to his boys. Got a pesky female who's simultaneously carrying your team and destroying your sport? No problem! Just physically and sexually abuse her and then set her reputation on fire. This is how it's done, boys!

No. I did not go through hell for that jackass to win.

I push myself up and run after Coach, catching him at the door of his office.

"Conversation over, Manning. I'm not doing this with you."

"I worked my butt off for you, Coach. You can't listen to me for two seconds?"

"I made my rules clear. You broke them."

"Did you kick Daniel off the team?"

He drops into his desk chair. "No. Your boyfriend is safe. It wasn't his fault you came on to him. You put him in a difficult position, Manning, and he shouldn't be punished for that."

"I didn't come on to him."

"It's all over the place." He spins his laptop around so the screen faces me.

I'm on Coach's computer. I clutch my stomach, hurting worse than a fist to the gut. Worse than a boot to the ribs.

It's Daniel's Facebook page. Coach clicks on the video. It's dark, but it's obvious that's me, especially when Daniel murmurs my full name for the camera's benefit. We're sitting on his bed — and when I say sitting, I mean I'm practically draped over Daniel in order to stay upright. He puts his hands on my arms, presumably to steady me and I purr a single word unintelligible to anyone but me. Then I press my lips to his.

My throat spasms, as if trying to eject breakfast. I've replayed my hazy memories of that night over and over again but seeing it happen on the screen leaves me raw and sickened. "I said 'Jack,'" I croak. "I said my boyfriend's name. Clearly, I thought that's who was there with me."

"Clearly, you're so drunk you can't even get the name right of the guy you're throwing yourself all over." Coach clicks on the Play button, and the worst moment of my life begins again like a twisted Groundhog Day.

"Not drunk. Drugged." I slam the laptop shut. "I was drugged, Coach. Add it to the list of shit I have put up with from *your boys* this season. Coffee down my shirt, Gatorade in my bag. They cut my jersey, flashed me, walked in on me while I was changing. Punched me in the gut and then kicked me while I was on the ground. Tried to put me in the hospital so I couldn't play in the Showcase. And finally, drugged me at a team event where major hazing occurred. So explain to me again, why am I the one being kicked off the team?"

Coach gestures at his laptop. "Because I just watched video evidence of you kissing your teammate. And it makes me want to lose my breakfast. Out, Manning. Out of my office. Out of my team."

27

The Ice Cream Pit Stop doesn't open until 4:00. As if hearts only break during dessert-appropriate business hours.

Plan B: I pick up two pints of ice cream from the nearest gas station, trudge back to the school parking lot and sit on the hood of Jordan's car. Ice cream and it's thirty degrees. At least it's not snowing. I open the chocolate fudge brownie, holding the carton with a mittened hand while I scoop bites twice the size of my spoon.

Kendall slides onto the hood next to me. The car barely makes a dip.

With one finger, I hold out the plastic bag. She takes it and pulls the other pint out. Karamel Sutra. She takes the lid off and licks the underside.

"I didn't come on to him." I dig out a big chunk of brownie and lick the spoon clean before handing it to her.

"Duh."

"It's time to go to the cops," Jeannie says, appearing next to me.

I nearly fall off the car's hood. "You're ditching class!"

"Study hall," she says. "My teacher gave me permission to come find you."

That makes more sense.

"But I would have ditched," she says, sliding a finger through my ice cream and licking it. "I came as soon as I heard. And don't change the subject."

Jordan plops onto the hood and we bounce as if we're white-water rafting. "I'm offering up physical violence to whichever of them you'd like to direct it at." Called it.

"Does it matter anymore?" I ask. "I'm out. Even if one of the college teams still wants me, all they have to do is google me, and guess what's the first thing that will pop up. Not that it will matter, because my parents are going to bury me in the backyard. And Jack ..." A hot tear lands in my chocolate ice cream. "And it's too late to go to the cops, Jeannie. I couldn't prove anything if I wanted to. I have no evidence because I'm stupid and stubborn and ... and ... more stupid."

"I'll swear it in court," Jordan says. "I know what I saw and what I heard. We'll get Avery. Hell, I'll torture every one of those boys until they admit it all."

"Then what? Jack will say it's all OK, he doesn't mind that I kissed Daniel and we'll live happily ever after. Some amazing college will say, 'Hey, we love drama queens, come play for us!'"

It's silent as we eat ice cream. At lunchtime, the swimmers and Silver Lake defectors show up with reinforcements — two tubs of Jilbert's and a bottle of chocolate sauce. And a box of plastic spoons. We shift the team meeting to the ground, blocking an entire row of the parking lot.

The assistant principal shows up at the beginning of fifth period. She doesn't want to be liable if a texting teen careens around the corner and smashes into us. Also, she can't really permit truancy, especially when we're flaunting it right outside her office window.

We stand and brush off the bits of asphalt clinging to our frozen rears.

"What are you going to do?" Jeannie asks, as the rest of the group heads toward school.

I sigh. "Jack first. Then home."

*

He's disappeared. Completely dropped off the face of the earth. I stalk his afternoon classes but he's not there. By the time I return to the parking lot, his Wagoneer is gone, too.

I know exactly where he is.

I hitch a ride with Laura to swim practice at the Rec Center. And yep, Jack is climbing out of the pool when I arrive. Water cascades off his bare chest as he pushes himself out of the pool. He flips off his goggles and chugs from a water bottle on the pool deck.

"How is it possible that anyone in the world would think I voluntarily kissed Daniel when I could have had *that*?" I ask Laura.

She shakes her head. "Beats me."

Jack looks over at me and his expression darkens. Shame freezes me in place. Laura nudges me forward with her shoulder. "Go on," she says. "He's a good guy. It's going to be fine."

I wish I believed her. Jack walks quickly toward the locker room, so I have to scurry over the slippery pool deck to catch up with him before he disappears. I grab his arm and he tries to shake me off, keeping his back to me.

"You're not even going to listen to me?" I ask, angry now. "You'll listen to Daniel, that moronic jackass, but you won't listen to me?"

He turns. "Oh, I did more than listen. I saw the video, Michigan. I watched you kiss that guy."

I cross my arms. "So you saw the video. And what — you thought that looked like a normal Saturday night out for me? Did you actually look at me? Did you hear what I said before I kissed him?"

"You didn't exactly say, 'Get off me, jackass,' as you leaned into him. You just muttered a bunch of drunk shit."

"Drugged shit."

"Oh, that's better, Michigan. Nice. Real nice."

"No! Jack, he drugged me. And then got me into his room and had his friend video us. And it was your name I said. I was so out of it, I thought you were there. I thought I was kissing you."

His features freeze, a mixture of shock and revulsion. "Are you — are you serious?"

"Yes, I'm serious. Jesus, do you think I'd do that sober? Or that I'd joke about this?"

He runs his towel over his head before settling it across his shoulders, covering the goose bumps spreading over his chest. "No. I just — it didn't occur to me that it was anything other than what it looked like. They *drugged* you? Mich, you should be at a hospital. Or a police station." He suddenly doubles over, leaning his hands on his knees for support. "Oh, God. How bad — what did they do? To you? While you were …" He waves a hand like he can't say it.

"You saw it all in the video. Thankfully, one of the guys called Jeannie and she brought reinforcements immediately."

"Oh, thank God." Jack's arms are suddenly around me, pulling me to his cold, wet chest. He's shaking. His hand strokes the back of my hair. "I mean, I can't believe this happened but at least —"

"Yeah," I finish for him. "It could have been worse."

"So Daniel — is he going to jail? Is it just him or more guys on the team?"

I don't want to leave his arms, wet as they are. But this is the part I'm ashamed of. I realize it's the part he's going to judge me for. I can explain away the video and the kiss but I can't take back my stupidity.

"Ah, no," I say. "He's off scot-free and I'm off the team."

"What?!"

"I was an idiot," I said. "I didn't go to the hospital or the cops. Didn't tell my parents. Swore my friends to secrecy."

"Didn't tell your boyfriend."

"Didn't tell my boyfriend. And now it's too late. Coach saw the video, he believed Daniel, and I have no way to prove otherwise."

"But why? Why didn't you tell anyone?"

"Because. If I let it come out, I would have lost everything." I push back from him and he lets me, his arms dropping awkwardly to his sides. "I … God, do you know how many times I wanted to walk off that team? But I was killing it. On the guys' team. I was the one girl who did something big when our team got cut. Next thing I know, I've got colleges scouting me and a reputation at school. And a hot new boyfriend who never noticed me before that meeting with Belmont. Daniel knew all that. I threatened him that I'd go to the cops, and he made sure I knew I'd lose it all."

I try to remind myself that I'm not angry at Jack. But he is not allowed to judge me. He's the one person who should understand the stakes. He has a college scholarship, a collegiate swim career, on the line. I'd bet my skates he'd put up with hazing for that, just like those underclassmen on the hockey team. "I'd already put up with so much. I didn't want it all to be for nothing." I exhale and cross my arms, tucking my shaking hands against my sides. "You have no idea what I've been through."

"And why is that?" he asks, his voice hard.

"Because I'm not a whiner. I'm tough, I can handle it."

"But you couldn't handle telling me about it? What are we even talking about here?"

"Hazing, team stuff."

"No, I want specifics, Mich. I want to hear what you've been keeping from me because if I have to sit through another Facebook video —"

"Fine! You want to know? Breaker waved his penis at me from the locker room. Did you want to know that? Daniel called me a dyke. They beat me up."

Jack's eyebrows shoot up and he narrows his gaze, like he's looking for bruises.

"Our first date." I choke on my swollen throat, but the anger keeps my voice working. "I was in so much pain for our first date. Vaughn punched me in the gut, and then Daniel kicked me in the ribs. My whole side was purple."

Kind of the same shade Jack's face is turning right now, so I keep talking. "Let's see, what else? Daniel put me in the hospital, trying to keep me out of the Showcase. I drank a mugful of what turned out to be roofies. And then, when I was so out of my mind that I thought I was kissing you, they took a video. Got me kicked off the team and now anyone with internet access can watch the worst moment of my life. There. We're sharing. Feel better now?"

"All this has been going on and you didn't tell me any of it."

"What, were you going to punch Daniel? Politely ask Vaughn not to hit me again? What if I'd told you, or anyone else, what was happening before the Showcase? They would have suspended the team and I wouldn't have gotten to play. I never would have been scouted ... not that it matters anymore. No one will want me now, since I'm not playing, and bad shit follows me everywhere."

His jaw is clenching and unclenching and he stares at the gray tiled wall across from me. I give him a moment. I did just drop a ton of shit on him.

"I'm sorry," I say. "That I didn't tell you. That you had to see that video."

He blows out slowly, nodding his head at the wall. "Are you OK?"

I stutter. "Yeah, I'm ... I mean, no. I'm pissed as hell about losing my spot. But the drugging thing, I'm OK. Honestly, the worst thing about that was worrying that you wouldn't believe me if I told you and that I would lose you."

His eyes drop to the floor. "I think you were right."

The earth tips. "W-what?"

"I believe you. You were drugged and — and taken advantage

of, and that's not OK. But —" He jams his hands on his hips. "Mich. This is a lot of shit to process. Months of stuff going on when I thought everything was all sunshine and happy. And you —"

He finally locks eyes with me and points an index finger at my chest. "You need to get yourself figured out. You shouldn't even be here right now. I am not your biggest concern."

"You are, Jack. I came to find you as soon as I could. I don't want to lose you over this."

He shakes his head and droplets of water trickle down the sides of his face. "No. You messed up with me months ago. This" — he gestures between us — "this you could have fixed long ago, if you'd really wanted everything to be right between us." He shivers. "I'm freezing. And I have to go. Good luck with everything, Michigan."

He turns and walks into the boys' locker room. I'm half tempted to follow him, to cling to him, to kiss him into understanding. But I hear boys' voices in there and I can't stomach another locker room full of boys.

28

Not my biggest concern? I came crawling to him, apologizing and begging forgiveness — OK, there wasn't a whole lot of begging, but I told him things. Things I kept to myself for months. And he walked away. What was I supposed to do?

Goddamn males.

I have no ride home, but the only things waiting for me there are a set of most likely furious parents and a stack of homework that dates back almost two weeks. I sit on the bleachers and watch Laura and her team swim a gazillion laps. I keep an eye on the hallway to the locker rooms, but I don't expect to see Jack. There are two entrances to the Rec Center, and I guarantee he'll take the one farthest from me.

Swim practice sure is dull to watch. It's hot in here and I've been through hell lately. My eyelids sag and whatever motivation I had left goes with them. I remember wondering what Jack thought about when he swam. It's what kept me pushing, trying to be an athlete like him.

I'm not as mad at him as I would like to be.

Laura nudges my knee with her bare foot. I startle awake and rub my eyes. My hand comes away with a smear of black mascara and sandy-colored eye shadow. I'm surprised there was any makeup left on my eyes after today.

"Sleeping Beauty, do you need a ride home?"

"Yeah." I work my dry mouth. "You're done already?"

"Already? That was seven thousand yards. It was like an eternity."

My parents will be even more pissed.

"Ride home would be great."

"OK. Quick shower and I'll be back."

Unlike most of my teammates, when Laura says "quick shower," she means it. She's back in five minutes, long hair streaming water onto her clothes and an ice pack plastic-wrapped to each shoulder. I take her swim bag from her. It's the least I can do.

As she drives me home, I encourage her to talk about swim season so I don't have to get all teary over my breakup-slash-argument-slash-end-of-the-world thing with Jack. When we drive past the rink, I avert my eyes, fiddling with her car's heating controls so I don't have to look out the window. Practice will be ending in fifteen minutes. Despite the bruises and sabotaged equipment, it's the first practice I've missed all season.

Daniel is in that building right now. Back to his coveted position as Coach's Personal Ass Licker. He gets to spend the last few weeks of his high school hockey career being king of the boys' club. He got what he wanted. And I let him have it.

At my house, I thank Laura and climb out. "We're doing coffee and French vocab at study hall tomorrow," she says. "It's time you got caught up. Both on homework and on friends."

"Yes, ma'am," I say. She's right and I'm happy to comply.

My family is at the dinner table when I walk in, surrounding a bucket of fried chicken. The starchy smell of fake mashed potatoes and salty gravy sits heavily in the air. Mom turns her attention from her phone to glare at me. Dad tosses an empty chicken bone onto his plate so hard that it bounces back off. He ignores the greasy remnant and gives me his "Ma'am, do you know how fast you were going?" glare.

But it's Trent's stiffened back that hurts the most. He doesn't turn around, just slides out from his seat and brushes past me out of the room, leaving his nearly full plate behind. Trent loves those nasty potatoes.

Mom sets her phone down and crosses her arms. "You have a lot of explaining to do."

"Where do you want me to start?" I ask, dropping into my chair. I eye the chicken but I'm not tempted. The smell is never appetizing, and I already feel sick from eating nothing but ice cream today.

"I think we can start with the underage drinking," Dad says. "And then arrive at the part where you get kicked off the team."

"And finish up with coming home late without telling us where you were," Mom says. "Were you drinking again?" She leans forward and sniffs the air, like fried chicken smell hasn't already permeated every soft surface in the room.

"No, Mom. Geez." I cross my arms and focus on Dad. "So I'm guessing you heard Henson's side of it."

He wipes his hands and balls up his napkin. "You address him as Coach, whether you like him or not. And, no, I heard Coach Norman's side."

"Coach Norman? What? Why?"

"Because he called to let us know that you are not welcome to coach Trent's team anymore."

My insides sink. But of course. I can't believe I didn't expect it.

"The parents of Trent's teammates don't want their kids looking up to someone who got kicked off her team for drinking."

They don't know about the video? "I wasn't really drinking," I say. "It was a stupid team hazing thing. I wasn't the only one drinking, I'm just the only one in trouble."

"I'm sure that will make all the bantam parents feel much better," Mom says. "Coach put you on that coaching staff to be a positive role model. You let him down. You let those kids down. You let your brother down."

"How did the parents even —" Oh. Of course. *The parents* include a certain stepfather. Who doesn't want me influencing his stepdaughter. Goddamn that man.

"So obviously there will be grounding involved," Mom says. "For the drinking. And certainly extra chores to make up for disappointing your family. And then there's getting kicked off your team." The team she never wanted me on in the first place.

Dad's face has a new expression, one I've never seen before. He's not angry about the drinking, not really. In a cop-dad/want-you-to-be-safe way. But at the mention of the team, I realize how proud he was of me. His disappointment guts me. And Trent can't even stand to be in the same room as me.

"Don't you dare punish me for getting kicked off the team," I snap at Mom. "I lost something I loved. Don't you dare pretend vacuuming or shoveling snow makes it all better. You're thrilled I got kicked off the team."

"And don't you sidestep the issue. Being sad about your team doesn't give you the right to break laws and make poor decisions."

"Oh, good. Here comes the consequence line."

"Well, maybe you should listen to it this time."

"Kind of hard when it's coming from you, Mom." I hold out my arms, encompassing our cluttered eating area off the kitchen. "Here's your consequences for slacking off in high school. A job you hate, nasty fast food for dinner and a daughter you can take it all out on."

"Michigan," Dad warns. One word in that tone and I know I've gone miles too far.

"What, was that 'uncalled for'? Fine. My consequence for mouthing off will be solitary confinement in my room." I snatch my backpack from the floor and fly up the stairs.

"No social media!" Mom yells at my retreating back.

*

After Dad's tone, I'm not stupid enough to slam my door. But I do fling my backpack at it once it's closed. Then — middle finger to Mom — I open up Facebook on my laptop and check my texts at the same time. I've got a ton of messages on both. The hockey girls are all rightfully pissed for me and loving the opportunity to be vocal about it. But it doesn't make me feel better.

So not fair. I would be so mad if I were you. *Yes, thanks. I am.*

Want me to take Daniel out for you? *Nice sentiment. But you're not actually going to.*

This sucks. Let's blow off first period tomorrow and get donuts. *So we can rehash painful crap over and over while I get even further behind on schoolwork? Oh, and ditch class, which will equal even more grounding and/or chores from Mom?*

There is nothing here that will make me feel better.

Nothing from Jack. No obituaries posted for Daniel.

I can feel worse, though. Trent's playing his "angry music," i.e., Dad's old Metallica CD. Strains of "Don't Tread on Me" seep through our shared wall. He doesn't know how appropriate that song choice is. It hurts me like Daniel never could.

Jack was right. He's not my first priority.

I stand up and finally take my first steps toward making things right. Straight to Trent's door.

*

Knocking would be a waste. Trent can't hear me over that music. But Officer Dad took the locks off our doors years ago, so I let myself into Trent's bedroom. Step over the fermenting piles of laundry clumped around the empty hamper.

Trent sits on his bed, his back against the Dylan Larkin poster on his wall. With a frayed hockey blade in each hand, he drums against his black bedspread. His eyes are closed and he swings his head along with the music, false-screaming the occasional favorite lyric.

I hit Pause on the aging stereo, and suddenly the only sound in the room is Trent's fading voice.

He frowns and crosses his arms over his chest, hockey blades still clutched in his hands. "Put my music back on and get out."

"No. Trent, I'm sorry about the team."

He shrugs. "Whatever. You were just an assistant coach — it wasn't a big deal."

"I want you to know, it wasn't right for me to get pressured into drinking. I want to be a better role model than that."

"Je-sus. The peer pressure speech? Don't even try to tell me where babies come from because I'll puke all over you."

"I just don't want you to think it's OK because I did it."

"Alcohol is bad," he says in a robot voice. "Drugs are bad. Got it." He scoots to the end of the bed and reaches around me to turn his music back on.

"I'm sorry ..." But I'm drowned out by Metallica.

I'm at the doorway when I'm hit with the memory of that first hat thunking off my helmet. Practicing face-offs in the garage. The key Trent stole from the rink manager. *We're number sixteen now.*

Threats and bruises and insults — they are great motivators. Pain and anger make you skate faster, shoot harder. But this is a different anger, a new determination bubbling out of the painful hole in my chest.

This wasn't supposed to be about me. Sure, I wanted to play. But then it turned out I was good. Suddenly it became about blazing a trail for future generations of girls, like Megan. It was about being a girl who was the public face of high school hockey. It was about being the kind of big sister who could show Trent and his teammates that a girl can be on the receiving end of their passes, can beat them at a face-off, without taking anything away from their game.

It is time to make this about me again. What happened to me is not OK.

I hit the music off again and this time I eject the CD so he can't turn it back on.

"I didn't let you down," I say. "I got a lot of shit coming my way and I need you to be there for me."

Concern flickers across his face. "What do you mean, shit?"

I let out a shaky breath. Yep, we're doing this. I straighten my spine. "I'm taking down an asshole and I can't do it myself."

I pull him by the wrist, out of his room and down the stairs. Dad's sweeping the garage, tall silver beer can in one hand and the Wings–Oilers game on the radio. He still wears a look of disappointment that makes it impossible for me to make eye contact with him. His head slowly swings back and forth between Trent and me. My hands tremble and I cross them over my chest against the chill of the garage.

Trent's warm hand comes down on my shoulder, steadying me.

"I need you to take me to the station," I say to Dad.

He studies me for a long breath. "What's going on?"

"I … I don't want to talk about it here. Please?"

His brows pinch worriedly. "OK," he says. "Of course. Whatever you need."

And there's no going back.

29

I give my statement to Officer Graves. Dad said this kind of thing is her specialty. How one specializes in girls who have been tormented by their male teammates when I'm the only girl hockey player in the U.P., I'll never know. But I should probably look into degree programs for it.

I'm hyperaware of Dad and Trent sitting on either side of me, clenching their fists and jaws. But any time I stop talking, my teeth start to chatter. So I don't stop. For an hour, I spew poison, going back to the beginning, the very first team meeting where Daniel took my phone and changed my wallpaper to a half-naked chick. There are spots in the story where I hesitate, not wanting to indict myself. Or anyone else — I don't want Trent to get in trouble for making me a key. I fully expect that I'm going to be in trouble for drinking and I'm ready to own that. But when I get to that part, Officer Graves doesn't stop me to slap on the cuffs. She doesn't even give me a dirty look.

Instead she quizzes me on every step I can remember taking,

every symptom I felt. Every sentence I can remember someone saying. She takes down contact information for Jeannie, Jordan, Kendall, Whit and Avery. She pulls up Daniel's Facebook page and watches the video.

I can't. I study her orderly desk instead. Trent's knuckles grow white on the chair arm next to me. Dad growls. Shame floods my veins.

"Mm-hmm," Graves says, nodding. "Yes, this fits exactly. Your behavior, your movements, your eyes. You didn't even say the right kid's name."

"You understood that?" I ask. "You believe me?"

She takes her eyes from the screen to meet mine. "Of course," she says. "This video is evidence in your favor."

"It is?" I thought it was in favor of my damnation.

"Yep. Although I still want to see Whitney's footage as well. And you said you have photographic evidence of the physical assault and battery at the rink?"

Geez, it sounds like a criminal offense.

Actually, that's exactly what it was.

I find the photos on my phone, with Dad and Trent peering over my shoulders. Trent inhales through his teeth. "Shit." No one corrects his language.

I hand my phone to Officer Graves and she manages to keep her poker face. Always a good sign when your bruises don't rattle the cop.

"This is good," she says, indicating the picture. "We'll pursue it, although we're more likely to see consequences for the drugging and attempted sexual assault."

The words pelt my chest. All of us Mannings try to breathe.

"So what's going to happen?" I ask.

"We'll press charges. Against Daniel Maclane, Vaughn Gaines and William Breaker. No, it's not a lot of evidence. We may not see a courtroom for any of these charges. But what we're doing is forcing the issue into the public eye, forcing the school to tighten their policies on hazing and hopefully opening the eyes of their parents. Some of the other boys may face minor charges for hazing, both against you and the other younger members of the team."

"And they'll be suspended from school. The team will be suspended from play. Season over." I think of Avery, of Winston puking his guts out because he so badly wanted to be a part of this team. I don't know if any of them had a hand in pranking me. Maybe they deserve it. Maybe they don't.

And I will be strung up from the scoreboard.

I slump in my seat.

Officer Graves leans forward and taps my wrist with her pen. "Michigan, you took the heat. And it doesn't feel good right now. It will probably get even worse. Your story is going to end up in the local paper. You're going to get talked about at school. Dirty looks in the hallway. You'll be trolled online."

"Is this supposed to make me feel better?"

She continues. "But."

I exhale. Thank God there's a but.

"This weekend," Officer Graves says, "there's going to be a girl out there. And she's going to go to a party, and a boy she doesn't know, and doesn't trust, will hand her a drink. And she's going to pour it into a potted plant and walk out that door. All because she's been bombarded with your story."

I purse my lips.

"You have to believe that," Officer Graves says.

I want to.

I was trying to pave a way for the girls who will come after me. Like Megan. And maybe the way to blaze a trail for them isn't by being silent and taking the abuse. It's by stopping it.

Trent clears his throat. "It's like prepping for a game, right? So you're about to drop all this ... stuff. But you know it's coming. So ..." He turns his gaze to Officer Graves. "How do we pre-game?"

I could hug him for saying "we." And he's given me an idea. Several, in fact.

"May I make a call?" I ask. "I know it's late and his office will be closed, but I'm guessing you can find a home number for me? Mr. Eric Johnson. He's the hockey commissioner of the Michigan High School Athletic Association."

*

I'm so sick of my own story. I lived through it and I didn't exactly enjoy it the first time around. Repeating it multiple times today does not make me happy. First to Jack, then to Officer Graves, although she asked so many questions that really I feel like I told it to her more than once. But I call Mr. Johnson from the police station, on his home phone, at nine at night, and I repeat the story.

And then, even though it's a school night, when we get home I call every coach who has been recruiting me, whether for camps or college. It's late, so I leave the same message on each person's office voicemail. By the time I'm a third of the way through my list, I no longer have to read the notes I wrote myself on the drive home because I've got my speech memorized:

Hi, Coach [insert name here]. This is Michigan Manning. I wanted to let you know that my high school team is under investigation for hazing, and as a member of the rookie class, I was on the receiving end. We're not sure yet how this will impact the end of our season, but I am looking forward to playing a lot of hockey over the summer and next season, of course. I am still very interested in your program and hope that everything I do in the off-season will be enough to retain your recruiting interest. Thanks, and have a good night.

I don't mention Daniel's Facebook page because Officer Graves got the page taken down immediately. I'm guessing anyone skilled in computers can still find the video — nothing on the internet is ever truly private — but I'm relying on the fact that most college coaches are (1) too busy with actual coaching to hack Daniel's Facebook account, and (2) too old to accomplish it successfully. No offense to my potential future coaches.

Mom is in pajamas and her bathrobe when we finally arrive home. Her face is scrubbed clean of makeup and she looks at least three a.m. tired.

"I got most of it from your father's texts this evening," she says. "But I want to hear it in your words. And I want to know why you didn't come to us earlier. Why we're just hearing about this now."

Jack said the same thing and I could barely stand to look at him. I know that if I look over at Dad right now, my heart will crack like pond ice in spring. But I have no problem staring straight at Mom.

"Because I got drugged by a teammate. I could have been raped. And the first thing you say to me when you find out is that you want to know why I didn't tell you about it when it happened."

I push past her and trudge up the stairs. Sit on the end of my bed and untie my shoes, dropping each to the floor. My parents' voices drift up the stairs. I can't understand the words, but the angry tone is obvious. So I'm responsible for screwing them up as well. Rubbing my eyes, I force myself to the bathroom to brush my teeth.

Trent beats me to the sink. I reach for the toothpaste. He hip-checks me out of the way. Despite the day I've had, a tiny grin tugs at my lips. Knees bent, I dig in and brace myself against the sink while I snatch up my toothbrush. Trent digs in harder, toothpaste foaming out of his mouth as he strains. But I've gained a helluva lot of strength in the last few months. I get a foot against the wall and push even farther into him as I crane for the tube of toothpaste. When my fingers curl around it, we both release.

"Ha," I say, as I squeeze a line of toothpaste onto my brush.

"Ha," he says back, dropping his toothbrush into his cup. He turns the lights out on me as he leaves the bathroom.

Eventually, everything is going to be OK.

30

It's overkill, but this is what happens when your dad arrests people for a living. Two uniformed police officers loom at the school's entrance the next morning. Between them, looking very small and unarmed, Principal Belmont checks names on his clipboard. As each member of the varsity hockey team arrives for school, they are directed into the same classroom Coach Henson used for our first team meeting. Rumor has it that Coach Henson is in his office, calling each kid's parents. Shitty way to start his morning, but in my opinion he deserves worse.

I'm in the bathroom coaxing my lungs out of hyperventilation when I get a text from Jordan. It's a picture of Daniel eyeing the policemen nervously while Belmont checks his name on the clipboard. Caption: Best start to the day EVER.

Any second now, the bell will ring and I will need to sprint to the meeting room. I'm shaking so badly that I can barely shove my phone back into my jacket pocket. I lean my hands on the laminate countertop and stare myself down in the mirror.

Years of pre-game jitters. And every time, I put my armor on, trusted my strength and focused on the goal.

So I put my armor on: Trent's hat, the one he threw on the ice for my hat trick. Breaking the school's no-hat rule is the least of my worries today.

I trust my strength. And maybe also the strength of the Owl River Police Department.

Focus on the goal. This shit ends right here.

I beat the bell to the classroom. Assistant Principal Marteaux and a bear-sized officer greet me at the door.

"Are you sure you're supposed to be here?" the officer asks me.

"My name was on the clipboard."

"Yes, but —" He looks at Mrs. Marteaux and lowers his voice. "We can't put the victim in the same room as these boys."

"Victim?" I set my hands on my hips and glare up at him from under Trent's hat. Of all the names I've been called this year, that's the one I like the least. "I am not a victim. Let me in there."

He turns to Mrs. Marteaux again, the big, armed officer looking for backup from our five-foot-two assistant principal.

"I'm sure it's not standard procedure," she says. "But if you need to sit in that room, Michigan, I understand."

I nod at the cop.

"I will be in there with you the entire time," Mrs. Marteaux says. "You tell me if you need anything. Anything at all."

"Thank you." I follow her into the room.

She motions to a box on the table inside the door. "Phone, with the ringer off," she says. She flips through a file and pulls out a folder with my name across the top. "World history and French III assignments. We hope to have you back in class by third period, but if not your teachers will send in that work as well."

I head to the front of the room, to my solitary female confinement table, feeling the stare of twenty pairs of eyes. Most of them look confused as to why I'm here when I was kicked off the team. But Daniel flexes his fist, clenched so hard that his entire arm is shaking. Someone's got a good idea of what this meeting is about.

I miss being ignored.

As soon as I sit, I open my folder and attempt to read the note my world history teacher has included. It may as well be in French.

Actually, it is. That's second period's assignment from Madame Kowalski.

There's a hushed whisper behind me. I tense, bracing for an attack. I doubt that Assistant Principal Marteaux can defend us both if Daniel goes rogue.

She clears her throat. "Absolutely no talking," she says in a steely tone. "Take out the classwork your teachers have sent for you and begin studying." The woman has a future in refereeing if high school administration doesn't work out.

I can't concentrate, but I'm smart enough to keep my head bent over my books. In the silence, I listen to the breathing of my teammates. The room smells of stress sweat, and I can feel the nervous jiggling of a knee against the table behind me.

One by one, they're called to Principal Belmont's office. I risk a peek at Winston's face as he returns to the room. His hat is pulled low over reddened eyes and his gaze stays straight ahead as he beelines for his seat and buries his face in his math textbook. I'm dying for Daniel's reaction but too chicken to attempt a sneaky glance.

"Michigan Manning."

Every breath in the room catches audibly. I try for a confident gait on the way to the door, where Officer Graves meets me. She's in full uniform: polished boots and name tag, crisp blouse stretching over her broad build, fingers inches from the arsenal on her belt. With her icy glare, she looks a hair away from tasing whoever forgot to put cream in her coffee.

But once we're in the hall, she relaxes and pats my shoulder. "Hang in there. You're the last one and then comes the fun part."

"Oh, you mean we're not at the fun part yet?" It does feel nice to be out of that room, finally able to speak and move and not have a spotlight on me.

Principal Belmont's office is cramped. Assmont sits behind his desk, flanked by Mr. Johnson and Coach Henson. There's one plain chair set in front of the principal's desk, presumably for the victim to sit in during the interrogation. No bright lights or needles for truth serum, at least not that I can see. I balance on the edge of the seat, but a rustle at the door makes me jump up again.

Brie's father swooshes in. A force like gravity pulls every head in his direction.

"Michigan, hello." He claps me on the shoulder.

"Hi, Mr. Hampton." I gulp. This is the guy who usually averts his gaze and mumbles around Brie's friends. But like Officer Graves, he's dressed in battle gear, his being a sharp suit and briefcase. Clearly, I am in his arena today. Suddenly I'm the one in need of blood pressure meds. I have an attorney?

There are introductions all around. Brie's father pulls a chair over from the conference table in the corner and sets it next to me.

"We've all been briefed on Miss Manning's story," he says. "I read Officer Graves's notes and spoke to Officer Manning."

"I've already spoken to Michigan as well," Mr. Johnson says, giving me a sympathetic smile.

"So I don't have to go through the whole thing again?" I say, relief clear in my voice.

Officer Graves smiles. "I don't think that's necessary."

"I do," the principal interjects. "How can I properly interview the team without getting the facts from the one person who has brought all of the allegations?"

"You have been provided with a copy of Officer Graves's report," Mr. Hampton says. "Any other details are to go through Miss Manning's legal counsel — me. I'm sure you wouldn't want to interfere with the judicial process."

He aims a glare at Coach Henson, who visibly shrinks in his seat. Judicial process? I feel like hiding under my chair. It was bad enough visiting the police station, and now sitting here in the principal's office. But going to court? Armed officers at school, an attack-dog attorney? It's Dad, I think. He isn't going to let the school sweep this under a rug. Coach Henson, Principal Belmont, Daniel. They are going to be held accountable.

I raise my hand. "Am I allowed to ask a question?"

"You just did," Mr. Hampton says. "So the answer would be yes."

"What's going to happen to the team?" I ask.

Mr. Johnson steps in, leaving Principal Belmont with his

mouth open. "I have made the decision to suspend four members of the team."

"So did I," Belmont counters. Mr. Hampton smirks.

Neither of them names the suspended players, but I can guess. "They are in violation of the tenets of the MHSAA for hazing and sportsmanship." Mr. Johnson's stare intensifies. "I cannot do anything else besides suspend them, Michigan. I'm horrified to learn of the claims that you've had to make, and I think we can all agree that the details of Officer Graves's investigation are shocking. But the rest of their punishment will have to be determined by a court of law."

"What about the season? Playoffs?"

"We regret to punish the entire team for the actions of a select few, but for safety's sake, the regulations state that each men's hockey program must carry a minimum of seventeen players on the roster."

For the first time ever, Coach and I share a sympathetic frown. But he stays silent. His face looks more lined than I'd ever realized, and his eyes seem shrunken today.

Of course. Coach's ass is on the line.

"Bring in your JV players," Brie's father suggests. He opens his briefcase and powers up a slim laptop. "Unless Coach Henson can be persuaded to reinstate Michigan, you're down an entire line."

Somehow I'd forgotten I'm no longer a part of the team. I'm here, aren't I? Doesn't this absolve me of all guilt? But, really, it doesn't. I put a glass of liquor to my lips and that fact has probably been verified twenty times by now. I broke Coach Henson's team rules, and for once I can't blame him for his actions.

But by now, everyone in this room understands that I wasn't the only one who broke Coach's rules. If we're all held to the same standards, Coach should suspend every member of the team. Eric Johnson folds his arms and studies me. Belmont leans forward on his desk, waiting. Coach's glare dares me to do it, to call the boys out on drinking during season. To suspend the team and cancel playoffs just because I no longer get to participate.

I look to my attorney. "Are we done here?"

"Actually, I've found your loophole," he says, handing his laptop to Mr. Johnson. "As commissioner, you can deem a judicial case a special consideration and allow the team to hold a limited tryout to fill the roster for playoffs. As long as none of the candidates have played for another men's team in the league this season."

Coach's spine straightens and his face lightens. He'll have to take JV or previously cut players, but at least he can attempt to salvage his season. Belmont seems to waver. Mr. Johnson seems embarrassed that Brie's dad is better able to navigate his own policies. He scans the screen furiously.

Mr. Hampton shrugs. "It's buried. The language is confusing. But it's there, I assure you." He snaps his briefcase shut, like a badass TV lawyer. Seeing him like this, I can definitely understand where Brie gets it from. "Michigan, I think we'll leave these men to discuss this option."

I'm out the door before Mr. Hampton finishes his sentence. In the hallway, I tell him, "Thanks for doing this." I assume it's a favor to his daughter. His aversion to all things drama queen probably means he doesn't realize Brie and I haven't talked since the Showcase.

Now that we're in the hall, he seems uncomfortable being in the presence of a teenager again, even with Officer Graves and her semiautomatic handgun present. "Well, your mom is a good court staffer," he says. "I was happy to help when she called me."

"Mom?" I was sure it was Dad getting my back. But of course Mom wanted to make sure I didn't say anything stupid in there.

"You and I will be talking very soon, Michigan. Get those grades back up." Yeah, he's definitely Mom's henchman.

Officer Graves escorts me back to the team classroom. "I don't think they'll jump me in the school hallway," I tell her. I try to make my voice sound like I'm joking, but I'm actually quite happy to have a uniformed, armed policewoman next to me. If she's not busy for the next two months, I could use a bodyguard.

A grim grin settles over her face. "We're done with our interviews," she says. "I've just heard accounts from two dozen people verifying the charges you brought against Daniel. I have a warrant for his arrest."

My jaw slips open. "You're taking him in now?"

She inclines her chin. "Yes."

Dread and pleasure fight each other for a spot in my chest. This I want to see. This I do not want to be present for.

"Breaker and Vaughn?" I ask.

"They're both still seventeen. I'll handle them privately once their parents arrive."

I pause at the classroom door. I spent four months fighting this war by myself. And now it's all out of my hands. Mr. Hampton, Officer Graves, they've completely taken over for me. Which is nice, but I never got to finish my own fight. I never even took the gloves off.

"Can I have one minute?" I ask the officer.

She doesn't bat an eyelash. "I'm going to retie my shoelace for the next thirty seconds and then I'm coming in."

I open the door to the classroom and stride through. Mrs. Marteaux is not at the front of the room; she must have taken advantage of my absence to step out. Not that I was expecting her to throw down punches as my backup, but it means I'm truly on my own here.

Every head snaps up to stare at me, at my straight back and my fierce expression. I walk straight up to Daniel, who has the newest *Hockey News* open inside the textbook in front of him. When I stop next to him and fix him with my glare, the bravado on his face fades. I hardly recognize him without it.

"Stand up," I say.

He stands up, lazily closing his magazine and crossing his arms over his chest.

I open my arms wide, mirroring my stance when I let Vaughn hit me. But this time, instead of the noisy hum of the rink innards, it is silent in the room. Instead of four on one, it is an entire team facing off against me.

"One punch," I say, lifting my fists. "You took my spot on the team. I get to throw one punch."

He snorts and aims a smirk toward his buddies.

"What if I told you it would keep you on the team?" I ask.

His eyes raise to mine, one brow cocked with interest.

"Isn't that how it works here?" I crack my knuckles. "Come on, Daniel. Take it like a fucking man."

His hands fall from his chest to his sides, as if he's considering it.

"Better yet," I say, "I'll play fair. I'll fight you one-on-one, right here. Then there will be no question who comes out on top. Right here, in front of your boys. You can show them what a hero you are. What a fucking winner you are."

His fists fly up and he steps forward. I'm immediately ready; my chin is tucked, my fists protecting my face, my stance low and balanced like in a face-off. His right arm swings at me in a sloppy haymaker, and the room around us is suddenly a blur of action. Chairs crash to the floor. Feet pound and bodies swirl around me. I brace for an impact that never comes.

A sharp whistle splits the air, and the entire room freezes. Well-trained hockey players that we are.

Officer Graves stands in the open doorway, shoelaces tied tight, her taser pointed at Daniel's chest.

At least that's what it looks like through the tiny crack between Avery's shoulder and the arm of Sanders's green-and-white letter jacket. There is a line of boys shielding me from Daniel, arms outstretched and fists up. Only Vaughn and Breaker remain behind him, Vaughn's fists raised and Breaker's arm encircling Daniel's torso, as if to pull him back.

"Mr. Maclane," Officer Graves says. "Before you speak, it is my duty to inform you that you have the right to remain silent. Anything you say may be used against you in a court of law …" She continues, but all I hear are the gasps and "holy fucks" slipping out of the mouths of my former teammates. Vaughn's mouth hangs open and Breaker pales, clutching the back of the nearest chair.

Mrs. Marteaux hurries back into the room on Officer Graves's heels, trying to shoo stunned boys to their seats.

Daniel's face burns red, the entirety of his furious glare focused on me. Clearly, he blames me for his arrest. I'll take that blame. Proudly. *Yes, you are a gigantic douchebag and I called you out on it. Enjoy jail, asshole.*

The room gasps as Officer Graves cuffs Daniel's hands and leads him to the door. His eyes stay on the floor for the entire walk of shame. The second they're out of the room, it explodes into four-letter words uttered in shocked tones. Even Mrs. Marteaux looks too stunned to issue silencing orders.

And I sag against the wall, my body suddenly heavy. This isn't the end. It's actually more of a beginning. There will be meetings with lawyers and court dates and, honestly, I'm not sure what. I've always preferred NHL Network to *Law & Order.* Playoff series can go seven games. I may be up a game now, but the series isn't over and I'm going to have to clinch on the road.

Avery whistles over the crowd. "Hey! D-bags! Shut up. Just like on TV, right? No big deal." He lopes to the front of the room and addresses Mrs. Marteaux. "Since we've all answered our questions, can we suspend the no-talking rule? For a few minutes. You can supervise, I promise we'll be cool." He smiles sweetly. Apparently this charm has worked in the past.

She presses her lips together. "I'll be listening. Keep it clean."

"Yes, ma'am." He winks at her. "May we excuse any persons who aren't members of this team anymore?"

She nods. "Yes. They've finished their questioning." She aims her voice over the room. "Principal Belmont will meet the suspended young men in the hall."

Breaker stands, pushing his chair back until it crashes over. He stalks to the door and slams it on his way out. Vaughn punches a table before flinging the door open. Ouch.

With his eyes on the floor, Carson stands and slips out the door after them.

I move slowly to the door to give them time to clear the hallway.

"Mich," Avery says. "Stay."

I shake my head. "I'm still kicked off the team."

He takes a deep breath. "We did a shitty job for you this season. At least let us come out of this smarter than we went in. Please." He gestures to the front table.

I walk to the front of the room. And I tell the story one last time. I'm still sick of my story, but I think this is probably the most important telling. So I make sure not to leave anything out, not to dumb it down or explain it away. I start with my eyes on the floor, then they drift to Avery, who nods in encouragement every so often. When I finally get brave enough to look out over the room, I'm shocked to find that every set of eyes is on me, every body leaned forward in his seat. Not a single boy is whispering to his neighbor or bemoaning the temporary loss of his phone or even pretending to study while really reading *THN*.

When I reach the part where Coach booted me from the team, I run out of words. Sanders raises his hand immediately. I call on him. "Yeah, Scott, what's up?"

"Michigan, I'm really sorry. It was my idea about Breaker flashing you. I dared him, I thought it would be funny because he made me moon my sister's basketball team's bus. I'm really sorry. It totally wasn't cool."

"Wasn't cool your sister had to see your ass either," Avery says.

"Yeah, no, I'm aware. Already got that lecture from my dad."

Winston raises his hand. I'm not sure I need all this confessional. But maybe they do. "What'd you do, Winston?" I ask.

"They, uh ..." His face turns deep red and he pulls his hands up into his flannel sleeves and tucks them into his armpits. "Daniel and Vaughn, they roughed me up a bit. After the first game. They said I played like a, um, pussy. Like I was afraid of being hit."

Well, he kinda did. Not that it makes it OK.

"So anyway, they kind of punched me in the gut a bit and Vaughn hit me with his stick a couple of times, on my back. And I got a bunch of bruises and stuff. So I told the cop. Mrs. ... Officer ... whatever. Anyway, so it wasn't just Michigan, if you all are thinking she's the only one that got those guys thrown off the team. You can be mad at me, too."

T.J. stands up. "After I got that double minor against L'Anse, when they scored on both penalties, Daniel and Breaker offered to give me a ride home and then dumped me on the side of the road. I had to walk two miles and it was twenty degrees out and they said if I called anyone to come get me, they'd be watching and they'd beat the shit out of me." He starts to sit back down and then rises up again. "Oh, and I told the officer that, too. Put some of the blame on me."

"You guys all remember," Ethan says, "That night at Vaughn's house when I told them I don't drink and they told me I'd be off the team if I didn't. So I did, and they kept giving me shots until I puked. And I told the cop that, too. And she didn't get mad at me for drinking because she said I'd been punished enough."

"Yeah, she was pretty cool when I told her about that sludge they made us drink," Winston says.

"Agh, that was the worst," Sanders said. "I think she was trying not to laugh when I told her that I had to run around the house bare-assed and it was freaking snowing."

There are a bunch of snickers around the room. "Frostbit junk!" one of the guys calls out.

Mrs. Marteaux clears her throat loudly. More snickers. No more junk references.

Sanders clamps his hand over his mouth. "Oh, shit, Manning. I just realized that I flashed you, too. I'm as bad as Breaker is."

"No, you aren't," I tell him. "But I'll send you a bill for my therapy."

"I'm sorry," Avery says to me. "That you went through all that."

"Why are you sorry?" I ask. "You're the only one who was ever cool with me."

"I was cool with you," Winston says. "I just didn't want them to know it. They hated you so much, Michigan. You should have heard them talking about you in the locker room. I didn't want a beating for being nice to you." He shrugs. "Guess I really am a pussy."

"No, you're not," I say. "But you're a dick for using that word."

Around the room, jaws drop. Including Mrs. Marteaux's. Oops.

"Where did you think that slur comes from?" I ask, scanning the faces of my teammates.

"Um. Fuzzy kittens?" Sanders says. "Because in sports, they're all … you know … cats …"

"Wow," Avery says. "I never thought about it before."

Winston stutters. I'm sure he's working up to yet another apology that I don't need. I hold up my hand. "Now you know. And I don't blame you for staying quiet. I didn't want a beating either. Or to get lectured and grounded by my parents or hear 'I told you so' or be the quitter who couldn't hack it. So I kept my mouth shut. Until now."

Knocking on the door interrupts us, and Mrs. Marteaux opens it. Mr. Johnson and Principal Belmont step into the room.

"Boys," Belmont starts, and then he catches sight of me and stops. "Miss Manning, we are about to have a team meeting. Mrs. Marteaux will write you a note back to fourth period."

Assistant Principal Marteaux digs my sparkly phone out of her crate and ushers me up the aisle and out the door. As I glance back, Avery mimes texting. I nod.

The real team meeting has already concluded.

31

Johnson is allowing tryouts for 5 open spots on the team. Tomorrow. We can still have playoffs.

I breathe a sigh of relief at Avery's text. He's got a lot riding on this season, too. He needs to finish strong so he can get invited to all the good camps this summer and impress the juniors' scouts.

I reply, That's great. It'll be weird to have new people for only a few games but at least you won't be shorthanded.

What about you? Need my best center back.

There's no way Coach will let me back on the team.

Coach is GONE.

I stare at my phone. Reread Avery's text until it sinks in.

Tryouts are tomorrow. I'll be there.

*

I stalk him. Yep, I'm that girl. Dark sunglasses, Jordo's red knit beanie. Waiting outside in the parking lot after school, crouched behind Di's sporty red coupe so he won't see me and run the other way.

As Jack tosses his bag into the Wagoneer's back seat, I lean against the driver's side door. So he can't escape without listening to me. Unless he climbs over the seat. God, I've become creepy.

"I wanted you to hear something from me before you hear it from the school," I say.

He jumps and cracks his head against the doorframe. "Shit! Michigan!" He rubs his head. "What?"

"Sorry! Sorry! Are you OK?"

"I'll live. What's up?" He's not looking me in the face, but maybe that's the possible concussion. Or maybe it's because scaring him into whacking his head isn't a real apology.

"I'm sorry I lied to you. And I wanted you to hear something from me," I say. "And not Facebook or the rumor mill or the back of the boys' bathroom doors."

He shrugs. "Eh. The stalls don't get used all that much. They write on the wall over the urinals, though."

Please let that mean he's teasing me.

"OK. So anyway, here's the real version of the news. I'm trying out for the boys' team. Again. I got Daniel arrested for drugging me. A bunch of the other guys came out about the hazing and abuse Daniel and his buddies pulled on them. Coach is also out. And I think I'm officially failing French by now. But keep that last one quiet."

"You're failing a class?" he asks. "You know Laura can tutor you."

"I'm on it. So … are you still mad at me?"

He sighs and rubs the spot on his head that's probably

growing a lump from the doorframe. "It wasn't that I was mad. More like hurt. We talked a lot, Michigan. I thought I knew you. But you were keeping some pretty heavy things from me." I nod along. This is not new information. What I need to know is, can I fix it?

He looks so wounded. "I would have been there for you, Mich."

That's the moment my heart actually cracks. "I know that."

He's silent. And then, "Do you want to tell me about it?"

"All of it. Which parts do you want to hear first?"

"Start with Daniel getting arrested because I think I'm going to enjoy every detail of that. The urinals didn't do it justice."

I grin and start right in, finally on a new story.

*

I expect Assistant Coach Peters has been promoted. He was pretty much Henson's protégé. The other assistant coach mostly worked with the goalies. Can't say I have much love for Peters, but I'm sure the admin is watching him like a hawk.

I want to call Megan; she loved being our manager and I don't know if Henson getting fired will mean she loses her position. Or if her mom and stepdad would even let her be around the team now. But I don't want to make trouble for her. Coach Henson wanted me away from her so bad that he got my coaching position pulled. Whatever her family is going through right now, I don't want to make it worse.

"With Henson getting canned, I'm afraid she'll move away," I tell Trent, as we drive to the rink. He has a rare evening off from hockey but insisted on coming to watch tryouts. "She probably hates me for getting her stepdad fired."

"She's fine," Trent assures me. There's something under his voice that I don't recognize, though. He's staring out the window at the giant red-and-white snowfall sign awful hard.

"Define *fine*."

"She's playing great. Kicking butt."

"Duh. Does she hate me?"

"No." There it is again.

"You're not convincing."

"I promise she has no bad feelings toward you."

"But how do you know that?"

"I'm smart. I know everything."

"So you talked with her about me?"

"I talk with her about a lot of things." He tries to hide it but a huge grin takes over his face.

I gasp so hard that I brake for a green traffic light. "No! Trent! Are you dating the coolest eighth-grade girl I've ever met?"

"Shut up," he says, shoving me. His face resembles the red goal light. *Ding, ding, ding* — score!!

"I have new respect," I say. "And maybe I'll start knocking before I enter your room."

"Shut. Up," he repeats. So I do, even though we're both grinning like idiots.

With Henson gone, I'm totally shocked to see Megan in the hallway when we get to the rink. She takes a running leap and flings herself into my hug. "I'm so sorry," I say.

"No, I'm so sorry. I wish I'd known …"

"Don't you dare apologize."

"Don't *you* dare apologize."

So we don't. I unlock my broom closet, giggling at the urge to yell, *Honey, I'm home!* to the spiders.

And I truly am home. Open hockey bags crowd the floor, spilling out pink sports bras and socks. Lady Gaga blares from phone speakers. It smells like a Bath & Body Works exploded.

My broom closet is jam-packed with hockey girls.

32

Jordan pulls her breezers up. This simple action takes up too much space in our sardine can of a changing room and she bonks elbows with Kendall. “Sorry.” She looks up as I attempt to maneuver into the room. “Hey, Mich. I know, I know. I’m more than a long shot. But I’m really only here to be your bodyguard.”

I reach over Kendall, who’s tying her skates, to hug Jordan. “You’re hired.”

Kendall looks up from her seat on the only chair in the room. “If I make the team, I’m taking Vaughn’s number.”

“Be careful. That’ll earn you two punches to the gut and a slap on the ass,” I say.

The door swings open again. “Bitches!!!!”

Illuminated in the doorway, like a hockey angel, is Brie. She drops her bag on the floor, which is already a puzzle of hockey bags and gear. So really, she drops her stinky gear on top of all of mine.

"Dibs on the only chair," she says, wrinkling her nose at the mop wagon with its well of dirty water. "Ew. Seriously?"

"Get Daddy to build us a better locker room," Jordan suggests.

Jeannie, tucked in the corner, once again reminds us of our missing manners. "Brie! Welcome home! We're so glad to see you."

"What are you doing here?" I pick my jaw off the floor. I almost lean over to hug Brie, but then I remember that we aren't talking. Weren't talking. But she's here.

"You have got a lot of explaining to do," she says, hands on her hips. "I can't believe I had to hear this from Twitter. My *dad* knew what was up before I did."

"Yeah, join the club," I say. "What's with the bag?"

"As soon as my season ended, I got sooooo tired with Wiltshire. Ugh, dorm food. And dorm beds. And all those privileged boys running around flashing their wallets and Audis and yakking about their summer homes. Uh, hello, it's *Daddy's* summer home, not yours."

"Uh. Huh," Jordan says.

"Oh, yeah. Audis are the worst," I echo.

"And then I hear there are spots available on this team and I think, I've got a couple of games left in me this season. Especially if Mich's pulling in the college scouts."

I roll my eyes. "I've got college *hockey* scouts watching me. Not sorority scouts."

"They have those?" she asks. "Whatever. I'm legacy, I'm totally in."

About 15 percent of me wants to deck her, but I laugh instead. This is what a team is. A family to fight over the toothpaste with, to share the only chair in the closet with. My throat swells up and I swallow hard, concentrating more than necessary on taping my stick.

The swimmers aren't allowed to try out because they have regionals this weekend, but they're in the stands cheering. The Silver Lake defectors also aren't eligible and have their own practice, but they made a poster for the swimmers to hold up for us.

And, sitting in the stands next to them, is Jack. My heart bangs against my chest protector and I try not to freak out that my little brother is sitting like ten feet away from him and God knows what they'd talk about if guys do that kind of thing.

Our fan club hoots and shakes their poster as we girls take the ice. At the bench, I peel off and stretch out on my own.

Avery skids to a stop next to me and drops to the ice with a thunk. "What are you doing out here?"

"Making sure you get some decent shots on you. Can't have you getting soft before playoffs."

He smirks. "Not a chance. I meant, why are you trying out? Can't you just tell the new coach you want back on?"

I laugh out loud. It never occurred to me to ask for my spot back. I lean on my knee until my hip flexor stretches. "Guess that's what I'm doing here. Telling Coach I want back on."

Avery tilts his helmeted head up to the stands and I follow his gaze to Carson. I'm shocked to see him here, but it's not like getting kicked off the team comes with a restraining order. He's way up at the top of the stands, his knit cap pulled low over his brows. If it weren't for those obnoxious high-top skater shoes he always wears, I wouldn't have recognized him at all.

He leans on his knees and focuses on the rink. It's too far away to see his face, but I feel his regret all the way to the ice.

"He asked if he could try out for his spot," a new voice says next to me.

It's an older man in a dark blue USA Hockey warm-up suit and skates. With a whistle around his glove.

"Ah … Coach?" I ask, hopping to my feet.

"Coach Norman," he says, holding out his gloved fist. I bump it with my own.

"Coach Norman's dad," I say in awe. Coach Norman, Sr, coached junior hockey for twenty years. He has some administrative position with USA Hockey now — duh, the warm-up suit. I've never met him before but everyone knows who he is.

"Nice to meet you, Michigan."

"Is Coach Norman still mad at me?"

"He never was. He said to give you his best and to return his calls."

I hang my head. "I know I should."

"You didn't let him down," he says. "Quite the opposite, in fact. So. This Carson kid. I can't let him back on the team. Athletic Association ruling. It's out of my hands." His blue eyes bore into me.

For the first time I realize that Carson wasn't standing with Daniel in the meeting room when Daniel got arrested. When the team took sides, he was on mine.

But I can still feel his fingers squeezing my wrist in the rink's garage, ready to hold me in place for Vaughn. He stood there while Vaughn punched me. Was he there when Winston got hit? Was it his idea to leave T.J. on the side of the road?

Avery said these guys need to come out of this smarter than they went in.

"*I'm* getting a second chance," I admit to Coach Norman.

"Ah, but that's different. Your expulsion was the decision of a coach who is no longer in charge of this program. Not the governing association." He absently toys with a puck on the ice. "I considered giving him a position on the bench, as a second team manager. But I wouldn't feel comfortable doing that without permission from you."

I meet his eyes. "You could put it to a team vote. An anonymous vote. If the team unanimously votes to let him be a manager, he could have a chance to earn his way back next season when his suspension is over."

It would hurt me hard to stand on the bench and support my team when I'd let them down so badly. To not let my skates touch the ice, to watch others making plays and scoring goals. If Carson is willing to put himself through that in order to regain the team's trust, it would mean he's truly changed.

A small smile breaks Coach Norman's stern gray mustache. "I have a lot of respect for you, Michigan. I hope you skate hard today."

"Yes, sir."

"Now go warm up."

*

Sanders scoots over to give me a spot to stretch out next to him. The ice is crowded today; the remaining team members are practicing, plus there are fourteen extras here to vie for a spot.

Besides the six of us girls, there's a handful of freshmen from the JV team and two sophomores who got cut earlier in the season. If the coffee guy is here, I don't recognize him in gear.

My stomach twists and flips worse than it did before my first game with these guys. What if the season-long scoring leader can't earn her own spot back?

From the first drill, it's pretty clear that Jordan and Whit aren't going to be able to keep up. Jordan's method of staying in shape has included daily Slurpees and smoking the occasional cigarette. She swore she'd stop if she made the team, so we'll have to find some other way of motivating her. A cute asthmatic, maybe. And Whit's always spent more time on the bench than the ice. She's red-faced and huffing by the end of warm-ups but she powers through.

"Lookin' good, Manning!" Ethan yells as I effortlessly stride through a passing-skating drill. I've only had five days off. Frankly, if you don't count the stress of this week, it's been healthy to give my body a break. I feel strong and ready to skate.

The usual pressure is missing. I no longer have to look over my shoulder constantly, to stand apart from my teammates at water break, to keep my eyes on the ice when they talk trash. There's a part of me that thought without that fire igniting me, I'd fall flat.

But, hell, this is actually fun.

When I dish passes to my teammates and they score, they meet me to celebrate. When we sit next to each other on the bench, we heckle each other and share Gatorade. Guys actually pass to me now. Shout encouragement when I'm fighting for the puck in the corner, defend my back in front of the net if I take a hit.

"Dang, girl," Brie says, as we plop onto the bench during the scrimmage. "Playing with the boys has done you some good."

"I'm pretty sure you've seen me play this season."

"Yeah, but that was just a Showcase."

"And?"

"And what?" she asks.

"Would it hurt you to admit I kicked ass at the Showcase?"

"You know you did."

"Is that why you came back?" I ask. "Because I was taking all the attention you thought you deserved?"

She grins and nudges my shoulder pads with hers. "Mich, I'm supposed to be the attention whore of this friendship. Not you."

"Yes. You called that title years ago. But as your best friend? Stop being an ass."

She rears back. "Again, dang, girl. Not only are you faster and more skilled than you've ever been but you picked yourself up a spine this season. Looks good on you, too."

"Thank you."

"Feel validated now?"

"Yes."

"Thank God. Can we go back to talking about how much faster and more skilled I've gotten this season?"

Sanders taps her on the shoulder. "So, uh, how do you feel about dating sophomores?"

"No intrateam dating," I remind him.

"What?" Jordan shrieks. "If I have no chance with Michigan, what am I even doing here?"

Brie and I laugh but Sanders slides down the bench, closer to Jordan. "This is called hockey. See, there's this black thing? It's called a puck. And that cold, white stuff — You're going to hit me, aren't you?"

Jordan's glaring at him. He ducks his head and bats his eyelashes at her. She settles for a helmet-noogie instead, aided by T.J., who holds Sanders's gloves down.

Winston sprints to the boards for a line change. "Mich, you're up!" I hop the boards and he holds out his glove for a fist bump as I hit the ice. "Nice shot last shift," he says. "You got this."

"Thanks," I say.

This feels like a hockey team. It feels like *my* hockey team.

*

The embroidered A is an exact copy of the one I never got to wear with my girls' team. Sparkling gold threads glint even under the dim lights of the rink bleachers. I hold the puck-sized A up to my shoulder. Yes, this looks good on me.

"You earned it," Coach Norman says. "Those boys look up to you, Michigan."

"I won't take that for granted," I say.

"I know." He hands me a laminated sheet of paper with large letters typed in black: Women's Locker Room. I grin. I am a woman with a locker room. Watch out, world.

"You are to use Locker Room A for the rest of the season," Coach says. "Hang this on the door when you're in there. The rink manager offered to give you a key …"

I look up from the sign. "I won't need a key anymore."

He nods. "If you do, I'd better be the first person to hear of it. Now, get out of here. I've got thirteen kids to meet with and they're not all going to be this easy. I'll see you at practice tomorrow."

"Yes, sir. Thanks, Coach."

"And Michigan? Get that French grade up. Yesterday. Got it?"

"Yes, sir," I repeat. My mother is going to love him.

*

Mom's at the kitchen table paying bills. I linger in the doorway, my jersey in one hand, A in the other. She glances up but doesn't meet my eye. We've been tiptoeing around each other ever since I got home from the police station. Her gaze stops on the A.

I shrug. "I'm no good at sewing."

She sighs and holds out her hand to examine the A. "It's iron-on. No sewing involved."

"Oh." They should make that obvious.

"But I'll do it," she says.

"Really? OK. Thanks." I hang my jersey over the back of Trent's chair and set the A on the table, assuming she'll get to it eventually. I turn toward the door.

"Don't you want to see how it looks?" she asks, standing.

"You don't have to do it now," I say, gesturing to her paperwork. "That looks important."

She doesn't smile but her face eases. "No. This is. I may not understand it, but it's important to you."

I follow her to the laundry room. She closes the door behind me and pulls down the ironing board from the back of the door.

She lifts the iron from a hook on the wall and plugs it in, spinning the dial.

"Guess I should learn to do this," I say, thinking of college in a year and a half.

"Nah. You'll have an equipment manager to take care of things like this," she says.

It's the first time she's ever made a positive comment about me playing college hockey. Something lifts in my chest, making it easier to stand tall. Mom smooths my jersey over the ironing board, taking special care with the spot on the front of my left shoulder where the A will go.

"Do you feel better about me finishing the season now that I'm not the only girl on the team?" I ask.

She huffs. "Brie's not much in a fight, unless it's verbal." She holds her palm out an inch from the iron, testing to see if it's hot. "No, Michigan, I feel better about you finishing the season knowing that you can take care of yourself. You've certainly shown you can."

I eye the linoleum floor. "I don't know. My teammates had to come rescue me."

"You took on a lot by yourself. And you handled it all. But if you surround yourself with the right people, they'll be there when you need them. Might be one of the most important things you can learn in life."

I watch as she presses the A onto my jersey. "Here?"

"Perfect."

She holds the iron over it.

"What else?" I ask. "Besides ironing, what else are the most important things to learn?"

"Nah," she says. "You'll figure them out."

She lifts the iron and gently flexes the edges of the letter to see if they lift up. The A stays strong on my jersey.

"French homework, maybe," she says.

"Geez, Mom. I just finished up the last of my worksheets. Grade will be back up when I give them to Madame K first thing tomorrow morning."

She lifts the jersey over my head and I slide my arms through the loose sleeves. The gold A gleams proudly from my chest. It's the hardest I've ever worked for an A.

GAME OVER

ACKNOWLEDGMENTS

Thank you to the many anti-Daniels I've known in hockey. For helping a poor college kid with skate sharpening and jobs at the rink, for staying late to practice one-timers, coaching my teams or having my back when I wore stripes and a whistle. You gave me the opportunity to fall in love with hockey.

Thank you to my dream agent, Kate Testerman. I still freak out when I see your name in my inbox. Fist bump to all of the KT Lit family, and a hug to Hilary Harwell for her excellent feedback (on this and all of my manuscripts). Thank you to Kate Egan for making me cry with your lovely emails (it's OK; there's crying in hockey). Thank you to the girls in your life who inspired you to say yes to Michigan.

Kids Can Press and KCP Loft, I am so grateful for the opportunity to champion the girls who dress in broom closets and endure jerks for the love of their sport. Thank you for giving them representation on bookshelves.

To my critique partners and beta readers, so much love: Laura McFadden, Edna Pontillo, Martha Sullivan, Niki Lenz, Sabrina Lotfi, Megan Orsini. Shout-out to all my YAAMS for their love and support and emails full of exclamation marks.

Officer Graves is a fictional character, but when it came to naming her, she just couldn't be anything but Officer Graves. I hope I've done the name proud.

Barb Diehl Richardson, if I had never known you, this book would have been set somewhere way less cool. (Also, I'd be sad.)

Becca Cales, for a girl who wouldn't be caught dead with a pair of pom-poms, you are one helluva cheerleader. Thank you for your endless support and belief in this crazy dream of mine.

Thank you to my writing buddies: Ani for years of quiet company next to my desk and Ivy for working through plot problems on our early morning walks. Yes, I just thanked my dogs. Obviously.

Maddie and Lauren, you are the inspiration that brought me back to writing. I hope I've shown you how to dream big and then work hard for that dream. I love you so much.

Most of all, thank you to Kevin. For being my rock, and for believing on the days I couldn't believe in myself. For you, in print, those three little words: You. Were. Right.

CARRIE S. ALLEN grew up in the Colorado mountains, at 10 000 feet elevation. She put herself through a bachelor's degree in biology and a master's degree in sport science by driving the Zamboni machine. She worked as a certified athletic trainer, first in a high school, and then in collegiate sports medicine. She lives in Colorado Springs with her husband, kids and dogs. When she's not acting as unpaid chauffeur, she writes about athletes. Not female athletes, but athletes who happen to be female.